PRAISE FOR THE ROYALS

"Geneva Lee convinces with fluid writing that's full of drama, ups and downs..."

— PEOPLE MAGAZINE

"Romance and drama...when it comes to dirty talk, the British heir to the throne can hardly be topped..."

— THE HUFFINGTON POST

"Sexy, sinful, and downright delightful! Geneva Lee is the queen of writing drama, angst, and the heroes of your dreams."

— CORA CARMACK, NEW YORK TIMES
BESTSELLING AUTHOR OF LOSING IT

"A royal tale unlike any other. Heart-stopping, mesmerizing, a delicious treat with every page turned. I only wanted more."

— AUDREY CARLAN, #1 NEW YORK
TIMES BESTSELLING AUTHOR OF
CALENDAR GIRL

ALSO BY GENEVA LEE

THE RIVALS SAGA

Blacklist

Backlash

Bombshell

THE ROYALS SAGA

(IN READING ORDER)

Command Me

Conquer Me

Crown Me

Crave Me

Covet Me

Capture Me

Complete Me

Cross Me

Claim Me

Consume Me

Breathe Me

Break Me

CLAIM ME

CLAIM ME

Ivy Estate Publishing

www.GenevaLee.com

First published, 2019.

Ebook ISBN: 978-1-945163-24-1

Cover design © Date Book Designs.

Image © Vasyl/Adobe Stock.

GENEVA LEE

CLAIM ME

THE ROYALS SAGA: NINE

ESTATE
PUBLISHING + ENTERTAINMENT

To Josh,
Who carries my heart

CHAPTER 1

CLARA

The creak of the door alerted the nurse to Alexander's presence, but I'd felt him coming long before that. I'd known he would come. An hour ago, I'd felt a prickle along my skin. Moments ago, goosebumps had broken out on my arms. Before the door opened, a shiver ran up my neck. My body responded to him like air surging before an approaching storm.

But today Alexander wasn't the reckoning.

I was.

I didn't turn. It wasn't that I couldn't face him, but rather that I refused to look at him. Instead, my eyes stayed on hers, briefly closing when I heard him speak.

"I don't have any secrets from my wife."

I would have laughed if I'd had it in me. Another lie. It was getting harder to decide which I hated more, the lies or the secrets, although it didn't seem like there was much difference between the two.

She glanced up, drinking in Alexander's words before her eyes darted back to me. Now she was piecing it together. I hadn't explained who I was. It felt wrong, somehow, to be the one to tell her. She had missed so much of Alexander's life. How was I supposed to tell her that I was his wife? That we had a child together? That I was expecting another? There were years of information to relay, and I had started my relationship with her by keeping secrets.

Maybe my husband and I weren't so different after all.

There hadn't been much time to tell her anything before Alexander arrived, anyway. First, the nurse panicked and checked all her vitals. I remained off to the side, largely unnoticed. Then the doctor had arrived. I was only alone with her for a few minutes. She had only asked one question.

"Where is my family?"

I'd told her he was on his way. I had known he would find me. It was one way he never let me down. After that, the uncomfortable silence set in. I'd offered her my name and told her I was a friend.

When Alexander clarified who I really was, she continued to stare at me.

"Wife?" Her voice was still weak, feeble from years of silence, but the tremble of pain in that one word had nothing to do with it. I couldn't bring myself to meet her eyes and look into their shadowed, blank depths.

I only nodded. I couldn't do this. He had kept this from me for a reason. Later, I would make him explain why. Now? I didn't want to be here. I had no place in this family reunion. She was as much a stranger to me as I was to her. Alexander had seen to that.

Rising to my feet, I forced a small smile. "Excuse me."

I moved quickly, refusing to allow myself time to reconsider. I needed to get away from her. I needed to be away from him. I needed to be able to think.

Alexander reached for me as I passed, but I skirted away, shaking my head. Even now, my body fought against me, tempting me toward him like a bee to honey. He'd thrown on jeans and a t-shirt that hugged his powerful body, stubble peppered his jawline, and his black hair was a chaotic mess. Apart from the clothing, this was the man I would have woken up to if I had stayed in bed. We would have made love. I could almost feel the scratch of his stubble on my thighs. I'd come here instead, lured into the darkness of his past and the mistakes we couldn't seem to escape. It's what kept me from going to him now—even a bee could drown in honey.

"Clara," he said in a hollow voice, his blue eyes flashing with regret. He didn't speak again as I reached the door. He didn't try to stop me.

We both knew it wouldn't matter. There was nothing he could say. I thought he'd given me all of him — body, heart, soul. I was wrong.

CHAPTER 2

ALEXANDER

"This can't go on," Norris said firmly. My trusted advisor and friend had become my personal alarm clock of late. He scanned me, his eyes skimming over my rolled up sleeves and wrinkled shirt. My tie was abandoned on the ground. Yesterday's suit jacket slung over the back of my chair.

I hadn't slept alone in years and since Clara had refused to come to our bed, I had taken to falling asleep in my office. It was Norris's unofficial duty to wake me before morning meetings.

I glanced at my watch, surprised to see he was a bit late today. He made clear his disapproval of how I was handling the situation with my wife. "Can the lecture wait? I need to grab a shower before I have to meet with some important person about some important thing."

Norris raised an eyebrow at my glib attitude. There was no use in pretending that most of the meetings I took weren't largely ceremonial. I was expected to approve or disapprove as needed. I was to have an opinion and support charitable causes. I was to play the role of the benevolent king. Anything more than that would be overstepping my bounds, or so Parliament had made clear over the last few weeks. This attitude was due, no doubt, to arrangements my father and his father before him had made. The monarchy had been gradually modernizing, or, as I saw it, pawning its responsibilities off on someone else. I'd been testing those previously sanctioned limitations. Now, it was becoming clear things would have to change. But I wasn't going to be the one to give in. Not while my family's safety was at stake. It was why I woke up and sat through the sodding meetings. I needed to play the part—for now.

"Today's meetings are the least of your worries. The staff is beginning to talk." He adjusted the knot of his tie, looking slightly uncomfortable about bringing up the topic.

"The staff is always talking." I ran a hand through my hair. I had learned from a young age to accept that the walls had eyes. Very little of what I said and did behind palace walls was private. Sometimes, I wondered if even my own bedroom was safe.

"Yes, but someone is bound to leak to the press that there are problems in your marriage."

I flinched at his words. I hated the way he made it sound. Mostly, because Norris had a clarity in viewing problems that most people lacked. When he coupled that with the blunt edge of truth it was harder to pretend he wasn't right.

I wasn't going to admit that to him, though. "It's just a bump."

He didn't question me on this, but his silence said more than enough as he took a seat across from me. One of us was right and one of us was wrong. I knew which was which, because I couldn't lie to myself even if I tried to lie to him. This wasn't a bump.

"I don't have to tell you that we have a delicate situation developing," he said, changing the topic to an equally unpleasant one. "Sooner or later we must make the announcement. It would be best if the revelation didn't come on the heels of news that Clara is sleeping in another bedroom."

Maybe we hadn't changed the topic of conversation after all.

"I don't want to push her," I said softly.

"She's not going to leave you."

I sucked in a breath and shook my head. He couldn't be certain of that. I'd chosen not to marry some idiotically bred aristocrat who would place stock in title and appearance. This wasn't a political marriage. It was a marriage of love and trust and passion—and I'd cocked it up.

"She doesn't trust me." It felt as if my chest might split open saying it.

"She will, but you have to talk to her," he said pointedly.

"I know, but I have to catch her first." I hadn't been trying very hard. Usually, our fights ended in angry, nearly violent sex. I suspected this one wouldn't. I'd be lucky if she let me touch her again. "Why didn't I tell her?"

"I don't know." His words were heavy as if he'd asked himself the same question.

I swallowed, unsure if I was ready to spill the truth into the open. Norris knew me and he'd stood by me through worse, but it was still difficult to admit the truth. "It never even occurred to me."

A muscle in his jaw twitched slightly, which was the only

indication he'd heard me. Part of me wished he would berate me, or yell, or punish me in some way.

"Nothing to say about that?" I pushed. It felt even worse to have it out in the open than I'd imagined.

"What didn't occur to you?" He measured each word, speaking through gritted teeth. He already knew the answer.

"It didn't occur to me to tell Clara about..." I buried my face in my hands, unable to continue. I didn't know what it said about me that I hadn't kept this a secret from my wife so much as I had ignored it altogether. It hadn't been important to share this with Clara, because for all intents and purposes, the woman in that room was dead to me.

And now she wasn't.

The truth was, I'd had plenty of opportunities over the past few weeks to tell her. When my father died, I'd taken over the responsibility, which meant getting occasional updates from Norris, but not much else. After another attack on my family, I'd increased security on everyone, including her, but I still hadn't told my wife. When Clara suggested Windsmoor as Edward's wedding present, I'd had another opportunity to come clean. Life had given me chance after chance, and I'd thrown them all away. There was no one to blame for this mess but me.

"Clara is your life now. She gave you a chance to start over and you took it," Norris said, finally breaking the silence dragging between us.

"That doesn't excuse what I did."

"No, it doesn't. But you can't change what happened in the past."

"That sort of thinking is what got me into trouble in the first place," I muttered.

"Not thinking is what got you into trouble," he corrected me.

He had me there.

"If I may," he began. I suspected whatever he was about to say wasn't going to be gentle. "Some space between you and Clara isn't terrible."

"It isn't?" I sat back in my chair, shaking my head. "It feels terrible. I haven't so much as touched her in nine days."

"Exactly. You two need to work on your communication."

"Our communication is fine," I snapped.

"Your communication is unique and not always effective." He folded his hands in his lap looking positively ecclesiastical.

Maybe Norris couldn't bring himself to say it, but I knew what he was driving at. "You mean fucking? We fuck too much."

"That you see that as a form of communication proves my point. You need to talk more."

"Well, she won't talk to me *or* fuck me," I exploded.

"You should clean yourself up." Norris directed his attention to the window, not rising to my bait. "You don't have long before your day starts."

I got the impression I was on his shit list, too.

THE HOUSEHOLD WAS BEGINNING TO WAKE AS I MADE MY way upstairs to our family's private rooms. Everyone was avoiding me. Housekeepers backed into walls, dipping into low curtsies and averting their eyes as I passed with a nod, but I felt their gaze on me as soon as my back was to them. Norris was right, something was going to have to change.

There was no pretending that nothing was wrong. The air felt too heavy, the whole palace seemed to be weighed down by the trouble lingering between me and Clara.

I stopped at the door to my bedroom, wondering if this would be one of the lucky times that she was here. She seemed to have guessed my schedule and managed to skirt me most mornings. Norris would have realized that as well. Now I knew why he'd been late this morning. He was determined to force us together. I opened the door and found our bed perfectly made. Either the maids had already been here or no one had slept in this room. It was wishful thinking to even consider that there were two possibilities. I knew in my heart that Clara hadn't slept there. I started to step inside, but my feet didn't seem to work. I couldn't stand it – being here near our empty bed. Instead, I turned and crept into the room across the hall.

Muted sunlight filled the nursery and fell over a rocking chair in the corner. Elizabeth was sprawled across her mother's chest, angled to allow for Clara's growing 'belly. My breath hitched at the site of my wife and child. Clara was beautiful in her sleep, her face glowing in the early-morning light. Her dark hair was piled on top of her head and her nightgown had slipped from her creamy shoulder. I thought of the freckles there and how much I wanted to press my lips to her pale skin. But the dark circles under her eyes drew my attention to a bigger problem. Had she been here all night?

I crossed the room quietly and lifted Elizabeth from her mother's arms. Both of them startled but neither woke.

Gently rocking my little girl, I carried her to her crib and lowered her cautiously. Slipping my hands out from under her, I breathed a sigh of relief when she didn't wake up.

For a minute, I stayed there and studied her sleeping form. She had no idea the trouble between her mother and me. All she knew was love. I would never allow her to know anything else. Whatever problems Clara and I faced had to be dealt with sooner rather than later. I wouldn't allow our children to suffer parents who were always fighting.

When I finally turned, Clara was watching me through hooded eyes. Silence stretched between us. This couldn't be our new normal. Nothing to say to one another. Avoiding each other at every turn. Had I broken things past the point of repair? And how the fuck was I going to fix this?

She sat up and her nightgown shifted farther from her shoulder, dipping low enough to reveal the swell of her breast. I locked my knees, forcing myself not to go to her and rip the rest of the flimsy excuse for clothing off her. Clara shoved it up quickly as though reading my thoughts. I bit back a smile.

But there wasn't even a glint of amusement in her face. When she spoke, her voice was cold. "She's teething."

"Why didn't you find me?" I asked, keeping my voice low so I wouldn't wake the sleeping baby. "She's not your sole responsibility."

Clara's eyes flashed and I realized I'd said something wrong. Again. "You weren't in our bedroom. I didn't know where you were."

It was a lie. She hadn't checked our bedroom and she'd known exactly where I was. I wasn't about to challenge her, though. Her lie was innocent and carved from anger over my own lies—lies that might have finally destroyed us.

"You have more important things to worry about." I didn't

miss the sharp edge her tone had taken, but before I could respond she stood, stumbling a little as she yawned widely.

I knew what I had to do whether she liked it or not. I went to her, lifting her in my arms before she could process what was happening. Clara didn't fight me as I carried her across the hall to our bedroom. Her arm looped around my neck as though she might fall—as if I would let her—and I could swear I felt her fingers trail softly down the back of my neck. No doubt that was wishful thinking again.

I brought her to the bed, wondering how far she would allow me to go. But she needed to rest and I needed to give her time to find her way back to me, even if it killed me to lower her onto the bed alone. I yanked the bed coverings down, drinking in her perfect body as she wiggled under the sheets.

Without thinking, I cupped her face, running my thumb along the curve of her cheekbone. I didn't dare kiss her and it was taking every ounce of restraint that I had to keep the rest of my body to myself. My thumb strayed to her full lips, tracing them and remembering her taste. I missed her. I needed her. I had to find a way to tell her that.

Her lips parted slightly and a sigh escaped before she moved her face away from my hand. I reached for her again, unsatisfied. She belonged to me and if she'd only remember that, we would find a way to make it through this.

"Don't," she murmured, her voice thick with sleep even though her eyes clenched shut a bit too tightly.

I yanked my hand back like she'd bitten me. I couldn't blame her for saying no, but this time, unlike so many others, she meant it fully. There was no room for another interpretation, and as if to prove it, she rolled to her side, turning her back to me, before curling into a ball. Part of me wanted to climb into bed with her, take her into my arms, and force her to talk to me. Most of me wanted to climb into bed and take what was mine. I doubted she would stop me, but I couldn't brush away the finality of her tone. Reaching down, I drew a blanket over her, allowing my fingers to brush over her shoulder softly before walking away.

She was back in my bed, but there was a wall around her —invisible but felt. She'd built it between us. I couldn't blame her. A good man would bring it down brick by brick. I found myself looking for dynamite.

CHAPTER 3

CLARA

As soon as the nurse closed the door behind us, Belle turned her patented best friend glare on me. It went well with her crimson lipstick.

"Fess up. What is going on with you and Alexander?" she demanded.

I shrugged, painfully aware that she wasn't going to buy any excuse I gave for his absence. She didn't know about what had happened. No one did. I hadn't even told Georgia what was waiting for me behind that closed door and she hadn't asked. Because she understood sometimes a girl needed time to process having the rug pulled out from under her. That wasn't a trait that Belle shared.

"Clara," she pressed. "Talk to me. I'm worried."

"Everything's fine," I lied, wishing I had more energy to sell it. I hadn't been able to sleep after Alexander had carried me to our bed and abandoned me there. Did I wish he had stayed? I'd told him to stop. Why did he only listen to me when I didn't really want him to?

"Bollocks. You are practically comatose, and I would

know, because I've seen you actually comatose." She fell
silent for a minute, her blue eyes narrowing. "You haven't
told him."

"No," I said quickly, "and I'm not going to. This has
nothing to do with that."

"He should know," she started but I shot her a look that
shut her up.

"No good will come of him knowing something might
be wrong with the baby." My husband was a mystery to me
in many ways. This wasn't one of them. I knew with absolute certainty how he would react to that news. I couldn't
stomach the thought of him trying to coddle me and protect
me, not after what he'd kept secret for all this time. It would
only add fuel to his belief that I was too fragile for his
world.

"You shouldn't face this alone."

"I'm not," I reminded her, "unless you're going to..."

"Of course, I'll be right here." She dropped into a chair in
the corner. "I just don't understand how you deal with it. You
two are like a roller coaster—up and down and bloody crazy.
Sometimes it makes me nauseous just to watch."

"That might be the morning sickness," I said dryly.

"No, it is definitely *e*-motion sickness and I caught it from
watching you." She crossed her arms and I noticed for the
first time the slightest hint of a baby bump as her shirt
stretched from the movement. "The stress isn't good for you
or the baby."

"I know." I took a deep breath and forced a smile that I
hoped was reassuring. "Everything is fine. We just had a little
fight."

"Stress bad," she repeated defiantly.

"Got it." I needed to change the subject because *she* was beginning to stress me out now. "You're showing."

That did the trick. She flipped her blonde hair over her shoulder, her other hand sliding down to the tiny swell and rubbing affectionately. "I know. Smith hardly lets me leave the house now."

"Getting overprotective?" I guessed. Belle didn't like to admit it, but I knew her husband was every bit as macho as mine was.

"No, he can't seem to keep his hands to himself," she said with a giggle.

"Oh that! Yeah, it's a real problem for men like ours."

"Men like ours?" she repeated.

"Cave-dwelling, beat-their-chest types. They enjoy seeing us knocked up as much as they enjoy knocking us up," I said with a smile that was actually genuine, if a bit rueful. "Alexander won't stop until we have an army."

I said it without thinking and then I remembered that wasn't possible. One complicated pregnancy was chance. Two was a sign. It felt like someone had hit me in the chest with a hammer. I gasped for breath and blinked against tears. A house full of babies wasn't in our future, because I was damaged goods.

"Hey," Belle said softly, coming to sit next to me. "We still don't know that anything's wrong and there's no reason to think—"

"One caesarean might not be a big deal," I sobbed, "but I'll probably need another if the baby's heart..." I couldn't finish the thought. It was bad enough confronting the possibility that I would have to tell Alexander we shouldn't have more children. When I had to face that something could happen to the baby growing inside me now I felt like I was going to crumble. I swiped at my eyes, embarrassed to have broken down so easily. "Sorry, I'm just..."

"*Stressed,*" Belle finished for me. She wasn't accusing me just making me see the truth. "Clara, what's going on? Do you need to talk?"

I wanted to open up and tell her everything, but I couldn't. Not yet. Not before I had real answers about why Alexander had kept secrets from me. I still didn't know if Edward knew, and until I found that out, it wasn't my secret to share. "We're fighting," I admitted. "It's normal stuff."

"You're the Queen of England," she pointed out. "I'm doubting it's normal stuff, but I understand if you don't want to tell me."

I bit my lip, trying to keep everything from tumbling out. This was my best friend. I told her everything. "I want to tell you, but I can't. Not yet."

"Like you can't tell him about the baby?" she asked softly.

I opened my mouth to explain that this was different, but there was a knock on the door. Belle gave me a tight smile and went back to the chair in the corner as the doctor entered the room.

"Your Majesty," he said as I swallowed a sigh.

"Clara," I reminded him. Any man who had been face to face with my nether regions should probably be on a first name basis with me.

He nodded as though he might consider using my real name, but I knew better. We'd been through this dozens of times when I'd been pregnant with Elizabeth. It wouldn't stop me from trying, however. I would never get used to being present but apart. It was no wonder Alexander was screwed up.

"I've spoken with the specialist you saw. I know he wanted to look into your scans and your charts further," he continued, his finger skimming over a chart.

"He didn't tell me much." I smoothed down my dress nervously. I'd thought I would know much sooner than now, but even though I was panicked over the results, I hadn't sought them out. Even now, I wasn't certain I wanted to know what he had to tell me.

"He took a cautious approach given..." he trailed away, and I filled in the blank: given who I was or, more importantly, given whose child this was. He flipped open a file and drew out a black and white image.

The doctor wasn't volunteering much and his obvious hesitance wasn't very reassuring. He moved closer and held out the image, pointing at a spot that had been circled digitally. "This is your baby's tricuspid valve. It connects your baby's right ventricle with the right atrium. While it's a bit early to be conclusive, it appears to be a bit too narrow."

My own heart plummeted into my stomach as I tried to process what he was telling me. "What happens if it is too narrow?"

"It would be difficult for blood to leave the baby's heart and get to its lungs. In most cases, we can keep the ductus arteriosus open with medication. Normally that valve closes when babies begin to breathe on their own."

I couldn't think. I had too many questions rattling around in my head. I looked to Belle for help, only realizing I'd begun to cry when the movement made hot tears hit my cheeks.

"So we keep it open with medicine," she jumped in, nodding to me. Thank God for best friends. "Then what?"

"It will depend on a number of factors. Likely the baby will need a surgery not long after birth. We will continue to monitor this very closely, Your—" I shot him a look and he fumbled for a second before shifting gears "—Clara."

Belle glanced at me, clearly torn about her next question. Our eyes met and I knew she was wondering exactly the same thing I was, but she couldn't say it. She shouldn't have to, I realized. Swallowing against the ache in my throat, I forced myself to ask it instead. "What are the baby's chances?"

"Very good," he answered quickly. "We're quite fortunate to have caught it. Early intervention means a very high survival rate."

Survival rate. Early intervention. Words I'd never expected to hear about my unborn child. I was cracking slowly, breaking under the weight of my life. I needed to be strong for the baby, but that was the only thing holding me together. One wrong word might be all it took to shatter me.

"There are a few other things you should know," he began and I braced myself, wondering how much more my own heart could take.

A HALF HOUR LATER I WAS ON INFORMATION OVERLOAD. Norris was waiting with the car as Belle and I exited the private entrance to the clinic. I would never know how he always managed to keep the paparazzi at bay, but today I was especially grateful for it. He eyed me without comment as I gave him a tight-lipped smile and climbed into the backseat.

Belle cast furtive glances at me but kept quiet, massaging her own baby absently as we drove.

"Home?" Norris asked, and I realized I'd fallen into a daze.

"Don't I have a schedule?" I said coldly, immediately regretting my bitchy tone. It wasn't his fault that this was happening. It wasn't his fault that the baby was sick. It wasn't his fault that he was here and Alexander wasn't. No, that was all my fault.

"I believe you're free this afternoon, if..." he said without a hint of sarcasm or annoyance. Of course, he usually had to put up with Alexander and his whiplash-worthy mood swings. The man was a saint—the father Alexander had never had and the man most likely to talk sense into my often irrational husband.

"Why don't we go somewhere?" Belle offered.

"Where?" I asked her. I wanted to, more than anything, but I couldn't just go out to lunch or to shop. I wouldn't know where to go, even if I could.

Belle searched for an answer, clearly understanding my unspoken need for privacy. "My house? I'll send Smith out for some curry and we can chat. Norris can sweep the entire building if he needs to."

"That won't be necessary," he said, his eyes following our conversation in the rearview mirror.

"Look, I'm on the approved list!" Belle clapped her hands like she'd won a prize, earning a laugh from both of us. I didn't tell her that I suspected she was more than on the approved list. It wouldn't surprise me if Alexander had security checking in on her regularly. He was overbearing like that.

Smith met us in the foyer, giving me a quick hello before wrapping his arms around Belle. He was one of the few men in the world completely nonplussed by my presence and I loved him for it. No fawning over me. No awkwardness. Then again, he didn't seem to notice much when my best friend was around. He gave her a swift kiss, and the look on his face sent my thoughts to Alexander.

Alexander looked at me that way. He didn't notice anyone else when I walked into a room. That wasn't what I missed, though. I missed his kiss. I missed his arms. I missed a thousand little things that I hadn't even known I missed. I missed *him*.

"Can you go grab us some curry for lunch?" Belle asked Smith in a low voice.

I blinked at the sound of her voice, realizing only then that I had started to cry again. Smith cast a worried look in my direction but nodded. Thank God for men who could take a hint. He grabbed a jacket off the hook by the door and slid it over his broad shoulders. Giving Belle one more quick kiss, he left.

"Let's talk." Belle took me by the shoulders, obviously not trusting my dazed state, and led me into the parlor.

"I don't want to talk about Alexander." I barely processed that we'd changed locations. I was too busy holding back tears. Taking a seat on her cream-colored sofa, I grabbed a pillow to clutch to my chest. It felt good to hold something. Later I would go home and cuddle Elizabeth.

Nothing really mattered to me now but her and this baby's health. I didn't care about the secrets Alexander had kept. I didn't have room to stress about that in my life. There were more important things to consider. At least, I kept telling myself that. I only wished I believed it. "I don't know how I'm going to do this."

It hurt to admit it, but I knew if anyone would understand it was Belle.

"Well, to start with, you aren't going to do it alone," she said.

So much for not talking about Alexander.

"I can't tell him," I said forcefully because she didn't seem to be hearing me on this point. "He will make this stressful. He won't be able to keep himself from worrying. This is about the baby, not us. Alexander knowing will only make things worse than they already are."

We weren't just talking about the baby's health anymore and we both knew it.

"Clara," Belle said my name with some hesitation. "What happened?"

"You know." But she didn't and that was the problem.

"Something else is going on." She took a deep breath and then rattled off the last question I expected from her. "Did he *hurt* you?"

"No! Nothing like that." I shook my head at the thought. "Alexander would never hurt me physically."

"Would he hurt you other ways?"

"Not intentionally." I knew what she was driving at. Both she and Edward worried about my often tumultuous relationship with Alexander and their concern had been mounting lately. "He doesn't seem to know how to be honest with me."

One of Belle's expertly shaped eyebrows arched into a question mark. "It seems like you both have that problem."

"It's complicated." I was aware of how stupid that sounded. Yes, Alexander and I had more to worry about than your average couple, but, at the end of the day, should things be this hard between a husband and his wife? Belle didn't say anything as I stewed. "Maybe it shouldn't be, but I don't know how to change it."

"It would help if you started talking about things." There was no recrimination in her voice — no edge of accusation. This was my best friend trying to remind me of a simple fact: if I wanted things to be less complicated, I should make them easier.

"Look," she continued. "Alexander frustrates the shit out of me. He always has. Sometimes I don't know how you put up with him, but I'm sure people wonder the same thing about Smith." Her accompanying laugh was hollow. "You know why you love him. I'm just worried. You're hurting. I can see that."

"Love increases our tolerance for pain," I whispered.

"Maybe it shouldn't," Belle echoed me earlier.

"It has to," I said. She didn't argue with me.

Love made people stronger. That much I knew. In a world where it was so much easier to hate, love was defiant. But love — true love — also broke hearts and tore people apart —then pieced them back together. We were all scar tissue masquerading as people. I'd seen Alexander's scars. The ones that marred his body and the ones that marked his soul. There had been no one around to love him through it then— to help put him back together. Under his strong body and dominant exterior he didn't have the layers of protection that loving him had given me. I'd developed a thicker skin with every lie and every secret. Every time a tabloid shared a vicious rumor that hit too close to the truth, I'd gotten stronger and with that strength, I'd shielded him. But maybe that was where I had gone wrong. I'd kept no secrets from him even while I guarded his from everyone else. We were caught in an endless cycle—my love protecting him from pain by enduring it myself. I'd fooled myself into believing that he carried the weight of the world but if we were going to be stronger together, we both had to change. I had secrets from him now—secrets that were going to hurt him. Secrets that could change everything. They were enough of a burden to carry. I couldn't carry his anymore.

I knew what I had to do.

"There's an estate outside of Windsor," I began. It was time to tell someone the truth.

CHAPTER 4

ALEXANDER

I was waiting for Clara when she came home. It took every ounce of self-control I had—and I didn't have much—to keep calm. "Why didn't you tell me you had a doctor's appointment?"

"You have more important things to do." She kicked off her heels and headed toward the closet, her eyes studiously avoiding me.

"Nothing is more important to me than you." I followed her inside, hovering by the door. She glanced at me warily, her gaze darting around me as she realized I'd trapped her inside. "I want to be there. I want to know about these things."

My words landed like a bomb complete with a warning siren blaring in my head. That had been a mistake—a big one.

"I guess I'm keeping secrets. You must be rubbing off on me." Clara kept her back toward me as she searched through a number of hanging garments.

Bringing up the doctor's appointment had been stupid. If there was anything I needed to know about the pregnancy, she would tell me. I didn't like that she'd left me out, because I wanted her to know it was important to me, too. But I knew she was making a point: she could give as good as she got.

I decided to change tactics. "There's going to be a press conference. I'd like you to be there with me."

She snorted, but she still didn't look at me. "Why? It's a bit late to include me."

"I don't want people to think…" I trailed away, instantly realizing my blunder. It was like I was planting land mines and then jumping on them. My self-preservation was clearly off. Of course, everything was off when she was shutting me out.

Clara abandoned her search of the closet and whirled around, planting her hands on her hips. "Don't want them to think what? That you kept secrets from your wife? Do you want them to think I knew about—"

"I want to be a united front." I was still in dangerous territory, but I meant what I said.

"You have a funny way of showing it." She returned to her search.

"Are you ever planning to speak to me again?"

"We're talking now."

"That's not what I meant." All of our conversations had been short these last two weeks. She shut me out almost as soon as I started speaking.

She shrugged as she reached for a silk robe. "Are you going to tell me the truth?"

"I don't have any more secrets from you." Even saying it, I knew it was too little, too late. Still, I was growing tired of this song and dance. We needed to talk. I needed to explain. Since the moment she'd walked out of that room in Windsor, she'd had no interest in my explanations. I couldn't blame her. But I wasn't going to let my past and the mistakes my father had made take my wife from me now.

Clara attempted to move past me to the bathroom, but I stretched an arm out to stop her.

"Really, X?" She pushed at my arm and tried to squeeze past me. Considering she was eight months pregnant, she wasn't going anywhere if I didn't want her to.

And I wanted her to listen.

"We need to talk," I repeated more forcefully.

"No, you need to listen." She glared at me with such intensity that I dropped my arm.

I didn't care how I got her speaking to me. She could yell at me, rant at me, berate me—I would take it all. I deserved it. "Fine. I'm listening."

This stopped her, but only for a moment. It didn't take her long to recover before she launched into everything she had been holding back. "Things are going to change around here. If I find out that you so much as went out to lunch without telling me, I'm gone. Also, Georgia is my new head of security. No arguments. I am not dragging another man to the obstetrician."

I clenched my jaw shut, forcing myself to listen rather than argue with her. I wanted her to talk. If she thought I'd let her walk out on me, she was very much mistaken. Now wasn't the time to tell her that, however.

"Anything else?" I was in no position to question her, but I couldn't be sure if she was thinking clearly. Not since she'd stopped sharing what she was thinking with me entirely. No matter how much she might push back, I couldn't allow her to place herself or our child in danger just to prove a point.

"I don't want to talk about it. I'm going to take a bath."

I grabbed her shoulder and spun her around, moving her backwards against the wall before she could dodge me. "I *do* want to talk about it. What changes?"

My arms bracketed her in place as my body began to calculate how long it would take to get her dress off. Maybe I didn't want to talk at all. We had more effective ways of ending an argument—ones we both enjoyed. If I could touch her, she'd remember why she loved me. Then she'd be able to forgive me.

"It's not going to work this time," she murmured, her lashes fluttering.

"What isn't it going to work?" I asked absently as I lowered my face closer to hers.

"Fucking this out," she said harshly. But even as her eyes blazed, her body began to respond to mine. Her belly was an unfortunate barrier between us but not insurmountable. She breathed in soft, shallow pants, a flush creeping across her fair cheeks. The hand planted on my chest was soft, not firm. She wasn't resisting me exactly, but my Clara was far too stubborn to admit she missed me, too.

"Poppet," I whispered as I angled my lips to her ear. Catching its soft shell between my teeth, I sucked it gently before lowering my lips to the curve of her neck. "Don't you miss this? I'm sorry. I want to talk. I do. But maybe this is what we need."

"Alexander." There was a warning on her tongue and I stepped back, heeding it. She pushed past me into the bathroom without so much as a glance back at me. I watched as she started the shower.

"I thought you were going to take a bath."

"I changed my mind. A bath doesn't sound relaxing anymore." She still wouldn't look at me. "I'm tired. I'm going to shower."

She was driving me crazy. She dropped the robe and when she reached for her zipper, I couldn't stop myself. Moving behind her, I took over. "Here. Let me."

Clara froze as I drew the zipper slowly down, revealing inch after inch of porcelain skin. I wanted to slip the dress off her shoulders and wrap my arms around her. I could almost imagine her full breasts in my hands. I could almost taste the sweet, wet heat between her thighs. My cock hardened painfully, reminding me of exactly how long it had been since I'd buried myself in her. She shifted slightly, pressing her ass against me as though she was thinking the same.

"Do you miss me?" she whispered, wriggling slightly against my erection.

"Fuck yes, I do, poppet." My hands went to her hips and gripped them, yanking her back against me so she could feel how much. "Do you miss my cock? Do you miss it when I fuck you? Tell me how much you need to feel me inside you."

"Yes, please."

I barely caught her whimpered reply, but it was enough. I released her hips and shucked her dress from her shoulders, helping its progress to the floor with impatient hands. I needed to taste her. I needed to be inside her. I needed to fuck her.

The scrap of lace she called underwear snapped easily with one tug. Clara's answering moan was like a lightning rod to my crotch. I left her garter belt, fastened low on her hips below the swell of her belly, on, enjoying how the garters crossed over her skin to hold her silk stockings. She was a masterpiece, sinfully beautiful. I drank in the sight of her full, round ass and long legs. I would never have enough of her. But as I began to unfasten my belt buckle, she pulled away.

"Clara," I said in a strangled voice.

"What?" She reached around and unfastened her bra. "I want to, but that doesn't mean I will."

"How long are you going to punish me?" I exploded.

"I haven't decided yet." She didn't seem the least bit moved by my outburst. Instead, she unpinned her hair and it tumbled to her shoulders. I forced myself to stay put as she undid her garter belt and rolled her stockings off one by one. When she was naked, she looked me in the eye, her gaze full of challenge.

She knew how hard it was for me to be near her after going so long without fucking her. It was a test, but I didn't know the right answer. She was trying to make a point, but Clara also craved domination. She had since the moment I met her. Taking her might be the proof she needed, proof that I would always choose her. Choose us. But answering incorrectly was a big gamble when I was playing with my heart.

"Clara, I need you. You need me. Let me love you." I took a step toward her.

"You seem to be confusing sex with love." She opened the shower door.

"Don't do this." I was begging now, but she stepped under the water and closed the door between us.

I wasn't the one who was confused. I knew exactly what she needed and I would show her. Whipping my belt off, I unfastened my pants and freed my cock. Fisting it, I began to stroke my shaft, my eyes on my wife. She was watching me.

The glass between us began to fog and she hadn't so much as touched the soap.

"You do this to me," I said. I had no idea if she could hear me over the running water, but she could see my lips moving. Let her hear what she wanted to hear—what she needed to hear. "You drive me fucking insane."

Clara was finally moving, her own hand snaking down between her legs. I pumped my cock harder as she began to knead her cunt. I knew the sounds she must be making—the sharp intakes of breath, the needy little moans.

"You're mine. You belong to me." I moved closer until we were face-to-face with the glass between us. "Play your game. Pretend you have the power. Nothing will change that. You are mine."

She could hear me now. I could tell by the way she swallowed back her pleasure and grimaced as if pained by it. I couldn't hear what she said, but I saw the words on her perfect lips. "Fuck you."

"You will, Poppet." I groaned as I felt my balls tighten. My hand sped up, urging me toward release. "*Soon.* You'll fuck me soon. You gave yourself to me, and I'm running out of patience. I will take what's mine."

Her eyes shuttered on this final warning, her body trembling slightly as her orgasm rolled through her. I came, watching her unravel, my release spraying the glass as my knees buckled from the force of my climax. When I looked up, she turned away and shut off the water.

But when she stepped out, she grabbed her robe and drew it on quickly.

"Clara, it's inevitable. Stop fighting it. Nothing will change what's between us."

And then in a low voice, she found the three words that did. She found the three words that ripped my heart out and changed everything. Three little words that carried the weight of everything—our future, our family, our marriage—and made me realize I was wrong.

"I hate you."

CHAPTER 5

CLARA

"Where are you?" Edward asked as soon as I answered my mobile, jamming it between my ear and shoulder as I narrowly avoided dropping my teacup. Across from me, Elizabeth frowned at the interruption, her tiny legs splayed in front of her and a teapot wobbling in her hands.

"Home," I said as I held my cup out and she pretended to fill it.

This earned me a laugh. "In case you haven't noticed, your home is rather large. Palatial, some would say. Where are you in it?"

"Are you here?" I struggled to stand up, getting off the floor was proving trickier these days. Nodding to Penny to take over my spot at Elizabeth's tea party, I mouthed to her that I would be right back.

"I've been summoned for an official meeting, which is never a good thing. I figured you would be there."

Heading into the hall, I started toward the offices. "Not today. When is the meeting?"

"A few minutes. Although I'm told he's with the Prime Minister, so who knows? You should come."

"Shit, I just left the nursery. I might not make it before..." It occurred to me that I might not want to make it. Alexander had slept in his office again. If he'd returned to our bedroom, I hadn't seen him.

"Language," Edward said in mock horror. I could almost imagine the goofy grin on his handsome face. "It's just downstairs."

"The lift is acting up, and it takes me twice as long to get anywhere at the moment," I grumbled. "I want to see you before your meeting."

"David is here with me. Why don't you just come?"

He suspected something was up. I couldn't blame him. Things were usually up between me and Alexander. Still, life was about to get messy for my family. I knew why Alexander had summoned him here. With the press conference looming, he had to come clean to his brother. A strange mixture of annoyance and relief churned inside me as I realized that Alexander had left me out of this meeting. After last night we had been avoiding each other. I had no idea if my husband was hurt, but I was. He'd been smart to avoid me, given the number of violent fantasies I'd entertained in the intervening hours.

"I'm on my way." I needed my best friend right now, even if it was just to see him for a few minutes.

"Well, waddle a little faster," he said.

"Did you just accuse me of waddling?" Did all the men in my life have a death wish?

"If the crown fits."

"Tell me. Why are Cambridge men such assholes?" I asked.

"Good genetics," he said without missing a beat.

I was almost there, so I hung up on him as punishment. The difference between Edward's behavior and Alexander's was that my husband's younger brother always had good intentions. How he had managed to maintain a sense of humor growing up in this twisted Royal cage, I would never know. But now he was about to face another secret his family had kept from him, and I wondered if this time his good nature would be irreparably damaged. He might hate Alexander. I wouldn't blame him for that. But what if he hated me, too?

Edward and David were laughing as I rounded the corner. Edward's hand brushed his husband's shoulder and I felt a twinge in my chest. They were newlyweds and it showed in how they looked at each other—like the whole world had been laid before them. I missed that. Not that I'd ever really had it. There had been no honeymoon phase for us. My marriage had been born in violence and danger. It was really no wonder that things were so messed up now.

We would never have this. Our lives would never be simple. I had to remind myself that they had their own troubles to deal with, especially when it came to battling public opinion. But as far as I knew, they didn't keep secrets from each other.

Edward turned and spotted me. "Happy anniversary!"

My heart plummeted at the reminder. I'd done my best to forget today was my wedding anniversary. Alexander obviously had.

His welcoming smile reminded me that being jealous of

my best friend was ludicrous. The important thing was his presence in my life. My pace sped up and I threw myself into his arms. They folded around me, holding me closely.

"How are things, Your Majesty?" His tone was light, but I heard the edge to it.

"We'll talk later," I promised. I didn't trust myself not to spill too much now. It wasn't my place to tell him the truth. Alexander could take responsibility for his choices. He could face his brother. I chose to ignore what was coming and the implications of it. I had shut Alexander out, but he hadn't volunteered much information. I didn't know if he would talk about it. I'd made it clear I wasn't interested in his explanations, not while I was preparing to deal with the fall-out.

If he wanted to be a united front, he shouldn't have divided us.

Edward's voice dropped lower so that only we could hear. No one appeared to be around, but with over a thousand people working here, prying eyes were never far. "How's the baby?"

"Fine," I said, clinging to him. It felt good to be held. It wasn't the same as being with Alexander, but it was a far healthier substitute.

"You're taking it easy?" he pressed.

I pulled away slightly and studied him. Guilt was written across his face. A slight sheen of sweat had broken over his forehead. He knew.

Closing my eyes, I searched for some inner peace and came up empty-handed. The only person in my life capable of keeping a secret was my husband, it seemed. "Belle tattled."

"Belle is losing it. She's really concerned," he said softly.

"Look," I began to explain, but the door to Alexander's office opened before I could. "We'll talk later. Don't say anything."

Edward's gaze flickered to the ground but then he inclined his head in agreement. He might be Alexander's brother, but his loyalty was to me. I didn't like putting him in this position, but technically, I hadn't been the one to do it.

Alexander stepped into view, stealing any further warning from my lips. A knot tightened in my stomach at the sight of him. Usually he wore blue or gray, but today he'd opted for a black three-piece suit. His tie was knotted at his throat and the lightest stubble dusted his jawline. I hadn't seen him this morning. He must have had his clothes delivered to him. Power radiated off him and I fought my body's response to it. Pressure ached in my chest until I was certain I might crack open and spill my heart at his feet. I belonged to him. I couldn't deny it. I knew it all the way to my bones. He was in my blood. His heart beat in my chest. He owned me.

We stared at one another, oblivious to anyone else. Alexander's face betrayed nothing. His eyes were cold, hard sapphires that contained none of the fire that usually ignited the moment we saw each other.

I'd told him I hated him. I'd meant it in the moment. I hated how I couldn't control myself around him. I hated that I would always forgive him. I hated how he consumed me.

And I loved him for all those same reasons.

But behind his detachment, the only thing I spied was venom. Our love had become poison, and it was killing us both slowly.

The world returned around us—seconds later, or

CLAIM ME 37

minutes, or hours—I didn't know how long the moment had stretched. It felt like an eternity.

Edward looked from him to me, staying silent. Did he feel the weight of the air as acutely as I suddenly did?

Alexander's head turned away from me, his nostrils flaring for a moment before he spoke. "I need to speak to my brother. Alone."

"I brought David and I think—"

"Just you," Alexander said, leaving no room for further debate.

Edward threw an apologetic look at his husband. He looked torn between accepting his brother's demand and refusing it.

"It's okay, babe. I'll hang with Clara." David gave him a quick kiss, his eyes shifting between all of us warily.

"Maybe she should be in there, too," Edward suggested.

"No," I said before Alexander could clarify what I already knew. He wasn't excluding David from this meeting. He was rejecting me. I'd been included until I'd opened my big mouth and said the one thing I should never have said to him. The one thing I'd promised I never would say. My throat slid over the ache of tears. I refused to cry in front of them.

Edward mashed his lips together and set his shoulders before striding into the office. He looked like a man going to his death. He knew bad news was coming his way. I knew that it wouldn't matter if David was in there or if I was next to him. Nothing was going to soften this betrayal.

Alexander paused at the door like he was going to say something. His blue eyes found mine, but instead of speaking, he shut the door between us.

"Walk?" David suggested softly.

"I need to get Elizabeth first." My voice cracked a bit, but I pretended to cough. I wasn't fooling him, but he didn't call me on it.

I didn't need to get Elizabeth. She was fine with Penny, but right now I needed a tangible connection to Alexander. The baby had been particularly calm today and I missed his wild kicks. My daughter would distract me from this mess. Being with her would remind me of what was really important.

It took us a few minutes to wrangle Elizabeth into a jacket and shoes.

"I'm sorry, ma'am. She wouldn't nap. She seems determined to stay awake," Penny said, as Elizabeth threw her body backwards in protest of being zipped up.

"Stubborn girl," I murmured to her. "Just like your father."

When I finally had her bundled up enough for the cool spring day, David was grinning from the door.

"Don't laugh," I warned him. "I won't have any sympathy when it's your turn."

"I might be borrowing yours," he said, a shade of regret in his words.

"If you want to talk," I offered as we headed through the western wing toward the gardens.

"I feel like I could say the same."

"I don't feel like talking about it," I admitted, watching Elizabeth as she ran drunkenly ahead of us.

"Neither do I."

"New subject then?" I asked. David opened the doors and I scooped Elizabeth up and carried her down the stairs, plopping her down when we reached the grass.

"How are you feeling with the baby..." he trailed off. "Sorry, Edward told me. We don't keep secrets from each other. Hazard of marriage, I guess."

"How refreshing," I said dryly. "I'm fine. Honestly."

"We just want to help in any way we can. I know you haven't told Alexander. I won't ask you why," he added.

"Thank you." I could strangle Belle for telling Edward.

David thought for a moment. "How worried should I be about this meeting?"

I grimaced at the question. I'd been hoping to avoid what was going on behind Alexander's closed door. I opened my mouth and shut it again, not sure what to tell him.

"That bad, huh?" David gave a low whistle, which made Elizabeth clap. He smiled down at her. "What is it this time? Secret twin sisters in Sussex?"

"I wish," I muttered. It had been easier for us to forgive Alexander when he was struggling to come to terms with his father's secret child. This was entirely different. Alexander had known and he had kept it from us. I felt betrayed. I couldn't imagine how Edward would feel.

"Christ. Will this ever end?" David looked to the sky, shaking his head and Elizabeth mimicked him. The movement proved a bit too advanced, though, and she toppled head first into the grass. David picked her up before the crying got past the initial lip tremble.

"Thanks," I said, rubbing my stomach. The baby kicked me in greeting. "I don't think it will end."

"Too bad we're stuck for life." He grinned but it didn't light up his face like usual.

"Are we?" I asked absently.

"Ummm." His hesitation made me realize I'd actually said that aloud. "I guess not. Not like they are anyway, but... Clara, you're not actually..."

"Of course not." But my answer sounded forced, even to me.

"They're not easy men to love," David said in a quiet voice, "but isn't that why we love them?"

"I used to think that. I'm not sure anymore."

"I understand, Clara. I really do, but you and Alexander, you two have a love that only exists in poetry." David probably did understand better than anyone else what it was like to have your world upended by falling for a powerful man.

"That might be true, but poetry isn't real. It's only pretty words." Elizabeth reached out for me and I took her into my arms. She looked so much like her father with her dark hair and blue eyes. Her stubborn streak only cemented the similarities. Most days she was a beautiful reminder of our love. Today it physically hurt to look at her. I'd messed up. I'd pushed him too far. I'd destroyed us and she would pay the price for her parents' broken love.

"What did he do?" David finally asked. "What—"

The slam of a door interrupted us and we looked up to see Edward stomping toward us. Even across the gardens, I could see the anguish twisting his features.

"Oh God, what did he do?" David asked again as his husband strode up to us.

"We need to leave," Edward said in a clipped tone. He was looking across the lawns, but his eyes were trapped in the past.

"Edward, I'm so sorry. I didn't—"

"It's okay," he cut me off. "I'm not angry with you. He told me...he told me that you didn't know. I just can't be here right now."

He kissed Elizabeth on the forehead before grabbing David's hand. "We'll talk soon."

I nodded, not trusting myself to speak. I watched them leave, feeling a little piece of my heart slipping away. My family was crumbling all around me and I was powerless to stop it. I could only try to survive the fall.

CHAPTER 6

ALEXANDER

I dressed in the bathroom off my office, splashing my face with water in lieu of a shower. Shaving was trickier, but, unfortunately, a necessary evil today. A new suit had been delivered—one of Clara's favourites. I didn't ask who sent it. I suspected it was Norris, who would want to see me looking my best for today's press conference. I would have preferred it was my wife. But it wasn't as if making certain I had clean clothes was a sign that she'd reconsidered how she felt about me. I was a starving man searching for crumbs.

I'd considered sending her roses for our anniversary, but flowers weren't going to cut it this time.

As I opened the office door, I came face-to-face with Prime Minister Clark. His was the last face I felt like seeing this morning.

"Good morning," I said, feeling it was anything but. "I had no idea the Prime Minister attended press conferences."

Didn't he have more important things to do? Somehow, though, we were still locked in a battle over who was in control of this country. I'd hand it over to him in a heartbeat—if I thought he could handle it.

"I will not be attending, obviously," he said, as if the time and place for us to be seen together was definitely not a press conference. I couldn't agree more. "No, I wanted to speak with you about how you were going to handle it."

"Handle what?" I barely kept my voice even. If the news had leaked to Parliament there was no telling who else knew. I hadn't been made aware of the story spilling. Yet, here was the sodding prime minister come to advise me once again.

"I assume this has to do with the motion Parliament is considering." He glanced into the office as though he felt uncomfortable speaking of it in the open.

Relief washed over me. That was a problem for another day. I stepped to the side and beckoned him inside. Closing the door behind me, I chose my words carefully. "This is about another matter."

"The Sovereign Games? I should think a press release would do." He was needling me for information, but he wasn't going to get any.

I didn't need to see another disappointed face. Not before I was about to come clean to the world about my family secret. I also knew he'd make it worse by spouting off some fatherly bullshit that I didn't need or want to hear.

"It's a family matter." It was best to keep things as simple as possible. "I don't think I need to address the motion before Parliament. These types of legislation have been suggested before. They never gather steam and—"

"It's moving forward," he interrupted me, looking rather shocked that I hadn't heard.

"It won't continue past that." I sounded more sure than I

was. I'd made a few enemies in Parliament over the last couple of years. Since it had been discovered that I was holding one of their own on charges of treason there had been a sort of reverse witch hunt directed at me. Why, I couldn't fathom. I understood wanting to avoid suspicion, but this was something more. How many enemies had my father made inside Parliament that so many were now turning on the crown?

"You'll have to appeal to them," Clark advised. "You haven't done enough to court your father's allies and he had many of them in both the House of Commons and the House of Lords. If you want to retain your family's power, you're going to have to start playing the game, son."

"I thought the King was above games." I thought no such thing, but I enjoyed how Clark squirmed when I reminded him exactly who I was to this country—and him. Plus, he seemed to need the reminder.

Clark didn't squirm though, which was disappointing. "If your father had a fatal flaw, it was his arrogance. I'd hoped you wouldn't follow down the same path."

I bypassed the fact that the Prime Minister had just insulted me to my face, and did my best to shake off his comparison between me and my father. It was the last reminder I needed today. "If my father had a fatal flaw it was that he stepped in front of a bullet, Prime Minister."

"You don't seem to understand." He ignored the tasteless joke. "This motion would strip the majority of the powers the monarchy still holds. It would withdraw your right to declare war. It would significantly reduce your holdings and strip your family of a number of its estates. You would simply become a man living in a castle playing at being king."

"Better than a man who wishes he was King." I had no idea why I was pushing things so far with him. Maybe because I needed to get it out of my system. Maybe because I couldn't stomach one more person telling me that I was doing a shit job. None of them understood what was really at stake.

"Your father thought nothing could touch him, too. I suggest you remember what happened to him." He stood and straightened his jacket before walking out of the room and leaving me to my ghosts.

Not only was I running late, I was now in a foul mood. Rounding the corner, I took the private corridor that led between my offices and the state rooms. The press conference was being held in the white room where only a few weeks ago Clara had publicly announced her withdrawal as host of the Sovereign Games. At the rate we were hosting press conferences, we were going to have to rename the room.

Norris met me halfway there, looking unusually flustered. "I'm told the Prime Minister paid you visit."

"He was delivering a message," I said through a clenched jaw. My mood wasn't going to improve until I could let this go. "Or rather, a warning."

"Which was?" He pulled a handkerchief out of his pocket and wiped his brow. It wasn't like Norris to get this anxious. Then again, it wasn't every day that someone publicly came back from the dead.

"The measures limiting the monarch's power are moving to a vote."

"They won't pass without public approval," he said swiftly. I wasn't sure which one of us he was trying to make feel better.

"And he compared me to my father a bunch of times," I added.

Norris winced. If anyone understood how I would take that, it was him. Before my father married my mother, Norris had worked for him. Then, Norris was placed in charge of the family's security. I'd grown up under his watchful eye. More than once, I suspected he'd gone toe-to-toe with my father regarding his parenting choices. Norris had been more a source of guidance than he'd ever been.

"Tell me," I lowered my voice to a whisper. "Can I have someone killed?"

Norris's face went white before he realized I was joking. In fairness, my jokes were a bit off today.

"You wouldn't be the first King to do it," he said with a chuckle.

My mood was beginning to lift, but there was a ceiling on how far it could go. There always was, except for when I was with Clara. But I wasn't with her now. Not really. Not after she'd told me how she really felt.

"Will Clara be there?" I tried to sound casual.

Norris, who usually had no problem sticking his nose into my marriage, had been oddly silent the last few days. It was as though he—and everyone else—knew I'd finally gone and permanently broken my relationship with my wife. There had been no well-meaning lectures or attempts to force the two of us together. Deep down, I even knew it was him sending the suits to my office every morning. If Norris had given up, what hope was left?

"She's—" He stopped talking as Clara came into view.

Behind her, an entire press corps was waiting to discover the worst thing I'd ever done. The secret I never should have kept. But it didn't matter, because, right now, there was only her.

She was dressed in a blue that matched my mood. I would never get used to the sight of my wife. She was the most beautiful thing I'd ever seen. Delicate but strong. Fragile but unbreakable. We might be broken, but she never would be. She wasn't born a royal. She was born a queen.

Neither of us spoke, and Norris excused himself and ducked quietly into the white room.

"I didn't think you'd come." I had no right to expect anything of her. She'd made that clear.

Clara bit her lip, her lashes fluttering down for a moment, and I realized she was holding back frustration. "I'm always with you, Alexander, even when you think I'm not."

I extended one hand not certain she would take it. Clara laced her fingers through mine. It felt right to touch her. I kept this thought to myself, although I held her hand tightly.

"Ready?" she asked me softly.

"No." We walked through the door anyway.

Edward had already arrived and I was relieved to see him. I'd known better than to expect either my wife or brother to stand by my side while I faced the consequences of my father's decision. It was as much my mistake as his now, though. I'd agreed to it, coerced during my lowest point, but I had been a man when I'd continued my silence. I was as culpable as him.

Friendly chatter filled the room, none of the reporters aware of the scoop they were about to receive. It was best this way, having my family with me. It would lay to rest any speculation about troubles between us. Edward leaned over and kissed Clara on the cheek, whispering something I couldn't make out. Her soft laugh rewarded him and I felt a pang of jealousy. I couldn't remember the last time I'd made her laugh. All I received from my brother by way of greeting was a jerk of the head. It was a start.

Things would soon be different for all of us. One Royal, thought lost, had been found. I couldn't help but wonder what price we would pay for her return.

There were no table nor chairs set up for the event, but rather a podium. I wanted to keep this as brief as possible. There would be one million questions, and it wouldn't matter if I answered them all. Every paper from gossip rags to *The Times* was going to be reporting any information they could get their hands on—fact or fiction. We would sort out the truth later.

Clara's hand stayed in mine as I took the podium, my brother flanking me on the left. I paused a moment, allowing for conversations to die down before clearing my throat.

"I'm sure you're all wondering why we've called you here without any prior press release. There will be a handout distributed at the end covering a few important items. We will be limiting the number of questions we answer and we ask that you respect our family during this time. It is with equal parts joy and regret—" I paused, gathering the scraps of courage I had left after facing my wife and brother, before continuing "—that I must inform you that my sister, Sarah Cambridge, who was reported dead nearly ten years ago, has awoken from a comatose state and will be rejoining our family soon."

My words hit like anticipated. Instantly, the reporters were on their feet. Questions flew at me from every direction.

Cameras snapped. I'd been right to do this before we brought her home. This was my cross to bear.

One question rose above the others, coming from a dozen different directions: *why were we told she was dead?*

"If I may," I said loudly, holding up a hand and waiting for things to quiet to a dull roar. "Sarah's prognosis following the accident was hopeless. We were told there was no brain activity and that she would spend the rest of her life in a vegetative state. My father couldn't bear the thought of ever removing her from life support. Instead, he arranged for her to be attended by private physicians at a royal residence. She was not expected to ever wake up."

As soon as I stopped speaking, the questions started again.

Why lie about her death?

What was the cost of her life support? I was glad I didn't see who'd yelled that one out.

Will she make a full recovery?

I chose to answer this one. It would be better for them to hear it from me rather than have them try to hunt her down to ask. "Sarah's progress since awakening has been nothing short of miraculous. The doctors seem confident that she will make a full recovery. In the few weeks since she woke up, she has begun to talk again and to walk. As you can imagine, there has been a lot to catch her up on, which is another reason we ask for privacy for our family at this time."

I knew it didn't matter how many times I said it. There would be no privacy. There would be speculation. There would be rumours. There would be gossip. Ugly, terrible gossip. It was yet another thing I wish I could spare my family. I wanted to shield them, but there was no hiding from my mistakes.

A reporter called a question and I barely caught what he said. "Clara, were you made aware that Princess Sarah was alive?"

I knew my wife. I knew that her loyalty was unshakable. She was still holding my hand, so I didn't expect her answer. Clara didn't pull away, even as she abandoned me.

"I understand your surprise," she said, "because I didn't know, myself. Alexander never told me his secret."

CHAPTER 7

CLARA

I didn't stay for more questions. Instead, I fled to the Royal closet, the small room hidden near the White Room, which probably had a long and proud tradition of providing sanctuary to runaway queens. I made a mental note to avoid looking at any news source for the next twenty years. It would probably be that long before they stopped printing photos of me rushing out of the room.

I'd felt Alexander's pain the moment I'd spoken and I hadn't been able to stop myself from turning to see his stricken face. It was the second time in a week I'd wounded him with my words.

I couldn't seem to hold back whatever I was thinking. There were shades of truth in everything I said. We both knew it. But he didn't know why.

I couldn't keep lying. It was tearing me apart and I had no strength to fight it. Not while so much more was at stake.

The door to the room slammed shut and I jumped but didn't turn to face him.

"How could you?" he asked.

I'd expected the accusation, but it didn't make it any easier to face.

"Running off? Telling them..." he trailed away.

I spun to face him, blinking hot, angry tears from my eyes. "Telling them what? The truth? Sorry, X, I wasn't born and bred to lie."

"Unlike me." His face was a stony mask that even I couldn't see behind. It had been so long since he'd worn it in front of me that I forgot how breathtaking it was, like a great marble statue of an avenging angel brought to life. This was the man who had brought me to my knees. Now, he still had the same effect on me. But this wasn't the man I'd fallen in love with—the man I had married. That man had removed his mask. He'd put it back on and it was my fault.

"I don't expect you to understand," I said. He couldn't. Not when he was like this.

"Because you don't love me anymore," he spat.

"Of course I do!" The baby begin to kick and I was reminded that I needed to calm down. I rubbed my stomach comfortingly.

"But you hate me." His mask slipped for a second and I saw the confused pain he was hiding.

"Sometimes," I admitted in a quiet voice. "You're apart from everyone, even me. You have no idea how lonely it is to keep your husband's secrets knowing there will always be more. Because no matter how many of your secrets I keep, you'll never trust me with all of you. I can't do it anymore. I can't lie for you. I can't pretend we're a united front and risk losing Edward and everyone else. I can't tell a lie and let everyone believe I betrayed them, because they're all I have. I can't do this alone anymore. You forced my hand. You made me choose and I choose this family. I can't keep our family together if I'm trying to pretend everything is okay between us. We're not okay, X."

"You think you're alone?"

It was only a part of what I was trying to say, but at least he was listening. Finally. "I am. I can't be enough for everything that's missing anymore. I...I'm sorry. I can't."

His gaze drifted down to the hand rubbing my belly as he shook his head. His started to say something and then his mouth fell open.

"You aren't wearing your wedding ring," he said quietly.

I knew that. I felt its absence like I was walking around naked. "My fingers are swollen."

"Bullshit." His eyes were glued to the bare finger.

"Fine, I can't bear its weight lately. It used to stand for something and now..." I wanted to swallow the words back as I watched the beautiful, strong man before me crumble.

"You're carrying our child. You're my wife," he whispered, no longer speaking to me. Then his voice ratcheted up. "I told you. I warned you! You can't do this? You decide that now? I told you I couldn't do it. I told you I could never love you. I told you I didn't want children. I didn't want to get married."

His words were a slap in the face and I stumbled backwards a step.

He finally looked up at me, his blue eyes hollow. "Why did you give me everything I didn't want if you were only going to take it all away?"

"X, I—" But he cut me off.

"You should leave."

"Why? So you can sleep in your office? So I can go back

to a separate life in the North wing?" Tears poured down my face now, but I couldn't even find the strength to wipe them away.

"No," he said, his voice deadly even. "Here. Buckingham. London. *Me*."

"Alexander." I broke with his name on my lips.

"Leave," he repeated, but this time I heard it for what it was: a plea. "We know how this ends. We always knew, Clara."

"Where would I go? There's nowhere I could go."

"Take any of it. I'll make excuses." He ran a hand through his hair and my knees buckled. "It won't matter much longer, anyway."

I couldn't process what he meant. I couldn't process any of it. "It doesn't matter how far I go. Don't you see that? My life is your life. I gave it to you."

"And I am giving it back!" he shouted. He whipped around, turning his back to me. There was a moment of silence as his words settled around us and then his fist lashed out and went through the wall. He sank against it, his hand covered in plaster.

I couldn't breathe. It was as if all the air had been sucked from my lungs. I gulped desperately, falling to my knees, as the weight of what was happening hit me. My heart had been ripped from my chest and my hands pressed to the gaping wound. "Please," I gasped. "Please...I can't breathe."

Alexander was in front of me in what would be a heartbeat if I still had one. He knelt down, brushing tears from my face. "Poppet, inhale," he coached. "You are going to be fine. You are going to be better without...without me."

I shook my head against his words and grabbed his shirt,

afraid he would slip away. I couldn't do this. Not now. "Make me feel something else. Please, I need to feel something else. Please, X."

His lips were on mine in an instant, speaking a language only we knew. Maybe for the last time.

I knew then I would trade any of it for him. I would sell my very soul if it still belonged to me.

He pried my fingers free of his shirt, but before I could protest, he'd gathered me in his arms and lifted me to my knees. My arms tangled around his neck, drawing him back to me and he answered, cradling my head as he captured my mouth.

We were drowning together, each of us struggling for air and knowing it was a lost cause. There was no saving either of us now. It was too much to bear and I reached down, trying to find his belt past my stomach, but Alexander was faster. His fingers deftly undid it, releasing his cock. He grabbed my hips and urged me around.

"I'm afraid our options are limited," he said as he yanked my skirt to my hips.

"Take me," I begged, spreading my legs with the new freedom he'd given me. "Make me yours. Make me yours again."

I heard him shove his pants down and then an arm wrapped around me, guiding me over him. A grateful whimper rolled through me as I stretched over his cock.

"Shhh, easy," he murmured, his other arm snaking under my arm to press against my chest. It flattened over my heart, and I wondered if he felt how hard it was beating. "That's it, Poppet. I don't want to hurt you. Take it slowly."

Tears continued to fall as our bodies joined together. I

wanted to remember every inch of him, every brush of his skin against mine, every soft word from his lips. When I slid the final distance over him, a moan fell from me.

"You will always be mine," he whispered as he began to move inside me.

My hips joined him, moving in a hypnotic rhythm. I didn't want this to end. I didn't want to know what life was like on the other side of this moment.

"No matter where you are, Clara. There was only ever you. There will only ever be you." His lips pressed to the nape of my neck, sending shivers racing down my spine. "Let go."

His command carried me over the edge, shattering me as his next words destroyed me. "Let me go."

He held me until my trembling body stilled. I bit my lip, holding back the next barrage of tears that were making their way from my broken heart. When his hands lifted me away from him, I swallowed hard. He hadn't come. He hadn't claimed me. I knew then he'd given me up.

Alexander stood and reached down to help me to my feet. Bending down, he straightened my skirt, smoothing it with agonizing tenderness, his hand brushing over the place where our child grew. I caught it and pressed it there. The baby kicked and Alexander's eyes closed, his jaw tightening.

"I'm not leaving," I said softly. He could try to force me, but I was through taking orders. I was his, but he was mine, too.

His eyes stayed shut, his palm lingering on the swell of my stomach. He turned away, drawing his hand free slowly. "Yes, you will."

CHAPTER 8

ALEXANDER

The bourbon burned down my throat, but it didn't erase the pain. I poured another glass, wondering if a second one would. There was no way out of this situation. For years I carried my guilt like scars. With Sarah's return I should feel healed. I felt anything but. Without realizing it, I'd let her, and that night, go. Now she'd returned to exact innocent retribution.

It was never my place to forgive myself. Not knowing what I did. Not knowing the truth the whole time. Her life had been stolen from her. I'd failed to protect her and then I'd failed to stand by her.

For the first time in a long while, I wished my father was here. I'd accepted his order to keep silent that she was alive. After I'd returned home, we'd never spoken of it. I'd given my sister exactly two minutes of my time every month when Norris offered me an update on her condition. I'd abandoned her, and my punishment would be losing everyone I loved.

I'd become what I feared most. I'd become the man I hated—the man who'd put me in this goddamn impossible situation years ago. And the most terrifying reality was that I was nowhere near turning away from that path.

I understood secrets now. I understood how fear turned a man into something primal. I would do anything to protect my family—to protect Clara. I would hurt her again and again if that's what it took. There was no doubt in my mind. Every time I promised her that I would stop making decisions without her, I lied—and I was killing her. It had to stop.

She needed protection—from me.

"Drinking alone again?" Norris asked, entering my office.

Reaching over, I plucked a crystal glass from the tray some angel from the household staff had left me and poured another. "Not anymore."

He unbuttoned his suit jacket and took the drink without comment.

"No more lectures?" I asked. I wanted him to yell at me. I wanted someone to yell at me, so I wouldn't keep hearing Clara's broken sobs in my mind.

"You wouldn't listen anyway." He drank slowly like a man who wasn't trying to chase away ghosts.

"What's next?"

Norris raised an eyebrow. "Next?"

"On the list of messes I need to clean up." I would have thought it was obvious. I'd been setting fires everywhere I went for weeks.

"We will need to discuss your sister's return," he said carefully. "You told the press she would be coming home to London."

"I assumed she would be." I scratched the back of my neck.

"It won't be long," he informed me. "The medical reports

are astounding. The doctors have never seen anyone react this well after such a long vegetative state."

His information tickled at the back of my mind. If I'd been paying more attention to the reports, I might have seen this coming. I could have planned. Her body had been trying to wake up for a long time. "It's not normal?"

"She had the best specialists overseeing her care. One of them was using an experimental therapy to keep her muscles from atrophying," Norris explained. "It was your father's idea."

He'd never told me. Or maybe he had, and I hadn't been listening.

"Alexander," Norris called my attention back to him. "Her body may be strong, but it will take her longer to adjust to all the changes. Life has moved on without her. Are you certain bringing her here is the best option?"

"Where else would she go? You said it yourself. She left behind a life half-started. All she has now is here."

"Have you discussed it with Clara?" he asked, taking another studious sip of his bourbon.

"Don't ask stupid questions. It insults both of us," I snapped. "My wife and I aren't speaking. She's turned on me."

He inclined his head, narrowing his eyes to display a network of wrinkles. "You don't believe that."

"No," I said after a moment, "I don't."

"She's holding you accountable."

"Someone has to." But it wasn't what I wanted from her. I wanted her to remind me that I wasn't a lost cause. "I don't know what to do. I can't see past today. Every hour in front of me is a void. I haven't felt this since..."

I didn't have to finish the thought. Norris had been there during my darkest moments. He'd pulled me out of a private club nine years ago after I'd nearly killed Georgia Kincaid. He was the one who saw the truth. I wanted it to be me dying on the other end of a strap. He'd protested when my father had sent me to the warfront, but he'd put me on the plane all the same.

He couldn't send me away now. I had to face this.

"There are other matters." I took a drink, my throat suddenly dry. "She'll need a security detail. Brex?"

"He's keeping an eye on Anders," Norris reminded me.

I'd forgotten I'd assigned him to watch my bastard brother. It was mental to think that in the course of a few months, I'd gone from one brother to two and then topped it off with the return of my sister. It was worse to consider how much they all hated me. "I'm sure they're both enjoying that."

"Actually, they've become friends."

Of course they had. It was no use pretending that my issues with Anders had anything to do with him. Save for the fact that he'd tried to steal my wife, he seemed like an okay guy.

"Speak with him about it. We'll need to make a decision soon."

"There's also the next round of the Sovereign Games," Norris began.

"Sod the games." I had more important issues to worry about.

"You will need public opinion in your favour. Your grandmother and uncle will be returning to London to attend. It's an opportunity to show the Royal family is—"

"Not as fucked up as everyone assumes."

"United," he corrected me. "It's what you want. It's what your wife needs."

"I can't even see my wife," I murmured. "She's not here with me now."

"The only way to get out of the darkness is to move toward the light." He placed his glass on the desk, still half full.

"I can't see any light." Not without Clara, and she was going to leave. She had to, and I knew it. I had to be strong enough push her away, but I'd never been able to shut her out. I was addicted to her. Nothing would matter if she left.

"Keep looking, even for a speck. Follow it like the North Star and you'll find your way home."

"Where should I look?" I asked.

"Start where you found it before." Norris checked his watch, frowning at the hour. He stood and buttoned his jacket. "With your wife."

"I can't ask that of her. I can't—" I swallowed on the truth sitting like a lump in my throat "—keep hurting her and I will. I can't be the man that deserves her."

"Perhaps being the man that loves her is enough," he said gently.

"I don't know how to fix this."

"The only way to fix anything is to start. Your brother is angry as well. You've been making all the decisions without them. You will need each other more than ever. Don't make the decisions regarding Sarah without them," he said. "If you want your family you're going to have to fight for them, but might I suggest you start by talking to them?"

I grimaced, knowing exactly what he was proposing. "I guess it's time for another family meeting."

"Indeed." He picked up the bourbon and headed toward the door. "You have a country to rule."

And a family to win back.

It was harder to admit Norris was right when I received news that my grandmother and uncle would be returning to London the following afternoon. My grand-mother seemed to have a sixth sense for picking the worst fucking times to visit. Probably because she thrived on drama. I'd never made my mind up about Henry. My father's brother had been a fixture in my life as a child but I'd seen him very little since my return from Afghanistan. My grandmother had moved in with him after I'd become king, and he had taken my father's place in her life. It was no surprise that she had a leash on him, although he did have an unusual ability to keep her in line. I didn't relish either of them coming, though, especially with Norris's proposed family meeting scheduled for that evening. I couldn't risk calling it off. Not after getting both Edward and Clara to agree to come.

I'd just finished an unproductive call with one of the many MPs I needed to win back when Norris called.

"Yes," I answered.

"Your brother has arrived. He's gone to your private quarters."

I hung up and barked an order at the nearest assistant I saw to cancel my meetings for the rest of the day. The clock was ticking, and if I could deal with this before tonight's family reunion, all the better.

Norris met me at the end of the south corridor. "You hung up."

"I want to get this over with." I continued past him into our family's apartments only to stop when I saw the small gathering there. Edward was playing with Elizabeth on the floor while Henry and Clara watched. My grandmother was absorbed with something out the window, a sour expression turning her face.

She was the first one to spot me.

"How could you?" she called out. Every head in the room, even Elizabeth's, swiveled to stare at me.

"You didn't give me a chance to warn you that they arrived earlier," Norris said under his breath. He clapped a hand on my shoulder for a second and took his leave. Apparently, I was to face the firing squad alone.

"And in a mood," I muttered. I plastered a false smile on my face and moved to greet them. "Welcome."

I stopped myself from adding *home*. The last thing I needed was my grandmother hearing a perceived invitation to move back into the palace.

"You gave us no warning you would be holding that infernal press conference," Mary launched into her rant. "We were forced to come early to avoid the press."

"I am sorry," I said tightly. Weighing my options, I decided to get this family meeting over with, regardless of their presence. Neither my wife nor brother had rushed to acknowledge my arrival. In fact, Edward had joined Clara across the room. He'd picked his side: Team Queen.

Had she spoken with him? Had they planned to confront me?

I shook the thoughts from my minds. It didn't matter.

"And then there's the matter of your father's bastard. You told him." Mary cast a poisoned glare in Clara's direction. "What will we do when he goes to the press?"

"He won't," Clara and I said together.

"Let's deal with one thing at a time," I said. Clara finally looked at me, the sharp edge of disapproval in her eyes. I'd always thought they were the color of the sea on a cloudy day. Now they were a storm.

I decided to change my tone. "I need to speak with all of you, anyway. I came as soon as Norris told me you were here."

Edward rolled his eyes and shot Clara a frown. It was going to take a lot to convince them I was capable of reform, especially since I wasn't so sure I was, either.

"I made an assumption that Sarah should return home—that she would want to—but I should have discussed it with you." I forced myself to add, "With all of you."

I didn't give two fucks what half the people in this room thought, but saying so wouldn't endear me to the ones I did care about.

"I'm not sure that's for the best." Mary sniffed. "Perhaps, she should stay with us for a time to acclimate."

"Mother, we discussed this," Henry broke in. "We will be in London for a few weeks. The doctors say she is asking to see her family."

"You're receiving reports from the doctors?" Edward asked him while glaring at me.

I held out my hands wondering if there was any point in telling him that this was news to me as well.

"Of course we are," Mary said. "We've always been kept

informed of her care. The reports were more regular from Albert, though."

So much for digging myself out of this hole. My family had arrived with shovels to bury me deeper. And who was keeping them in the loop? I made a mental note to discuss it with Norris. I imagined it was some policy established before my father's death. If I'd known...

"Where would she stay?" Edward asked. "I suppose there's room at Clarence House."

He looked green even thinking about it. At first, I couldn't understand why. Then I remembered how young he'd been when Sarah had left. He barely knew her.

"You're newlyweds." Clara placed a hand on his arm. "Sarah lived here?"

I didn't miss the accusation in the question. She knew very well that Sarah had lived here until the accident, but she wasn't going to miss the chance to rub my nose in shit.

"This was her home."

"She can't come here." Mary looked around like we were in the middle of a shack.

"There are nearly eight hundred rooms in this house," Clara said dryly. "We can find room."

I fell in love with her a little bit more. Few people would stand up to Mary. Mary herself made it her mission to condescend to my wife at every opportunity. Clara no longer took any of it.

Then, I remembered that while I was falling in love, my wife had accepted a life of duty that no longer included feeling the same about me. My jaw clenched as I considered this, only partially aware of the bickering that had broken out between the group surrounding me.

Democracy was getting us nowhere. I should have stuck with being a king. "Enough. Sarah will come here. Clara?"

It was a statement to everyone else, but a question for Clara. Our eyes locked together, everyone else fading away. She could overrule me. She had that power, and she needed to know it. Norris was right. I might not deserve Clara, but I needed her. And I wasn't going to win her back by dealing her out. She had to have equal say.

"Sarah will come home," she repeated, changing the final word.

It was a little thing to notice—that simple word change. This was still Clara's home—our home. But I saw it for what it was: a tiny speck of light blinking at the edge of my darkness.

CHAPTER 9

CLARA

Sarah's room was practically a time capsule. I was surprised to find no dust when I drew back the curtains. Light slanted across a room that time might have forgotten but housekeeping had not. It was then I realized that Albert had never given up hope. He'd kept her bedroom ready, as if she might walk into it at any moment.

A copy of *Twilight* sat on her bedside table next to a long-dead mobile phone. Would she come looking for these things? She'd gone away a girl and she was coming back a woman who'd missed ten years. As far as I knew, Sarah had never fallen in love. She hadn't gone to college. She'd missed her brothers' weddings. Life had moved on without her. She was as frozen in time as her room.

I'd never come here before. It felt like a violation. Now it was up to me to prepare it for her return, but I didn't know where to start. I sat on the bed and stared at the remnants of the lost girl, feeling a strange kinship.

Except it wasn't the last ten years I'd lost, it was the present. I was going through the motions, caught in an endless cycle of doing as I was told and having the rug pulled out from under me. I understood feeling powerless. I didn't know Sarah. I actually knew very little about her. I'd always been hesitant to bring her up to Alexander and Edward. I regretted that now.

Was she the type of girl who wanted to pretend like nothing had happened? Would she walk back into this room and pick up where she'd left off? Or would being reminded of that stolen time sting and burn? I was an expert at pretending to pick up where I left off and that was getting me nowhere.

Taking out my mobile, I made a call.

"God, I haven't been here in years." Edward surveyed the room in wonder. "I snuck in after...after she died. I mean, after the accident."

"I think it's going to take us all a while to get used to her being back. I didn't know if calling you for help was the right thing to do, but I can't bring Alexander here. He blames himself for all of it—the cover-up and the lies. I can't make him face this," I explained.

"I want to help." Edward sat beside me and wrapped an arm around my shoulder. "But he is to blame. At least partially."

"I know that. I do, truly," I said when he made a clucking sound.

"Do you?"

"Yes, and he has to be held accountable, but he also has to be forgiven," I said softly. I'd seen the darkness growing in Alexander, threatening to consume him. It had been foolish to believe we'd vanquished it. Darkness was part of him—it drew me to him—and I was always waiting for the gates to open and let it through.

"I don't know if I can." Edward hung his head in shame. "I don't know how you can, either."

"If I stopped forgiving Alexander I wouldn't be able to look at him. It's part of the whole marriage package."

"I heard you two yelling after the press conference," Edward confessed, turning to study me. "I heard him tell you to leave. I thought about coming in, but..."

My throat slid as I considered what to say. I was glad he hadn't. That afternoon had been the first time I'd been with my husband in weeks. For the last few nights, I'd had to come to accept that it might have been the last time I would ever be with him again.

"I can't talk about that." The words came out as broken as I felt. "I'm sorry."

"I understand," he said quickly, his curiosity shifting to worry. He lifted his arms from my shoulder and pushed his glasses up the bridge of his nose. "But you know he doesn't want you to leave."

"I'm not so sure." Trying to figure out what Alexander wanted was like trying to fit two different puzzles together. Every time I thought I knew who he was, I'd turn over a piece to discover that it didn't fit.

"That's not what's really important. Do *you* want to leave?"

"No. Yes. I don't know." I cradled my baby bump and willed myself not to cry. It seemed like I should have run out of tears by now.

"I'm sorry. You said to drop it." Edward jumped to his feet and forced a smile, but it wasn't his boyish grin. The fun and games were over. There were no parties or private shopping dates. Even lunch out was impossible. The paparazzi had been insufferable since his wedding. I couldn't imagine how vicious they would be now. We'd blinked and our whole lives had changed.

"I thought we should get her room ready." I decided to take his cue and focus on why I'd asked him to come over. "But I have no idea where to start. It's clean. These are her things."

"But will she want any of them?" he asked, echoing my thoughts from earlier.

"I wouldn't," I said and his eyes flashed to me. "I've been thinking about it. I would feel trapped in a life that wasn't really mine, but..."

"She's not you," he finished for me.

"I knew you'd understand my predicament." I sighed with relief.

"So you called your GBFF." He turned in a circle, a frown on his face.

"My GB-what?" I asked.

"Gay best friend forever. Every fabulous woman needs one." His mouth twisted into a smirk. It wasn't his usual grin, but it was something. I'd take whatever scraps of humor I could find.

"Am I a fabulous woman?" I asked with a much-needed giggle.

"Hello! You're the *Queen of England*," he said. "You are the definition of fabulous."

I shook my head, wishing I could believe it. Being in here only reminded me that most of the time I felt like a fraud. "What if she hates me?"

"What if she hates *me*?" he repeated.

"You're her brother."

"That's no guarantee. My father hated me," Edward pointed out.

"Your father loved you," I said softly. Sitting here, I realized how much he had loved his children. I had to assume he hadn't reserved all his affection for his daughter. "I think this room proves that. He couldn't let her go."

"Maybe he should have," Edward said. "Clara, I-I feel angry. About Anders. About Sarah. My father changed all of our lives without a thought to how any of us would feel about it."

My feelings on Albert were beyond complicated. He'd stepped in front of a bullet to save his son's life. He'd treated me cruelly, but he'd given me a future. Death had taken him before I could ever know him, and now I never would. That was hard enough for me. I couldn't fathom what it was like for his children.

"I want to meet him," Edward's announcement called me from my thoughts.

"Who?" I asked, wondering what I'd missed.

"Anders."

"You have." I studied him for signs of a stroke. I'd been there on multiple occasions where both had been present. At least one of which that had been truly unforgettable.

"As my brother, not as a stranger," he said, pacing across the room. He got to the other side and turned back to do another loop, his hands behind his back. "But he..."

"Doesn't want anything to do with us?" I guessed. Edward nodded. "Give him time."

"Time doesn't fix everything." His eyes flickered around the room as if it was concrete proof of that.

"No, it doesn't, but he'll come around." I'd gotten to know Anderson Stone a little before Alexander's revelation had screwed everything up. He would probably never get along with Alexander—the two of them were too similar—but there was a better than decent chance he would give Edward a shot.

"I don't know how else to move past this." Edward paused at the window. "I'm so angry with my father. I had more family, and it's not just that he kept them from me, but that he let sadness take over his life."

"Losing a wife and a child..." I shook my head. I couldn't even fathom carrying that loss with me. I could barely handle this trouble keeping me from Alexander. It felt like my heart had been taken out of my body and locked up somewhere I would never find it. "If it came to that for me..." I stopped, realization crashing through me. "If it comes to that, I don't know what I'll become."

"You will never be like that," Edward said fiercely, lording over me in a way that made him look more like his older brother than usual.

"You don't know that." He couldn't. No one could. Not even me. "If Alexander makes me leave. If the baby..." I couldn't even say the words. My eyes found the floor, unable to look at him. How would I face it if the baby's heart couldn't be fixed?

"I do know." Edward dropped to the floor in front of me, his hand lifting my chin so I couldn't avoid him. "That won't ever happen to you because I won't let it. Belle won't let it. No matter what happens, we will be here."

They wouldn't let me fade away. They wouldn't let my heart turn as black and hopeless as Albert's had. I had best friends and they would be here to love me through it.

"You have to be that for Alexander, too," I said in a soft voice.

"I don't know if I can," he said with a sigh.

"Yes, you can. He's your brother and we can't let him become..." I couldn't even say it. What would it take to turn Alexander into his father? Had he already?

"Then, we won't," Edward promised. He pushed to his feet and held out a hand. "Come on. Let's get out of here."

"But I still don't know what to do with her room." I let him help me since getting to my feet was becoming a bit more of a task these days.

"Leave it," he said.

"But—"

"There are, what, a million rooms in this place?" He said. "You don't want her on the same floor as you two. You'll scar her with all the noise you two make."

"Hey!" I smacked him on the shoulder.

"I speak only truth." He held up his hand. "You two are like animals. It gives the rest of us inferiority complexes. Besides, I've been dying to burn down my grandmother's suite for years."

I raised an eyebrow.

"I'll settle for redecorating it," he reassured me. "It will give her space and piss Queen Mother Mary off."

"So it's a win-win?"

This time his answering smile was blinding. "Isn't diplomacy fun?"

CHAPTER 10

ALEXANDER

The new secretary was a nervous thing, scampering in and out of the offices like a lost mouse. Patience took effort, but since Norris recently told me off for scaring away household staff, I was doing my best. "Yes?"

"Your Majesty, it's the Prime Minister." She dipped into a curtsy, a habit she seemed to be forming.

"You don't really have to do that every time..." I waved my hand, realizing it was a lost cause to tell her otherwise. "Take a message."

"He's quite insistent," she continued, twisting her hands together as if torn between telling the Prime Minister no and questioning my authority.

"Take a message," I repeated through a clenched jaw.

"He did say it's the third time he's tried to reach you —"

"Take a message!" I roared.

She scuttled out of the room, throwing terrified glances back at me.

"There goes another one," Norris commented as he came

inside and shut the door. "We've posted more job openings in the last two months than the last two years."

"They don't listen." I settled back in my chair. Maybe it was something wrong with me. My staff didn't listen. Parliament didn't listen. My wife didn't listen. I was the common denominator. "I have wondered if we need so many people working here."

"You've been thinking," Norris said. "That's never a good thing."

"Would you prefer I didn't?"

"Not about the household staff. You have more important things to focus on."

"I looked over your security proposal. There's only one thing missing." Norris had drawn up a plan to minimize press interference when Sarah moved from Windmoor House to London. There was no way to avoid it completely, but my old friend had a knack for sneaking people in and out of buildings. It'd been a particularly useful skill when I was hiding my relationship with Clara. Now I wanted to see my sister safely home. Times had changed.

"What did I overlook?" He leaned over my desk, peering down at the memo I'd been reading minutes before.

"Me."

"That will require more skill than I have." Norris straightened, crossing his hands behind his back. "It will be impossible to sneak you out of London. The press are practically pitching tents at the exits."

"I don't care. She's been up there, mostly alone, since she woke up. She should have someone in her family by her side when she returns home." I'd stayed away—to protect her—as long as possible before the announcement. Visiting Windsor without official business would have caught the attention of the press. It was yet another thing I would have to apologize for. Sarah had been briefed on most of the major changes in her family's lives. She knew our father was dead. She knew I had a wife and child. She knew Edward had married. But knowing and confronting were two entirely different experiences. She shouldn't have to walk through the doors of her home by herself. It was still a lot to ask of Norris, so I thought it prudent to add, "Please."

Norris sighed and I knew I'd won. "I will need to redraw this. It will likely take me another few days to get the necessary security procedures in place and plan the timing of it."

He reached for the memo as the door to my office burst open. We both looked up, startled, before immediately moving into defensive positions. Norris stepped in front of me across the desk even as I rose to my feet, but the intruder was a friendly face—most of the time.

People rarely asked me about my time in Afghanistan. I'd taken a new role as King and that was all they saw. But even in a suit, Brex was a soldier. He still cropped his hair close to his head. The gun he carried in a holster was visible through his jacket. He never tried to hide who he was. It made him the perfect asset to my security team. That's when I remembered that he shouldn't be here.

"Why aren't you at Windsor?" I barked. He'd been reassigned from Silverstone and my illegitimate brother to head of Sarah's security detail. The move had raised a few eyebrows internally. Brex was a notorious ladies man, and Sarah? Well, Sarah hadn't seen a man in ten years. I could only hope her taste still skewed towards boy bands and not ex-military. Regardless, I knew I could trust Brex. He would never betray me by making a move on my sister. Plus, his heart was already spoken for, even if the woman in question didn't return his feelings.

"I'm not needed in Windsor," he said testily.

"Like hell you aren't." I rounded my desk, halfway to the door before Brex called out.

"You might want to hear what I have to say before you go running off to her."

"I don't have time for this." I whipped around to face him. "She shouldn't be left alone."

"Don't worry. She's got half the staff kneeling before her already," Brex said dryly.

"What is that, five people?" I snapped. We kept a skeleton staff at Windsmoor. It was difficult to ascertain who could be trusted with such a delicate secret.

"I think your staff is a little bigger here."

It took a moment for what he was saying to sink in, but when it did, my head fell back and I released a frustrated groan. "How could you?"

"Have you met your sister?"

My head swiveled to glare at him. "We haven't spent much time together lately."

"I don't know what she was like before," Brex said, stuffing his hands in his pockets, "but she's more demanding than you are."

"That hardly matters, since I'm your boss."

Norris cleared his throat meaningfully. I turned my glare on him and realized I was in danger of losing another staff member—and I couldn't afford to have Brex walk from this job.

It was a lost cause. I'd wondered what the Sarah who

woke up would be like and here was my answer. The same. No, she wouldn't be exactly the same. She would struggle with everything that had happened. But now? Why would she have changed? To her, she'd fallen asleep and woken up ten years later. From the sound of it, she was still the same bratty hellion I'd dragged out of the club that night.

"I just came to tell you that I delivered your precious sister safely and to ask for reassignment," he tacked on.

"I'll look into it. Who do you suggest? Georgia?" I called his bluff. We both knew Georgia would eat Sarah alive—if Sarah didn't get her first.

"If you two are done with your pissing contest, might I make an observation?" Norris broke in.

"Oh, but Poor Boy and I are just getting started." Brex's laugh was always easy, much like the rest of him. He was already over our squabble. "We were just about to get out a yardstick."

"I'm sorry to put a stop to that." His mouth only twitched slightly before he looked to me. "But if Sarah is here, might it be prudent to warn your wife?"

"Fuck." I stomped out the door and the mousy secretary dropped a stack of papers. I didn't even apologize.

I'd overlooked a number of things about bringing Sarah home. While I'd been concerned with getting her here safely, I'd never considered what I would do *when* she got here. Clara agreed that Sarah should come back to Buckingham, but to where *in* Buckingham? Her old room was down the hall from the quarters my family currently occupied. There were other concerns, as well. What would she wear? Should she go back to school? Now that she was here, it was real. Sarah was back. But what exactly did that mean?

Brex and Norris followed behind me, nearly matching my pace. They didn't have quite the same incentive I did to prevent a spontaneous meeting between my wife and my sister. It was something I'd planned to control. Now that was out of my hands, too.

Sarah had barely spoken the day Clara had found her at Windsmoor House. She's been as confused as my wife. Now that they both knew everything, the dynamics were likely to be a little different.

"By the way, Poor Boy, now would be a good time to tell me if you have any other dead family members stashed away," Brex called from behind me.

"Brexton," Norris said his name sharply.

"What? I'd like a little warning if his dad is going to come bursting through those doors next."

"There's no one else." I stopped in my tracks, realizing I'd made another blunder as the two caught up with me.

"I just think it's best to keep me in the loop on these matters." Brex masked pain well, but I'd known him long enough to see past it. I trusted him with the secret about Anderson. I'd made him head of my family's security when I'd moved Norris to my primary advisor. Why hadn't I shared this?

It was the same reason I hadn't told Clara. Shame. Guilt. I'd wanted to let that night go, but I never really had—or else I would have been honest with them. I couldn't do much about it now. "I'm sorry."

"I suppose you didn't tell your wife, either, or so she said to the press, which seems like a pretty good punishment for your cock up." He shrugged as if this was some comfort. "But, seriously, I need to know about these things. I should have been overseeing the security there."

Would it have happened differently if he had? Would Clara have ever found her way there? Would I have been given warning my sister had woken up in time to come clean? Did it matter?

It wouldn't have mattered. Besides, there was no point entertaining hypotheticals. I had real problems to deal with, and I smelled a shit storm brewing.

"Where did you leave her, exactly?" I asked.

"She went straight to the North wing," Brex told me. "She headed home."

"Christ." I started again, speeding my way toward inevitable disaster.

"Don't have a coronary. Clara and Elizabeth are out for a walk," Brex said, moving alongside me.

"Walks don't last forever," I said through gritted teeth.

"I know you wanted to be there when she got home. But what's the big deal? It's not like she doesn't know the place."

"She *doesn't* know the place," I reminded him. "Or my wife. Or my daughter. You said it yourself: have you met her?"

In my mother's absence, Sarah had been queen of the castle. Now, there was a new queen. I didn't have a clue what to expect when their paths crossed.

Then there was the matter of Clara. I was trying to be more open with her. I was trying to include her in decision-making. If my sister showed up in our front parlour, it was going to look like I'd failed again.

"I'm sure everything's fine," Brex said hurriedly, but now he was moving even faster than me.

I walked into my living room and I stopped the moment I saw her. In the hospital bed, she'd been so small and so pale. Her hair had hung around her shoulders as limp and lifeless as her last ten years. She had aged into someone unrecognizable. That wasn't the woman waiting for me now.

She looked exactly like our mother.

I shook my head, trying to process what I was seeing. My mother was a beautiful woman. Her Greek heritage had combined with my father's traditional British looks to create something entirely different in Edward and me. But where we shared a mixture of our parents' traits, Sarah was all our mother. Her dark hair swung around her shoulders, setting off her olive skin and dark eyes. Despite years of being in a hospital bed, she had the full figure of a woman. I'd expected a girl to come home. Only now did it occur to me how unprepared I was.

"Hello, brother," she said. She lounged back, legs crossed, and spread her arms over the back of the sofa with the air of a queen greeting her court. "I'm home."

CHAPTER 11

CLARA

After I finished my walk, I discovered my living room wasn't empty. The doctor suggested I take a "calming walk" when I felt stressed. I'd walked the better part of a marathon around the grounds over the last few days. As soon as I entered the room, I nearly turned around and headed back out for another lap. My pulse sped up as I took in the scene before me. Elizabeth squirmed out of my arms when she saw her father. I let her go without thinking. She toddled over to him and raised her hands in the air. Alexander picked her up, his eyes watching me the whole time.

"Clara," he said in an unusually calm voice, "meet my sister, Sarah. Sarah, meet–"

"Oh, we've met," Sarah simpered with a smile that didn't quite reach her eyes.

Until now, I thought she might not remember the day I found her in Windsor. It was a stupid wish. I'd sat there that day without telling her who I was, and then I'd kept my silence while my husband figured out how to deal with the fallout. But the bomb had finally fallen and she was here. She didn't seem the least bit aware of the rubble surrounding her. No—she seemed to be enjoying herself.

Her eyes scanned over Elizabeth, narrowing into catlike slits. "And this is your child."

It wasn't a question. She'd been updated on major events in her family's lives. Now, it would be up to us to find the blanks and fill them in. I'd imagined what she'd be like when she returned. I questioned how she would handle the world moving on without her. But seeing her obvious animosity, I had to remind myself that she had every right to be angry and frustrated and annoyed. The Sarah I'd painted in my mind wasn't a real person. She was a portrait drawn from memories Alexander and Edward had shared over the years. I remembered her accident and had been horrified like the rest of the world. But I hadn't exactly been a Royal watcher then. It felt morbid to watch media coverage and see photos of the mangled car plastered on newspapers. At the time, I'd been recovering from my first battle with an eating disorder, and I'd turned away from the news, looking for brighter spots in the world. It was like I had known then that it was different for me somehow, as if I'd had a premonition of what this family would come to mean to me. Instead of devouring details about them, I'd somehow known to wait until it was my time. All of which meant I knew very little about the girl in front of me.

And she was a girl. I didn't doubt that. She looked like a woman. She was gorgeous—the feminine equivalent of her brothers. But where Alexander was strong, sharp angles, she was soft and willowy. She looked like photos I'd seen of their mother. Still, she wasn't a woman. She'd missed the moments that would carry her into womanhood. Was she aware of it yet?

Sarah was born a Royal, so she had an armor she wore at all times. I saw it shrouding her. It was reminded me of when I'd met her brothers. To most, Alexander had hidden behind the cocky playboy reputation the world had assigned him and shown very little to anyone else. It had taken a lot to chip away his shell. Edward was the charming spare to the heir. They'd been hiding so many secrets for so long, both of them were more comfortable with illusion than reality. But they'd had the opportunity to grow into themselves. Sometimes, I saw them slip into that comfortable, old skin. Sometimes, it was easier for all of us to take a place on the board—the solitary King, the protective Queen, the loyal knight—than to face the truth that our true enemies weren't opposite us, but inside us all along.

"We have a room ready for you—Edward and I," I blurted, unable to stop the nervous chatter. "Or you can use your old room. We left it the way it was."

"Like a tomb?" She laughed, as if this was a ridiculous notion, but she stood up immediately. "This I have to see."

I left Alexander holding Elizabeth, looking to Norris and Brex for guidance, and followed her down the hallway to the room at its end.

"You weren't joking." She stepped inside and looked around. "I never thought I'd be back here."

"Were you...did you..." I didn't know how to ask what I was wondering. She spoke like time had passed. I'd wondered if it would be like coming home after a long night out. "I was in a coma—only for a few days—but I heard some of what was going on around me. Was it like that for you?"

"I guess we have something in common." She looked at me as though she was seeing me for the first time. "Something like that, I guess."

I wanted to ask more questions, but I held them back, staying near the door to give her some privacy. She walked to her bedside table and picked up her mobile. "Do you think my boyfriend's number has changed?"

I searched for an answer, wondering if I should laugh or comfort her.

"Relax." She rolled her eyes and dropped it. "I mean, I'm fantastic in bed, but I doubt he waited around." Her gaze fell on the book and she grabbed it, thumbing through until she reached a bookmark. "Does she wind up with the vampire or the werewolf?"

"Um, the vampire, I think." I couldn't believe we were having this conversation.

"That's a shame." She set it down and grimaced as she surveyed the space. "For fuck's sake, clear this out. I don't have to sleep here, right?"

"No, we have a space for you upstairs." I bit my lip. "I thought you might want some space."

"I wouldn't want to disturb your happy little family." She continued to act cool but her words sliced through me, cutting with a sharpness that I barely felt until air hit the wound.

"I'll show you."

Edward and I had spent the last few days sending off for fresh bedding and curtains. We'd settled on a blush color scheme that left the suite feeling light and open. It was neutral enough that she could add her own touches—if she decided to stay.

"I hope you like it. Edward thought you'd want light after..." I trailed away. Maybe I should have kept our reasoning to myself.

"Thanks." But she sounded anything but grateful. "It's cool if I change it, right? I'm rather accustomed to something darker."

"Of c-c-course," I stammered. "Whatever you want."

"You're sweet," she said, and I felt her making a mental note.

She thought I was sweet. She thought she could use that. She didn't know there was a lot more to me than that—yet.

Alexander joined us, passing Elizabeth to me when she held her arms out.

"I can't get over how weird it is to see you as a dad." Instead of sounding amused, she seemed disturbed. Something was off. Sarah's physical recovery might have been miraculous, but she had a long way to go before she was okay again.

"Thanks." Alexander grinned, completely unaware of the strange undercurrent to her behavior. "Do you like your room?"

She shrugged. "It's fine. Not like I'll stay. I'm old now. Don't you have to gift me a house or something?"

"One step at a time," he suggested. "Will you stay for dinner tonight?"

"I assumed I was. I invited a friend," she said, flashing her teeth. "I hope that's okay."

My eyes flickered to my husband as I set my shoulders and forced a benevolent nod. "Any friend of yours..."

. . .

AFTER PUTTING ELIZABETH DOWN FOR A NAP, I SOUGHT the sanctuary of my bedroom. I was flustered, completely overwhelmed by Sarah's sudden appearance, but if I was being honest, being around Alexander had more to do with how wound up I felt. He'd avoided our family's private quarters entirely since I'd agreed to let Sarah come home. For all I knew, he'd taken up residence in another wing of the palace. Seeing him had its usual effect. It was hard to be strong and gracious and *fucking regal* when the person who made my knees buckle was in the room.

"I'm sorry." His smooth voice startled me, and I whirled around to see him sitting in a chair by the fireplace. The curtains were drawn against the afternoon light, and Alexander had found the shadows in the corner—his natural habitat.

"For what? Scaring the shit out of me?" I rubbed my chest, sliding my hand down to soothe the baby who'd begun to kick with annoyance at being woken so rudely.

Alexander leaned forward, half his face coming into the light. He frowned and shook his head. "For springing this on you. I didn't know she was coming."

"No shit, Sherlock." I leaned against the wall while I waited for my heart to settle. Then I realized it wouldn't — not with him here. That was what he did to me. Sometimes, he didn't have to be present at all. I might catch a hint of bergamot or cloves in the air and find my body aching for him, recalling how his skin smelled when it was against mine.

"You're not mad." There was strangled relief in his tone. He stood, backing slowly toward the door. "I'll leave, then."

"Don't," I said suddenly, then bit my lip, feeling a bit too needy.

He froze in place and we studied each other for a moment. It was there in the space between us—a spectrum of feelings: anger and fear and hope and want. It only had one name: love.

"Have you thought..." he began slowly, clearing his throat and starting over. "Have you thought more about what I suggested?"

"Does your whole family speak in riddles? I already had to put up with the Cheshire Cat for twenty minutes. What are you talking about?" This was going well so far. We'd barely begun speaking to each other and we were already fighting.

He crossed his arms over his broad chest and my eyes zeroed in on how the seams of his jacket strained against his muscles. Nothing could contain him. He was more powerful than anyone or anything on earth. I could never resist him and I was getting tired of trying.

"I looked," he continued with some hesitation, "into our family estates. There are several within an hour that would suit you and Elizabeth. Some are more up to date than others..."

My heart plummeted, reminding me painfully that it was still there, splintered and in pieces. Every time I thought we were past this, I was proven wrong. I'd opened myself to him the day he'd told me to leave, showing him what that thought did to me. I'd thought he had seen that it was impossible—that we had to find a way through this together. Then, he left the room, telling me otherwise and leaving me confused again. When he'd included me on the decision about Sarah, I'd thought...

Maybe it wasn't a rational thought at all, but stupid, blind hope. I'd once clung to hope. I'd believed it was an inexhaustible resource but now my supply was dwindling. Soon there would be none left at all.

"Stop," I whispered as he continued with his plans. By some miracle, he heard me.

"We need to discuss this. The baby will be here soon. You should be settled, be—"

"I don't want to talk about this. I don't want to leave."

"You want to leave. You don't. You want to talk. You don't. What do you want, Clara?" he demanded.

"I don't know. I'm stressed and pregnant and horny—" I tried to swallow back this last confession but it was out of my mouth. I hid my face in my hands. How could I be embarrassed to admit that to a man who'd memorized every inch of my body?

"You're..." I heard the strain in his tone as he processed this. When I finally dared to look at him, he stepped back into the shadows. After a moment in which he didn't speak and I prayed I was about to wake up from this humiliating nightmare, he turned to the chair. With deliberate movements, he slid his jacket from his shoulders and laid it over the chair back. It was dim in the room, but I'd watched him do this a hundred times. He unknotted his tie and slid it free from his collar. He dropped it onto the abandoned suit coat. Then, he walked toward the nightstand, popping his cufflinks free one at a time.

"What are you doing?" I knew, but suddenly I wondered if I was dreaming.

He stalked toward me, unbuttoning his shirt as he came nearer, then tossing it to the floor.

"I can't take care of everything. I can't answer all your questions, but I can take care of that."

"I didn't mean..." I shook my head as my thoughts began to swim with the heady rush of his nearness.

"Shhh. This is what we're good at, Poppet." He drew his index finger down along my cheek, tracing my mouth and plucking my lower lip slightly. My mouth opened with expectation. "Tell me what you need. I can take care of you."

In that simple, self-assured statement I heard what he was really saying. He needed this, too. He needed to show me he loved me the only way he thought he could. As much as I needed this, he needed something more from me. We needed each other. And maybe we were slipping into an old cycle, but I was tired of fighting it. The last time we'd been together, on the floor, it had been short and desperate. It'd been over too soon. I needed more. He needed more.

"I want to be what you need—in every way," I added softly, feeling suddenly shy.

He stepped away, his eyes flashing on the surface with concern, but I saw what ran beneath it, unrestrained and dark. He'd been holding himself back for weeks. Maybe longer. We'd grown comfortable with our lovemaking. It had been too long since either of us had pushed the boundaries.

"Clara, I don't need—"

"I do," I cut him off. "I thought I needed to feel something other than this dull ache or this anger. Now I know what I really need, X. Release me."

"I won't take advantage of you." He shook his head, but I could see the war raging behind those words.

"I'm giving myself to you. No lovemaking. No angry sex. No hiding. Take me into the darkness, X. I'm not afraid." I brushed my hand down his face and he caught it. "No safe words. No lines. We're past that."

"You don't know what you're asking." His blue eyes were haunted as he studied me.

"Yes, I do. I'm asking you to take control for a few minutes so I can have peace. I want to feel what only you make me feel. I want to be owned. I want to be your every fucking fantasy." It was a dizzying revelation, even to me. There had been moments when he'd taken me to a place with nothing but sensation and sound and ache and want and freedom. A place that existed beyond pain and pleasure. A place only we could find.

"Fuck, Poppet." His mouth met mine with a groan and we devoured each other. He pulled away, breathless, and tipped my chin up so my eyes met his, clearer and brighter than I'd ever seen them. "I'll still stop if you ask me."

"I won't," I promised.

"The only problem is that you're still dressed," he said in a low voice that made my core clench.

"What about you?" I asked, reaching for his pants, but he slapped my hand away.

"Strip," he commanded. "If your cunt isn't bare in sixty seconds, you'll regret it. I can take you to the edge and keep you there for hours—and I promise *I* will enjoy every minute of it."

Yes, please.

I slipped my dress over my head, thankful it was nothing more than a simple cotton number without time-consuming zippers. I wanted hours, but I'd prefer if they came with multiple orgasms. Alexander stayed away, watching as I unfastened my bra and dropped it on the floor. Wiggling my panties down, I kicked them free.

His thumb brushed thoughtfully over his mouth as he circled me, eye fucking every inch of my body.

"Come here." He beckoned me to follow him with his index finger. My pulse sped up when he moved toward the bed. But instead of lifting me onto it, he picked up a pillow and placed it on the floor. "Kneel."

He offered me a hand, and I allowed him to help me get on my knees.

"That's a pretty Poppet," he praised me, leaning down to kiss my forehead. "You're so perfect—so fuckable. But you need more than that, don't you?"

I nodded. "Yes, please."

"Since you asked so nicely." He gave me a wicked smile. "I'm going to make every inch of your skin sing, but first, you will show me you deserve it."

I opened my mouth to protest, unwilling to wait for him to begin. I was on fire, ignited by his gaze alone. But he slapped my lips softly. "You don't need to speak. There's a place for your voice and while you're naked, it's when I tell you to speak. You may nod. If you've changed your mind, though..."

I shook my head quickly, my eyes turned up to stare at him. I could see the outline of his cock in his pants. I wanted to reach out and free it, but I didn't dare.

"You will wait." He shushed me gently when I whimpered. "Only for a moment, but try not to move." He bent over and caressed my belly. "Unless..."

I understood what he was saying. Nothing mattered more than the baby. Not my needs or his. I'd handed him total control over me and he wouldn't overlook that gift. Tears stung my eyes, but I didn't dare brush them away. Alexander walked to the closet and I felt them slip down my cheeks. When he returned a moment later, he drew a breath in sharply.

"You are always gorgeous, but you are breathtaking when you cry. Not always, of course. But now? I've never seen you look so beautiful, because I know what you're feeling. *Happiness*. Completion. This is right. I was always meant to own you." He stepped before me and unfastened his pants. Taking out his cock, he massaged it before my eyes. "Suck my cock and show me those pretty tears. Show me how grateful you are for it—for us."

I leaned forward, placing my palms on his thighs to steady myself. This wasn't about getting off. He wouldn't make it simple. He wanted an offering and I knew what I would receive in return. Drawing my tongue over the tip, he rewarded me with a growl. I wanted to tease him but I couldn't stop myself from taking him entirely into my mouth. Looking up to him, I let my final control slip and the tears streamed down.

"Oh God, my cock belongs in your mouth, doesn't it? Don't answer, Poppet. You've been hungry. I need to feed you." He rocked against my mouth, his taste mixing with the salt of my tears. I hollowed my cheeks, drawing him as deeply as I could, high on the pleasure I was giving him. Finally, he guided me away, his cock still hard. "I'm not ready yet."

He held out his hands and I took them, pushing to my feet. I swayed slightly, feeling a bit drunk on the moment.

"You've been very good and now I'm going to give you what you asked for: release." His head angled to my ear and he continued to whisper as his chest brushed over my nipples. "That's not just about orgasms. Although you'll have plenty of those. You want to forget—and we can—together."

I swallowed as his mouth continued down to my breasts and covered my nipple with wet heat. His tongue circled the furl until it pebbled into a hard point. He moved to the next one before he stood up and studied it. "Such perfect tits. I might have to come worship them daily. Would you like that? Would you like me to fuck your tits with my mouth until you come?"

I nodded, wishing he would do that now.

"That's not what today's about, though. I've been saving some things. We've never needed them. Making love to you has never required many *additions*, but it's time I take you into the dark. Are you sure you're ready?"

"Yes," I answered without doubt.

Alexander licked his lips and took my hand. Leading me all the way to the bed, he pointed to a pile of pillows in the middle. "On your knees. You may hold those."

He waited as I crawled onto the mattress, then oversaw my positioning until he was satisfied.

"I thought the point," I began when he adjusted the pillow for the tenth time to support my stomach.

"Shh," he cut me off harshly. "You have no opinion. Your only job is to be taken care of."

I sighed, feeling a bit frustrated by his considerateness. Then, he brought out the rope.

"Did you feel that little thrill?" he asked as he set it on the bed next to the pillow. "I saw it pass through your eyes. You were worried that I was going to hold back, but I won't. That doesn't mean, however, that I can neglect my duty to protect you. You will be safe and loved through every moment of this."

I nodded a little, letting go of any newfound resistance.

I hugged the pillow as he took the rope and wrapped it around one ankle. Then, I felt a slight tug as the rope pulled taut before he continued to the other ankle. He'd bound me to the bedposts, I was certain, though I couldn't risk looking and messing up the exact positioning he insisted on. I felt his weight shift onto the bed behind me and then cool fingers trailing along my seam.

"Your cunt is so swollen," he murmured. "You will never let it suffer this long again. Do you understand? Answer, Poppet."

"Yes," I whispered, fighting the urge to push against his touch. I wanted him to sooth the ache, not feed it.

"It's hard wanting something and holding back." He said, continuing to trace me. "I know. I've wanted you like this for so long. I don't know if I'll be able to stop. That's why we never have gone into the dark together. That's why I pretended I didn't need it. That's why I leashed the monster."

He thought his darkness was a monster. He thought it scared me. But I'd fallen in love with the monster before I'd fallen for the man.

"Let him free." Somehow I knew it was okay to speak if only to give him permission to shed this final mask—the one he'd worn so long.

"I need to see it. What your body looks like marked by me, but it won't be like the time with the belt. You tried to control that and you weren't ready. You were still scared."

"I'm not scared anymore."

The first smack stung. He'd spanked me before—playfully and forcefully, but this was different. Harder and driven by purpose. I bit the pillow determined not to cry out. His hand massaged the spot, dissipating the heat a little before a slap hit the other side of my ass. I sensed the difference. He'd found the same spot, spanking it exactly so that it stung across my entire rear. Again he massaged it away. He did this slowly, repeating it until I relaxed into the pillow, knowing what to expect: the rhythmic, measured force. Even as the heat built so much he couldn't caress it away, I found myself slipping into another place. I felt each strike and heard each whispered praise.

"Good girl," he said with reverence. "Strong girl."

I was in a dream—on fire, burning and alive. Then suddenly the flame began to fade, extinguished by the soft, wet lap of his tongue.

"Ohhh," I moaned, knowing it was okay, that he needed to hear it. A finger pushed inside me, curling and coaxing and I cried out into the pillow. All the sensations that had faded came rushing back. There was bone deep ache and shivers of promised pleasure and there was pain—and somehow together it had turned my entire body into a network of sensations that sang along my skin, just as he'd promised it would. The notes were building into a symphony and then the music stopped.

"Please," I cried out, only to feel his body move over mine. He kissed my neck as he sank his cock inside me with one powerful thrust.

"Fuck, you're tight," he said as he stroked in and out. "I need you to come. I can't hold it. Not now."

There was a strain I'd never heard before and something about the vulnerability of it sent a powerful swell through me that shook my entire body with its force. When the final notes softened, Alexander groaned and slammed into me before pulling out. I felt the heat of his release on my still burning rear.

The afterglow was almost as good as the place his spanking had taken me. There was nothing but pure and total bliss. Gradually I became aware of the ropes loosening, followed by his strong arms massaging where they'd cut into my flesh. Then a warm, damp cloth cleaned the spot where he'd spilled himself. I felt him linger there. I could almost feel the shift in the room.

"There's going to be a bruise," he said flatly.

I breathed deeply and pushed myself up. "I know."

"Clara, I'm—"

"Don't you dare," I stopped him, struggling to maneuver my pregnant belly and uninterested limbs. When I finally managed it, I found him with his head in his hands. Crawling to him, I sat beside him and moved his hands from his face.

"I went too far," he began.

"No, you finally went far enough." I pushed his arms down and attempted to climb in his lap. "Oh for fuck's sake, help me."

Despite himself he laughed, and whether he realized it or not, he'd never sounded more relaxed, even if he was beating himself up.

"This will all be easier in a few weeks," I said. "When I no longer feel like I swallowed a bowling ball."

"You would..." He stared at me in confusion.

"Of course. Why do you think I wouldn't?" I stroked his cheek, wanting to offer him some of the comfort he'd given me.

"You told me once that you could never...lose control," he reminded me.

I had told him that, but so much had changed. "And you told me that you didn't need it. That you weren't really a Dominant."

"I could be anything you need me to be. I will be."

"I need you to be open," I whispered. "I need you to give me all of you."

"I hurt you," he said in a quiet voice. "I left marks."

"You hurt me, but you didn't *harm* me. I would have stopped you if it was too much. You set a boundary line for yourself that was miles ahead of where you needed to take me, X, and you've been standing and looking at the distance this whole time." I understood that now. The anger, the frustration—he'd been trying to live up to some imagined standards. It didn't excuse everything he'd done, but it explained more than I'd ever imagined.

"I didn't want to need it. Not after I realized I loved you. Not after you told me you couldn't. My responsibility as your partner—as a dominant—is to make you feel safe. I had to respect those limits."

"I know, and thank you." I kissed him softly. "You gave me the space I needed to heal. In case you haven't noticed, I eat like a horse, because deep down I've always known even when you're trying to lock me up from dangerous people that you'll let me walk out the door. I've always known you respect me and my limits. I've always known that deep down you're just a puppy dog."

His eyes flashed and he gripped my hips. "I don't think I spanked you hard enough."

"Oh, you did," I promised him with a laugh. "But, seriously, X, we were different people then. We were falling in love. We didn't think we'd even stay together."

"In other words, we were idiots." He kissed me.

"This doesn't mean everything is okay, though." If we were being open, I couldn't keep that from him. "I trust you with my body. I always will, but..."

"I need to earn back trust in some other areas." He pressed his forehead to mine. "I know, Poppet."

"I just want to be clear that you can't tie me up, give me the best orgasm of my life, and just get out of jail free whenever you screw up."

"The best?" His boyish grin was so unlike him, carefree and happy. I melted against him, wrapping my arms around his neck, but it faded too quickly. "Then I should be clear. I still think you should consider one of the other estates."

"Alexander, I can't." I shook my head, my mood darkening.

"Hear me out. Just until we sort this shit out. With my sister. With Parliament. I want you focused on the baby, not my mood swings."

"I will keep that in mind," I said, crossing my fingers behind his neck.

"But you aren't going to listen, are you?"

"I think I've been pretty obedient today. Don't press your luck, X."

His hand slid under my stomach and his thumb found my clit. "Then let's work on our communication for a while."

"Yes, please."

CHAPTER 12

ALEXANDER

I caught myself smiling as I made my way to dinner that night. I wasn't looking forward to hosting my sister and her guest. But Clara would be there, and I'd walk through hell to sit next to her for a moment. A few household staff gawked as I passed and then rushed away like they'd witnessed the calm before a storm. I couldn't say they didn't have their reasons.

My brother met me at the end of the hall. For a second, I envied his jeans and Oxford. He looked comfortable. I was always forced into these infernal suits. Then I remembered how long he'd hidden in his own skin. I grinned at him, realizing he was finally happy. What more could I want?

"You seem to be in a better mood." Edward looked me over with suspicion.

"Would you rather I wasn't?" I was in an excellent mood. I couldn't keep a smug grin from my face as I considered how I'd spent my afternoon: buried deep within my wife.

"She just keeps forgiving you," Edward said ruefully, guessing why I was in such a good mood.

"Would you rather she didn't?" I felt like a broken record. Would I ever have a moment of happiness not chased away by my mistakes?

He thought for a moment before shaking his head. "No, but only because she's a better sister than you are a brother."

"Fair enough." I took the corner, heading toward the dining room and he followed. "Why are you here? Not that I mind your company."

"Some welcome."

"The last time I checked you weren't speaking to me."

"Would you rather I wasn't?" Now he sounded like me. I didn't push it. If my brother was ready to call a truce, I would accept his terms. "Clara called me. She wanted back up."

"Indeed." I paused and considered what he must be thinking. "Look, I didn't know Sarah was coming home."

"Clara said that, too. You two seem...better."

"Let's not get ahead of ourselves." I wasn't deluding myself that this afternoon meant we were past whatever problems we faced. The fact Edward was here was proof. I could only hope it was a start. If all I could give Clara was release—my body—I would, but I wanted to give her more. I wanted to give her all of me. I was finally ready.

"*You* might have invited me, though."

Maybe Edward wasn't taking this as well as I thought. "I was preoccupied," I admitted. "Sarah told us she invited *a friend* to dinner."

"A friend?" Edward chewed on his cheek thoughtfully, his mind somewhere else.

"I was trying not to think about it." I'd put it out of my mind immediately. I wasn't sure I wanted to know who my sister was cozying up to already, after a ten year absence. "Is that why...?"

"I didn't bring David?" Edward nodded so vigorously I thought he might sprain a muscle. "Any friend of Sarah's..."

"Is likely to be a snake," I finished for him.

"I didn't know she'd been in contact with anyone yet," Edward said.

"Neither did I." I would have to speak to Brex about keeping an eye on her *friends*. "I suppose it's to be expected."

We shared a look. None of us knew exactly what was to be expected, but we had a pretty good idea. We'd all run with the same crowd until Clara had saved us from them. Now, none of them had been around in a long time.

"I didn't think I'd have to deal with the brat pack again," Edward grumbled.

"Brat pack?" I raised an eyebrow. That was a brilliant term for them.

"Your beautiful wife coined that term back when you were *dating*."

It was a nice way to put it. Clara's and my relationship had started in a much more physical capacity. My first realization about what she truly meant to me occurred around the people my sister had called friends—not because I cared what they'd thought, but because I knew how cruel and manipulative and elitist they could be. I'd been glad to be rid of them.

"What did she think of her room?" Edward asked.

I shook my head. "I wouldn't bring it up."

I didn't have time to go into details, because we had reached the apartments. We'd chosen to dine in our family's quarters rather than suffer through the inevitable awkwardness at one of the many over-long tables in the overly formal state rooms. That was Clara's decision, and I'd agreed, wanting whatever made her feel comfortable. I hoped she hadn't put herself to too much trouble following our afternoon together, but knowing Clara, she had. Despite how angry and confused she still felt, I knew my wife would do everything to make Sarah feel welcome, even if my sister continued to treat her like some lowly commoner. I also knew Clara wouldn't put up with that treatment forever. If Sarah thought Clara was the type of woman she could walk all over, she was going to be very surprised.

The table was laid out formally. White roses, which I'd told Clara were Sarah's favourite, had been placed in silver urns down its center. She'd chosen her favourite china, one my mother had commissioned after she'd first married my father. Despite those choices, there were a reasonable number of forks and glasses. The effect was elegant but not stuffy. It had been a long time since we'd sat down as a family to have dinner. I looked around for Elizabeth's highchair, but it wasn't there.

"I thought we'd make tonight adults-only," Clara said from behind me.

I rather wanted to sit down with my wife and daughter, but turning to face her, I lost track of what I was about to say.

The dress she wore dipped low, putting her full breasts on display and skimming over the swell of her belly. The silky ivory material seemed to melt into her skin, nearly as soft and delicate as she was. While most of her was pale, her cheeks still held the flush I'd put there earlier today. My teeth sunk into my lower lip, remembering the velvet of her nipples against my tongue. Had she bathed and washed me from between her legs? I knew she hadn't. I could almost smell it clinging to her, and it made me want to bend her over the table and fill her again. I wanted to see the marks I'd left. I wanted to kiss them.

"Oh Christ, you two have made up," Edward muttered, looking away from us.

Both our heads whipped toward him at the same time. "No, we haven't!"

Edward held up his hands in surrender, chuckling to himself. "Sure. Sure. Let me know if I should leave."

"I don't know what you're talking about," Clara said, her cheeks deepening to scarlet.

"I'm talking about the fact that any moment now you two are going to start shagging on the table."

"Well, I'm not hungry anymore," a lofty voice said from the corridor.

I should have known exactly who my sister would invite to dinner. I should have put a stop to it. The lovely, flushed pink drained from Clara's face, telling me I was right.

Sarah was back, which could only mean one thing: Pepper Lockwood was back, too.

Clara recovered before I did, holding an arm out to the table. "We're glad you're here. Alexander told me white roses were your favourite."

"They were," Sarah said coolly.

"You look nice." Clara wasn't giving up on winning her over, even with Pepper's presence. She was a better person than me, because I wanted to cancel and send them on their way.

"We thought we'd go out after." Pepper smirked, her eyes zeroing in on Clara's pregnant belly. "We'd invite you, but..."

"Not really my scene." Clara took a chair at the table.

"We didn't realize this would be so family-friendly" Sarah said, gesturing to her outfit. She was overdressed for a family dinner—or underdressed, rather—in a tight, black dress that barely covered any of her. Pepper seemed to have drawn inspiration from her, as she was wearing a silvery scrap and sky-high heels. They were mirrors of each other: the bitchy, beautiful blonde and the cool, dark brunette. I pitied any man they set their sights on.

"I'm sure Brex will be happy to take you out." I chose my words carefully. My sister wasn't a child anymore, but she wasn't exactly an adult, either. Brex would keep an eye on them, but it might take Norris to keep the press at bay. After ten years, I didn't have the heart to tell her she couldn't go, but I would have to speak with her. For now, we needed to get through this meal.

"Is he the one who drove me here?" she asked. When I nodded, she licked her lips. "Pepper, you'll like him."

I tuned the rest out, my stomach turning a little, and sat next to Clara, dropping my hand on her thigh. Her eyes fluttered to me, surprised by the gesture, but she didn't say anything.

"You don't sit at the head of the table?" Sarah asked, watching us intently.

"My place is by my wife's side." I said it more for Clara's benefit than hers. Maybe we hadn't fixed everything between us, but I wanted her to know I still believed that.

"How modern of you." She rolled her eyes at her friend.

Pepper unfolded her napkin and placed it on her lap. "Tell me, Clara. Do you struggle with getting enough to eat for the baby?" She threw an anxious look at Sarah. "Clara has an eating disorder."

"Oh? They didn't tell me that." Sarah dropped her chin onto her hand, leveling her gaze at me like a dare.

"My wife —" I began, but Clara placed a hand over mine.

"It's fine. They're just concerned," she said meaningfully. "I struggled a little with morning sickness, but we're both healthy. I suppose not being able to eat makes you appreciate food more."

I was in awe of my wife. Here she was, sitting at her own table across from two vipers, acting like they were old friends. I'd always known Clara was magnificent, but she'd never seemed more like a queen. It wasn't going to keep the snakes at bay, but maybe they'd think before they tried to strike.

"I was sorry to hear that your wedding was called off," Edward said from the end of the table, turning on them. "Pepper was engaged to Philip Abernathy, but didn't he leave you at the altar?"

Pepper's nostrils flared and she nearly spilled her wine on the linen tablecloth. "I called off the wedding. He was still hung on that bitch ex-fiancée of his."

I closed my eyes, searching for strength. I was going to need it in about two seconds. But neither Edward nor Clara rose to the bait.

"Belle is a singular woman," I said when they didn't speak. This earned me a surprised look from my brother and a grateful one from my wife. In truth, I was certain Belle hated me passionately, but I would allow no one to speak ill of their best friend. Pepper might keep trying to challenge the Queen, but she needed to remember there was a king at this table.

"I'm surprised you noticed. I didn't think you looked at women that way," Pepper said to Edward, as though his homosexuality was some type of ammunition.

Sarah waved her off with a laugh. "I knew that before the accident."

"I was thirteen when you had your accident," Edward said flatly.

"It was a surprise to us," Pepper said. "None of us saw it coming. He always acted so *normal*."

"Normal?" I repeated. "Maybe I didn't hear you correctly."

"Oh, darling," Sarah said, sounding genuine for the first time, "I never judged. I only wish I could've been there for you."

She sounded like this proclamation warranted sainthood. I still couldn't decide if she was being sincere or making another dig.

"We all wish that." Edward picked at his salad and I made a mental note to have Pepper officially banished from the grounds.

Despite the sniping, we made it to the main course before things got really ugly. Clara's diplomacy had a limit, and she'd played her hand subtly by way of her choice of entrée: a thick steak surrounded by béarnaise sauce.

Pepper stared at it like she'd been served dirt.

"I don't eat red meat," she whined.

Sarah frowned, her fingers lingering over her fork and knife. "I asked the kitchens to prepare something light. My apologies."

"Some of us have to watch our figures, we haven't cornered our men yet." Pepper fluttered her eyelashes and smile sweetly at Clara like this was a compliment. I considered throwing my knife at her.

But Clara lifted her fork and knife to cut into her steak without blinking. "I spoke with them as well," she said, not the least bit apologetic. "I asked for the steak. The iron is good for the baby."

She hadn't apologized. It was a message. Here—in this palace—her decisions took precedence.

"I'll pass." Pepper pushed her plate forward and an attendant rushed in to take it to the kitchen. "It must be so nice not worrying about how you look anymore, Clara."

"Pepper," Edward said, his mouth twisting as if his food was bitter. I could see my brother's patience growing thinner by the minute. I'd already begun to visualize dropping the girl's scrawny ass outside the gates.

"I've never really worried about how I look," Clara said with a shrug.

"Alexander doesn't have any complaints," Edward said, backing her up with a good-natured reminder of his earlier teasing about our bedroom habits.

"He does already have you up the duff again," Sarah commented. "Although I heard she was pregnant when you married her. I wouldn't have thought that would work on you. It's convenient, really, to—"

"Sarah." This time it was me giving the warning. I could give my sister some slack. None of us understood what it was like to be her right now. But she was walking a dangerous path. If she wasn't careful, she would slip and hang herself on the rope I'd given her.

"I think that was her plan from the beginning," Pepper

jumped in, not heeding my warning. "She's like an animal. Every time I see them they've just shagged."

"This conversation needs to stop right now," I said in a low voice. Heat flooded through me, threatening to boil over.

"What?" Pepper said with mock innocence. She leaned closer to Sarah, as though to share some juicy gossip, but she didn't bother to whisper. "Clara knows what I'm talking about. Don't you remember the time I saw you? Well, Alexander didn't see, but she looked right at me. It was that hunting weekend in the country. I've never seen a woman act so filthy. She was giving it to him right on the balcony. He took her knickers and—"

I was on my feet, my fist slamming into the table before she'd finished sullying that memory. "Get out!"

"She is my guest," Sarah started.

"Consider this me rescinding her invitation," I growled.

Clara placed a hand on my upper arm. "X"

"Don't try to be diplomatic," I said, not looking at her. "My sister seems to be struggling with something. This palace is ours now. The throne? The crown? Mine and *hers*." I pointed to Clara to clear it up for Sarah. If she wanted to see how far she could push me, she'd find out that it wasn't far where my wife was concerned.

Sarah was on her feet, leaning across the table toward me. "Then why not leave me in Windsor? I see you have a nice thing going here. Who would want little sister to come fuck everything up?"

I opened my mouth to speak but there was a loud knock at the door. We all turned to find Norris standing there looking unfazed to find us already at each other's throats. "I apologize for the interruption, but I need to speak to His Majesty immediately."

"We're in the middle of dinner," I grunted out, willing him to understand that now was not the moment.

"Actually, we're through." Sarah stepped away from the table and Pepper stood, throwing her napkin down. They sauntered out of the room and back to whatever suite we'd arranged for her.

I looked to Norris, hoping for a reprieve. Now wasn't the time to leave my wife. Not after what they'd been saying to her. "Can this wait?"

He shook his head regretfully. "I'm afraid not."

"Don't worry," Edward said. "Clara and I are going to finish our steaks and then we're going to eat everyone's desserts while coming up with new nicknames for Pepper Spray."

Clara giggled, but it was half-hearted. "Go on, X. I'll be fine."

I hesitated, but she shoved at me playfully. We'd been putting on a show here tonight, presenting a united front, and at some point, it had become real. There was a real possibility that if I walked out now I'd come back to find that door has been closed. I tore my eyes away from her and looked to my brother. "Force-feed her chocolate so she forgets that Pepper was in our home."

"I'll consider it an order," he said with a smirk.

As soon as we were in the hall, I turned on Norris. "This better be good. I was in the middle of putting Pepper Lockwood in her place."

"About damn time someone did. Although it looked like

Sarah was getting an earful, too," Norris said. He heaved a heavy sigh. "But I'm afraid it couldn't wait."

"What couldn't wait—on the night my sister came home after ten years?" Riots had better be involved. Violence, at the very least.

"Parliament met for a special session," Norris said. I felt the world tilt on its axis at his next words. "They've overruled your decision regarding Oliver Jacobson."

"What does that mean?" I asked even as a flash of a bloody wedding flooded through my mind. Wish granted. Violence was involved.

"Alexander," he placed a hand on my shoulder as if it might provide comfort for what I was about to learn next, "they've released him."

CHAPTER 13

CLARA

"I can't believe Pepper was there." Belle grimaced and took a sip of her sparkling water, wrinkling her nose. "Just thinking about it makes me wish this was alcohol."

Edward surprised us with an afternoon private viewing at Tamara's. I'd been hesitant at first, until he'd told me that the designer had created an entire maternity line inspired by me. She'd been a go-to choice for most of my wardrobe since I'd started dating Alexander, and I more than appreciated the gesture. It wasn't the ego massage so much as the prospect of a day out with friends that made me say yes. I needed to do something normal—not an easy task considering who I'd married—and shopping would have to do.

"Me too," I said, my hand running circles over my belly. I was unnerved to put it mildly. Although I'd done my best to hide it last night, I needed to sort out my feelings with my friends now. "I've never wanted to steal Alexander's wine glass so badly."

"Now, now. Neither of you are drinking." Edward sipped his champagne while wagging his finger at us.

"You should abstain in solidarity," Belle pouted.

"I wasn't the one born with a uterus." He seemed to sense he was on dangerous ground with that comment and shifted gears immediately. It was a good thing since I was considering pouring my non-alcoholic beverage over his head to force the issue. He raised his glass to me. "You should have seen Clara. She was the perfect queen."

"What does that mean?" I demanded. It probably wasn't good form to take that as an insult given that Edward was Royal, but every example I'd ever been given of what constituted a perfect queen was usually coupled with how I fell short of it. Considering what it took, according to Alexander's father and grandmother, I was reluctant to fall in line. I wasn't interested in being obedient or demure. Edward squeezed my hand as if to say I was overreacting.

"You stayed completely calm. It was spectacular," he told Belle. "Pepper was trying to get a rise out of Clara and she didn't so much as blink."

That I was proud of, actually. "If you only knew. I was screaming inside. Plus, if she continued with that story..."

"Oh! What story?" Belle leaned forward, her pregnancy not yet making such things impossible, and I felt a little jealous. I would need both of them to help me out of the showroom's squat chair.

"Apparently"—Edward waggled an eyebrow mischievously— "she saw our lovebirds fornicating."

"*Fornicating?*" Belle repeated. "What are you? Eighty?"

Edward pushed his glasses up. "It's how well-bred people say she caught them shagging."

"Thanks for the translation." Belle's eyes were bright

with excitement at this news. "I guess you two made up. I mean, if Pepper is catching you in the act."

"A long time ago!" I couldn't keep from laughing. If Pepper had caught us in the act yesterday, I couldn't imagine what she would think. Then again, I had Pepper to thank for snapping a photo of my first kiss with Alexander. That picture had wound up in the tabloids. It was a good thing there was usually a safe distance between us.

Belle's mouth turned down in disappointment. "Then you two haven't made up?"

"I thought you were mad at him, too." When I looked at her, I realized the joke was a mistake.

"Yes," she said, her lower lip quivering, "but the pregnancy is making me all moody. I just want everyone to be happy."

"Wait for it," Edward muttered, and I gave him a questioning look.

A moment later, I understood what he meant. Her eyes rounded, filling with tears and she began to dig in her purse frantically. "Bollocks! I don't have any more tissue."

Edward produced a handkerchief from his suit jacket and handed it to her. "That's because you keep going through them."

"A handkerchief? You *are* eighty," she said between sobs.

He pretended to snatch it back, but she held it away.

"You try growing a human life inside you and see how easy it is." She dabbed her eyes and blew her nose. "I'm having a baby, remember?"

"Don't remind me," Edward said sullenly, "or I'll drown myself in champagne."

"Hey!"

"No," he said quickly, pulling off his glasses and wiping the lenses. "You aren't the only ones preoccupied with how I can't have a baby."

"David is still talking about it?"

Edward's husband had made no secret of how much he wanted a child of his own. Now that they were married, his interest seemed to have skyrocketed. He'd even volunteered to be an emergency nanny if we needed one.

"More than ever. Now just doesn't seem like a good time," Edward admitted.

"What? With all the Royal fuckupedness?" I guessed.

Edward downed the rest of his champagne. "Between my sister coming home and this Anders business—it never seems to let up. There was enough drama surrounding our marriage. You know how it is. My children will be photographed every time they go into public. Every mistake they make will be put on the cover of a magazine. Combine that with half the country thinking gay marriage is immoral, and I don't think I can do it. David doesn't see it that way, though. How can he think it's a good idea?"

"It is not half the country," Belle corrected him. "More like a third. The majority don't care at all who you married. Most cared more about the actual wedding. Half were mad you didn't have one to obsess over and the other half are glad they didn't have to pay for it."

"I did save the monarchy a pound or two," Edward said dryly.

I was still stuck on the other things he'd said. I cradled my bump, recalling all the times Alexander had said he would never have children. Edward was right. There would always be scrutiny and people judging every move our family made.

I hated that my child would have to deal with that. Part of me wanted to keep him right here where I could shield him from all of it.

"Oh no," Belle said, taking me from my thoughts, "you've got her thinking now."

"Christ. I'm sorry, Clara. I wasn't thinking."

I waved off the apology. "It's not anything I haven't thought about before. Alexander felt the same way you do, and then Elizabeth came along. I don't know if we'd have had children if..."

In reality, I couldn't imagine a world in which we didn't have a family, even knowing what our kids would have to go through.

"See? Alexander didn't want kids and now look at him." Clearly, Belle thought this should be the deciding factor.

"He is a great father," Edward admitted.

"You sound too surprised." I'd never doubted Alexander would be wonderful dad, because I knew his capacity for love.

"Well, he's a rubbish king." Edward grinned.

"Is not," I cried.

My friends shared a look. I'd fallen into their trap, and they knew they had me.

"I told you they made up," Edward said.

"Don't start," Belle warned.

"You were upset when you thought we hadn't," I said in confusion.

"She gets just as worked up when she's happy," Edward told me, taking another handkerchief from his pocket. "I stuffed the whole thing full of them this morning. Someone has to keep up with her waterworks."

"Am I interrupting?" Tamara asked.

I struggled to hoist myself to my feet. In the end, Edward leaned over and pushed me. "Thanks," I said dryly. "Chivalry is dead."

"Clara," Tamara said, spreading her hands in welcome. "I have lovely things for you. You're going to drive your husband crazy. Although it doesn't look like you need help with that."

She touched my stomach lightly. I responded with a hug. "Your hair!"

"Do you like it? My terrible sister told me I needed to look like a woman my age when I turned fifty." She cupped neon pink locks that had once been platinum blonde.

"I love it." Not many women could pull it off, but she wasn't like most women. "It suits you."

"Let me show you what I have." Tamara pointed at Belle. "And for you. I heard Bless is expanding to maternity."

"I have to find some decent designers," Belle teased. Her wardrobe rental company focused on high end fashion. Since she'd become pregnant, Belle had started adding maternity clothes to the line.

"I can help you there," Tamara promised. "I didn't bring models in. I wanted you two to be the first to try these pieces."

"I can't believe you went to the trouble," I said as she crossed the room and rolled a rack of gorgeous pieces to us.

"You two are the best publicity I could ever have. I should be thanking you." She picked an emerald green dress from the rack and held it out to me.

Edward coughed significantly. "I get no credit?"

"He wants a finder's fee," I muttered to her, running my

fingers over the dress' silky fabric. How was it possible that it felt as good as it looked?

"I'm sorry. Would you like a dress, Edward?" Tamara asked, completely deadpan.

"Not that kinda queen, babe." He poured himself another glass of champagne and continued to banter with Tamara as she picked out something for Belle to try.

The dress felt like butter and I marveled at how something so elegant could be so comfortable. It was cut to accentuate all the best curves pregnancy had given me. Rather than dipping at the bust, it rose to hug my neck. Slipping my nude heels back on, I strolled out to show them.

Edward stopped mid-sentence when he saw me.

"Well?" I asked, spinning around.

"Long live the Queen," he called, adding a low whistle. "How do you make that look so sexy?"

"The model helps," Tamara informed him. She bustled over and checked the fit, smiling with satisfaction. "I knew this color would suit you. How do you feel about the collar?"

My fingers drifted up to it, a funny sensation washing through me at mention of the term, but I nodded. "Every dress I own makes it look like I'm a bar wench. I like it."

"Don't worry," she whispered conspiratorially. "I have a few that will put the ladies on display for Alexander."

Belle joined us a moment later wearing a pair of white, wide-legged pants that rose high to sit over her tiny baby bump and a black shirt.

"I look pregnant," she announced, "and I love it!"

The outfit did an amazing job of accentuating her pregnancy while still being sophisticated. It was the perfect fit for a powerful female entrepreneur.

"I want a pair of those, too," I said, eyeing them. "Unless I'm too..." I ran a hand over my much larger bump.

"No, it's genius." Belle trotted over and showed me how the high waist, which looked tailored into a perfect waist, actually expanded where the fabric gathered. "And she has these nifty buttons that keep the shirt in place. Tamara, you are a genius!"

"I definitely deserve a finder's fee," Edward grumbled good-naturedly.

"I'll make you some silk pajamas," Tamara promised, pushing another choice into my arms.

By the time I said goodbye, Belle and Tamara were discussing how many pieces she could have produced for the website and arguing over colors, since Tamara had insisted our pieces be unique. I kissed everyone and headed to the door, feeling lighter than I had in ages.

"Is all that coming with us?" Georgia asked as an assistant carried a stack of bags and boxes behind us. "I should have brought a second car."

"You could have stayed," I told her. Norris had always sat out on shopping dates, but Georgia might have been interested. I'd rarely seen her wearing anything other than black, but on the occasions when she'd been dressed up, I knew she had style. She'd probably get along with Tamara, too.

"Not really my thing," Georgia said, waiting for me to get into the car. I hesitated before choosing the front passenger seat. Surprise flashed over her dark features for a second, but she didn't say anything. I usually rode in the back, but I had something I wanted to speak with her about. I'd been thinking about it since Tamara had mentioned the word collar.

"I wanted to ask you something," I said with a little hesitation when she started the engine.

"Sure." As usual, Georgia maintained a disinterested air. But she'd butted into my business enough times for me to know she wasn't as detached as she let on.

Over the years, I hadn't been very welcoming to her input, not since she'd revealed to me the nature of her prior relationship to Alexander. I'd been jealous, but not because she was an ex-girlfriend. She and Alexander had never been romantically involved. I envied what they'd shared—a place he'd been unwilling to take me. We'd dabbled. We'd played around before. Nothing had ever gone as far as yesterday. I had the sore spot to prove it. Now I had questions and I wasn't sure who to ask.

"The anticipation is killing me," she said dryly, maneuvering a turn.

"Can we go somewhere and talk?" I blurted out. There wasn't enough time between now and our arrival to discuss this and I didn't want anyone overhearing. Georgia had always been discreet. I knew she would keep my confidence.

"Is that what you wanted to ask me? On a date? You're not my type."

"Never mind." It was a stupid idea.

"You could just order me to take you somewhere," she said. "If you don't want to go home, just tell me where to go."

"That's not it." I shook my head, trying to find the courage to ask her about submission. "I want to talk to you."

"Really? I thought that was an excuse?"

"If you don't want to..."

"Your wish is my command," she muttered. Her eyes

searched the street until they landed on an open parking spot. "I guess this will do."

She parked the car and swiveled in her seat. "Hit me."

"Do you want to get coffee or something?" I asked, looking around for a café.

"Let's cut to the chase. We're busy women, and I'm guessing whatever you want to ask me is something you want to stay private."

She made a good point. I took a deep breath and called on my courage. It was easier to find than I thought it would be. Maybe because I'd already faced what really scared me. "You said something once about talking girl to girl."

I wanted her to fill in the blanks and remember that conversation. I wasn't quite ready to come out yet.

"You want to have girl talk with me?" she asked blankly.

I told myself to get over it and own it. "I need to know about submission."

Georgia leaned against the car door, a wicked smile curving across her face. "I knew you had it in you."

"Why?" I asked desperately. That was where I needed to start. She had known before I had. She'd made comments since we first met. Alexander had been drawn to me. He'd brought up submission and backed down when I'd balked at the suggestion.

"You want to know if there's something wrong with you?"

I nodded. I didn't know enough about true Domination to understand exactly what I was getting into or why. I suddenly found the idea easy to swallow.

"Not all of us are fucked up. Just some of us, like me."

"I'm not saying you are," I said in a rush, worried I had

offended her. "I never thought of myself as wanting something like that."

She gave me a hard look. "Let me ask you a question. Did you ever really stop to consider that? I mean, most people don't. Most people are introduced to submission by someone. Or they seek it out. I think you did a little of both. You've always known what Alexander was. I don't think he hid it as well as either of you pretended."

There was a dark edge to her words and I wondered, not for the first time, how Georgia had discovered this about herself. Everything about Georgia was domineering. She was cold and calculating and deadly beautiful, but she had made no secret of her own submissive tendencies. Her personality seemed at odds with that side of her. Still, she wasn't ashamed of it.

"I guess not," I admitted. "When he first brought it up to me, I couldn't imagine letting him have that power over me."

"And now you can." It wasn't a question but a statement. "I take it that you no longer have to imagine." Her eyes skimmed over me like she was looking for proof.

I crossed my ankles, keenly aware that a knowing eye might spot the slight rope burn on them. My cheeks heated at the reminder of red bindings and stinging skin.

"Good for you," she said, and I was surprised by her sincerity. "It's going to help."

"Help what?" It had certainly helped my horniness, but I didn't think that was the point.

"Your communication. He's always trying to control you and you're always trying to prove something. You two never *talk*."

"We weren't exactly talking yesterday," I said dryly. I'd

heard this lecture from pretty much everyone in our lives, but she seemed to think we'd found the solution.

"You want to know why he keeps secrets from you. Don't act surprised," she said when I stared at her. "Everyone on the security team knows that you two have been fighting. Probably most of the palace staff. You're not exactly subtle about it. Look, he's been keeping secrets from you because he's been holding part of himself back. Now you've erased those final boundaries."

And we had. I'd felt the subtle change.

"Of course, he loves you and that complicates matters."

"Complicates things? Shouldn't it make things easier?"

"Submission isn't just about sex," she said, "and it isn't about romance a lot of the time. You guys have that all mixed together now. It's going to be up to you and him to make sure that you're clear on the difference between those areas."

"How do I do that?"

"You should set some hard limits," she advised. "Things you won't do. Behaviors you won't tolerate. Decide if you're willing to submit to him full-time or if you'd prefer scenes."

"Full time? Scenes?" I felt like I was getting a vocabulary lesson.

"You're not a full-time girl," she told me. I opened my mouth to protest but she held up a hand. "Don't worry about it. I'm not either. I still want to choose when and how I submit to someone. I'm not interested in a collar and am not interested in being a slave."

"Slave?" My mouth went dry. There was a lot I had to learn.

"Taking orders. Humiliation. Not my bag." But her eyes darted away from mine. She might be willing to guide me, but something told me that there were layers to Georgia Kincaid she would never show me. "And Alexander will need some boundaries. He's a natural Dominant, but he's got some screwed up ideas about that. He thinks he was punishing himself, but he was discovering himself."

"I feel like I've been holding him back," I confessed.

"He held himself back, but I always suspected..."

"That he wouldn't be able to let it go," I said. How had I not seen it?

"My guess is that he's been training you without even knowing it himself. Pushing the line. Testing your limits."

"I let him...he..." It felt wrong to tell her what we'd shared, like I was betraying a confidence. Alexander had finally shown me that part of himself.

"You don't have to tell me what he did. I can guess." Her mouth twisted as if recalling a memory, and shivers broke out over me. I had to remind myself that this wasn't about her shared past with Alexander. It was about my future with him. "But you can tell me how you felt when he did it."

"Nothing," I said in a low voice, "and everything. It was like everything went blank and there was only this connection between him and I. I was more aware of him than I was of myself."

Her lips pressed together while she listened. When I finished, she said, "That's called subspace. Everything goes blank and you're..."

"Free," I said. "Is that why you do it?"

"I'm not going into details—unless you want them, you kinky bitch." It wasn't evasion, but I decided to respect it. Georgia didn't have to explain her preferences to me.

"It wasn't just sex, though," I continued. "I mean, I heard what you said about it not being about sex."

"It's different, but a lot of people enjoy sex as part of it. Considering the number of times I've had to pretend not to hear you two going at it, I imagine you will."

I ignored this comment. "What else? Do we need things?"

"You'll need a safe word."

The heat on my cheeks kicked up a few degrees. "We have one of those."

"I see what he likes about you," she said, laughing at my blush. "I wonder if the rest of you turns that red."

"Who's the kinky bitch now? Do we need other stuff?"

"Do you want me to take you shopping?" she asked flatly. "I'm discreet, but there's no way you're going to be able to walk into a shop and buy a whip without winding up on the cover of every tabloid in the world."

"Good point." I chewed on my lip.

"I'll see what I can do. Get you a starter kit. Consider it a baby present."

"That will definitely be the most unique one I receive," I said.

"I don't do pacifiers and prams," she said. "You don't really need much. I'm sure he'll take care of that."

"I want to show him that I want this," I confided to her. "He thinks I'm doing it for him. After, he apologized."

"That's his own head messing with him. Alexander never had anyone love him for who he is," Georgia said with odd insight. "You'll have to give him—"

"A little rope?"

"That's a start." Something like a giggle escaped her but she hid it. "I have to admit that I'm a little jealous."

"Should I not talk about this with you?"

"I'm not going to steal your husband. Don't get all hormonal on me, but I've seen what that man can do." She sighed as if it was a fond memory. She'd told me once that he'd left scars.

"I haven't," I said quietly.

"You will."

I couldn't tell if that was a threat or a promise. Georgia started the car and headed toward Buckingham. There was a lot to process, but, strangely, one point stuck out more than most. "I think we're in danger of becoming friends."

Georgia's eyes never left the road. "I wouldn't buy matching bracelets just yet."

CHAPTER 14

ALEXANDER

I threw the morning tabloids on Sarah's breakfast plate, which she was enjoying well past noon. That probably explained how the girl in the photos looked so well-rested after a night of drunken partying.

"I suppose it doesn't matter how perfectly they cook the eggs if there's newsprint in them." Yolk dripped from the pages as she picked them up with a look of disgust.

"I thought you'd want to take a look up your skirt, since half of Britain already has." The cover of the top paper included a rather unflattering photo of her on her ass somewhere in East London.

"Lighten up. You used to take me to that club." She shrugged, lifting her tea cup to her lips. "You sound like Dad."

I looked to the heavens. If there was a god, he would grant me patience. I felt like her father, because she was acting like a child. "I stopped going to that club years ago."

"When you got married, right? When you became boring. When you grew up," she spat the words at me.

"Yes, Sarah, life went on without you. I'm sorry we didn't all wait for you to come home."

"But you didn't even wait for me to wake up. You told everyone I was dead." She stood and put herself on equal footing. "I'm just showing everyone I'm not."

"You've been home one day—" I began.

"And I went out one night." She dropped back into her chair with a trembling lip. "Do you know what I did when they let me have a phone—and after they showed me how to use the damn thing? I looked up my friends. Married. Kids. Divorced. Dead. *I know* life went on without me. You can't imagine what it was like just to miss so much."

"Not all of your friends have moved on," I said. She was right. She'd been home one day and I'd jumped all over her.

"Pepper," she said with meaning, "and you've disinvited her to my house."

"She brought that on herself." I would listen to Sarah, but that didn't mean I wouldn't correct her.

"Did you know I had a boyfriend before the accident? He's married to some cunt in Devonshire." Tears swam in her eyes. "About the only thing I have going for me is that I have money and no responsibilities because I have no job, no education, and, oh, yeah, my dad is dead. But, hey, I'm second in line to the throne."

"Third," I corrected her gently.

"Of course," she said with a snort. "Soon to be fourth. Your perfect wife is procreating."

"She welcomed you into our home." My patience was wearing thin and bringing Clara into things stretched it further.

"She had no choice!"

"Yes, she did. It was up to her." If Clara had said no, that would have been the end of the matter.

"She really has you whipped." Sarah stared at me like she'd woken up with new eyes.

"First, no one says 'whipped' anymore. Allow me to catch you up on that. Next, I wouldn't underestimate my wife."

Sarah shook her head, frowning with what looked like sympathy. I realized too late that she'd misunderstood me. "I knew she had to be a conniving bitch. Married with two children—she tricked you. I did the math, she got pregnant so you would marry her. You don't have to lie. Are you sure the baby is even—"

"Shut up," I said in a low voice. She was teetering on the edge of saying something I couldn't ignore. "I don't deserve Clara or my daughter. They are the most important people in my life."

"Is that supposed to mean something?" she hissed. "No one else warrants much thought, do they? I notice you didn't come to visit me when I woke up. Every day, I learned some terrible new fact and all that information came from strangers."

"I wanted to keep the press away." Brex had told her as much, but my absence spoke louder than any message, it seemed.

"You wanted to keep them from finding out what you did, but you can't shut me up, Alexander, and you can't lock me away. I've had enough of that for a lifetime." She stood, grabbing her tea cup. "If I want to dance naked on the streets for the next six months, I will. I'm an adult now."

I wanted to tell her to act like it, but we were interrupted by Norris's arrival. A man in a navy blue suit followed behind him. I clamped my mouth shut, not wanting an audience for our disagreement. Their presence had a similarly stupefying effect on Sarah. She stared at our new guest with ravenous eyes until they fell on his wedding band.

"Excuse me," she huffed and sauntered down the hall.

"I'm sorry about that."

He shrugged. "Teenagers."

He wasn't wrong.

I stood and started toward my offices. This was definitely a visit that needed to remain private. Norris took his leave to check in with the staff.

We shut the door behind us and I reached for the Scotch.

"Thank you for meeting me." It was an overly formal greeting given our history, but Smith Price tended to put me on edge. I knew enough about the man to know we had similar predilections, but that was where our similarities ended. We'd been bred for very different lives. Him to cover others' sins and me to pay for them.

Smith took the drink I offered him. He swirled it around the glass thoughtfully. "I don't have much of a choice, do I?"

"If you want out, say the word."

He had been an integral part of my plan to find out who was behind the attacks that claimed my father's life and threatened my family. His actions had nearly cost him his own life, but he was no loyal servant to the crown. An ally, perhaps. I'd never go so far as to say a friend. As far as I could tell, he was a bad guy who'd developed a conscience. I hadn't fully trusted him until he became involved with Clara's best friend. I knew better than most that love changed a man. When his role put her in danger, he'd still seen it through.

Perhaps he knew, as I did, that he wouldn't sleep until we'd rooted out this evil.

"Clara knows," I warned him. "She may tell Belle." My instinct had been to keep the news from Clara, but actually telling her was easier than I'd expected.

"I wouldn't keep this from her. I thought we'd put this behind us," he admitted, showing an unusual amount of vulnerability.

So had I. Only a month ago, Oliver Jacobson had sat in a jail cell levelling impotent threats at me. Now he was a free man. "It's my fault. I assumed Parliament would see how dangerous he was."

"They have a confession," Smith said. He'd been privy to it. It wasn't technically ethical to share it, but he'd earned seeing it.

"They now claim it was given under duress." I'd followed the rules and been rewarded with accusations. Many times I'd imagined what I would do when I got my hands on the man who had tried to take Clara from me. I wanted to squeeze the life out of him slowly, to enjoy watching it ebb away. Somehow, despite keeping my hands to myself, I was the one being punished. If I'd had it to do over, there would be nothing left of Jacobson to walk free.

"Parliament was never going to see it for what it was," Smith said. "They can't admit that one of them turned. It would make the rest of them look bad."

But it wasn't only Parliament that had failed us. "I thought once the news broke, the public opinion would swing in our favour."

I'd been very wrong about that. The press had painted the whole thing as an overreach by the monarchy, and me as a man hell-bent on avenging his father's death. It might have been my duty to, but my motives were entirely different. "I guess Albert wasn't terribly popular."

"And Jacobson is," Smith grumbled.

"You met him before. What was he like?" I'd been completely unaware of the man until we'd uncovered his name. On paper he was the last person anyone would suspect.

"He made a few digs at your lot, but he seemed alright. Then again, he was doting on Belle's mother and she's a heinous woman. I didn't suspect him, but I didn't trust him, either," he added.

"But did he seem capable of this?" He'd grown up poor and risen through the ranks of Parliament. He'd put himself through University and earned chart marks. He contributed to charitable organizations. Frankly, he was boring.

"No, and that's always given me pause. Otherwise he would have a bullet in his head," Smith admitted, confirming a suspicion I'd had for a while.

"I'll admit I was surprised when we took him alive." I'd done Smith the courtesy of dropping the name before we went for him. I wasn't certain if we'd find Jacobson dead or alive, but I would have bet on the latter.

"You nearly didn't." Smith's eyes were cold emeralds as he levelled them at me. "Were you hoping I would?"

I should deny it. Even now, was I really certain I could trust Smith Price? He'd ratted out one ally and he was no fan of mine. The feeling was mutual. But my gut told me I could, because we both had something irreplaceable at stake in this game.

Instead, I shrugged. "Sometimes. It would have been an easier mess to clean up."

"And now he's untouchable. There might be ways..."

"Anything would be questioned. God help us, if that man hung himself tonight in front of an audience, they'd call it murder." I never thought I'd be a man who coolly discussed such matters, like a business transaction. That it was so easy made me feel uncomfortable.

"If killing him is out, it would help if we could pin the bombing on him." Smith appeared to have no hesitation, either, though I wondered if he'd always been that type of man.

"It won't matter. He was sitting in a jail cell during that symposium. That's all anyone sees. But he knew it happened," I told Smith, recalling the blood-chilling satisfaction on Jacobson's face when he discussed it. "He asked me what had happened, but he knew. He may not have ordered it, but he knew it was going to happen."

And then he had said there were more things to come. I'd chosen to ignore that, but I tried not to think about where Jacobson was right and what he was planning.

"I've been trying to figure that out," Smith admitted. "The bombing doesn't make sense. It felt like a—"

"Distraction." I rubbed my jaw, shaking my head. It wasn't a good sign if Smith was thinking the same thing. "The thought had occurred to me."

"What does Norris think?" Smith asked. Norris had been Smith's primary point of contact during the operation. The two had developed a respect for each other that I didn't understand. Then again, Norris was also a man who would act without hesitation to protect his own. It's why I kept him by my side.

But Norris didn't have any more insight than we did. "None of it makes any sense, which makes it even more worrying."

No groups had claimed responsibility for the attack on the Child Watch symposium my wife had been attending in January. No credible groups, at least. We'd had even fewer leads. The source that had warned us in time to get Clara out safely had vanished. "It's too convenient. The intelligence arrived with minutes to spare."

"Enough time to save everyone, but not to stop the device from going off." He paused, chewing on the thought. When he finally spoke, he chose his words deliberately. "Are we certain Clara was the target? If they wanted to hurt her, they could have."

"What else could it be?" I'd dismissed this idea outright before, but that was when I'd still expected answers.

"Why would you threaten a queen but not take her?" Smith asked.

"You'd only do that if you were..." My hands gripped the arms of my chair, my nails digging into the leather. Clara might not have been in real danger that day, but she would fall with the rest of us if the other player had us in check.

"She was a distraction. All the king's horses and all the king's men," he said in a hollow voice. "Everyone—all your men—were focused on that. What didn't we see?"

"You know as well as I do what it's like to be at war." Smith hadn't been an actual soldier like me, but he'd been on the front lines in his own way. He'd been raised by Jack

Hammond, one of London's most prominent crime bosses —
an old family friend and an old family enemy.

"This doesn't feel like war," Smith said.

"Because it isn't. We've been treating it like it is. That's
our mistake. We assumed they wanted us dead." It was much
worse than that. There was an honesty to war—a brutal,
violent truth. The enemy wanted to kill you. That was how
you won a war. The enemy didn't play with you. "If this is a
game, what is the prize?"

CHAPTER 15

ALEXANDER

"Aren't you ever coming to bed?"

I looked up to discover night had fallen and that I was sitting in a nearly dark room. There were papers in my hands that I'd been staring at for hours without seeing. Clara stood in the doorway, light silhouetting her from the waiting area. She was an angel sent to save me from my demons, but I wasn't certain I deserved redemption.

We'd taken a step in the right direction the other day, but where our relationship was concerned we often started sprinting before we were near the finish line. I couldn't bear to lose any more. I needed this to be right. I needed *us* to be right. The truth was, all was not forgiven, and it was up to me to atone for what I'd done. She needed to trust me and I needed to give her enough space to see that she could. "Do you want me to?"

"I thought you might last night," she admitted. She moved into the office, revealing she'd come down here in only a dressing gown. Its soft pink silk fluttered around her, caressing her curves in a way that made me jealous. "Of course, with everything going on, I understood why you didn't."

I'd filled her in on the details regarding Oliver Jacobson. In the past, I'd made the mistake of keeping things like that from her. Even now, I wondered if I'd made the right decision. Clara had enough stress to deal with between the baby and my sister moving into our home, but these things had a way of coming out. This morning, I'd woken to my sister gracing every gossip rag in the country and Jacobson's face headlining every legitimate news source.

Clara circled round my desk and leaned against it. Her hair was damp from the bath and faint traces of rose clung to her skin. My self-control slipped and I reached for her hips, drawing her body along the edge of the desk until she was in front of me. I wanted to bury myself in her and forget the last few days. I settled for resting my head on her stomach, listening to the miracle she guarded for us.

"I wasn't sure if you were ready for me to come back to your bed," I said in a low voice.

"*Our* bed," she corrected me, her fingers brushing through my hair. "First, I was sleeping somewhere else. Now you've been sleeping in your office. It's our bed for a reason, X."

"I should earn it."

"What?" she asked softly.

"My place beside you. In our bed. In our life." There were a million reasons I should stay here. I wanted her to go away from London and from me. To somewhere these twisted games couldn't touch her—and I couldn't hurt her.

"Earn? You earn trust. You earn respect." Her hand cupped my chin and urged me to look up. "Love isn't something you earn, X. My heart is a gift, and I gave it to you. You carry my heart inside you and I carry yours."

"You've done a better job of protecting mine," I whispered, drawing away from her as though breaking physical contact might help me resist the truth in her words.

"Stop punishing yourself for the past and be with me. We have to start somewhere." She held out a hand. It was an offering. Taking it was a beginning. It was up to us where we went from here.

I followed her to our rooms, promising myself I wouldn't push her too far. I wouldn't take more than she'd given. As soon as we were inside our bedroom, she headed to the bathroom, slipping off her robe as she went. She hung it on a hook and began her nightly routine. I watched her going through a handful of ordinary habits— brushing teeth, washing her face —the whole time falling more in love with her. When she was finished, she walked into the bedroom and gave me a funny look. "Aren't you going to get undressed?"

"I didn't want to presume." In fact, I did want to presume. I wanted to strip down and carry her to bed.

"Are you going to sleep in your suit?" Her eyebrow arched as she called my attention to the obvious. She moved to the bed, gliding past me in her slip of a nightgown. As she drew down the coverlets, I forced myself to the closet. Hanging my suit jacket, I considered the ridiculousness of the situation. She was my wife, I reminded myself as I unknotted my tie and tossed it on the bureau. This was our bed. I slipped my belt off, my thoughts drifting to how she would react to it now. An image of her flawless bottom covered in red stripes floated to mind and I shook it loose, but not before my cock showed a little interest. Was she ready for that? Not now. And that wasn't what this was about—it was about going to bed with her. We'd been there before. Multiple times a day, if I could help it. Even sleeping next to her was a luxury, but I couldn't stop planning what I would do to her once I got there.

Anxiety fed those fantasies in a way it never had before, because I finally understood what I had to lose. She'd given all of herself to me, even the parts she'd once protected, and I had shown her the darkness I tried to deny.

She winced as she sat on the edge of the bed and the sight squeezed my heart. "Are you okay? Is it...?"

"Down, boy," she said with a giggle. "My back hurts. In case, you haven't noticed I'm lugging a few extra pounds around."

It was a relief, but I needed to check on her. "It's my responsibility to ask, Poppet, but let's see what I can do. Where is it bothering you?"

Her hand reached to the small of her back. I placed my palm there, applying gentle pressure and began to massage circles against her tight muscles. A moan spilled from her, filling the room.

"I don't think you've ever made that sound before," I said dryly. I adjusted my pants with my other hand, my cock having gotten the wrong impression about what was happening.

"Clearly, you're doing it wrong," she murmured, continuing to groan with pleasure.

My self-control was slipping away with each noise she made, but I wanted to do this for her —to be what she needed in other ways. Still, I couldn't help but press my lips to the freckles dusting her shoulders. My mouth drew the strap of her nightgown down so I could continue to worship her.

"That feels so good," she murmured, leaning into me.

"Is anywhere else feeling tight?"

She angled her face so our eyes met over her shoulder. "Getting ideas, X?"

"Poppet, I always have ideas." With effort I pushed off the bed and knelt before her. Taking her right foot into my hands, I massaged it gently. "What about these?"

"Don't stop," she begged.

"Every night for the rest of your life," I promised, kissing her knee cap.

"I think I'll settle for every night I'm pregnant." She laughed softly and the sound of it settled on my chest like a warm light.

"Like I said, every night for the rest of your life," I teased. "In case you haven't noticed, making babies is one avenue we don't need to perfect."

Her smile faded a little, and I realized I'd overstepped. There were so many unsettled issues between us. Every moment with her I saw our future together more clearly but it was a mistake to assume she felt the same. "You probably don't enjoy being pregnant as much as I enjoy it."

"It is a little easier for you." She sighed as I started on the next foot. "There's just..."

"Yes?" I prompted.

"Nothing," she murmured. "You don't have to keep doing that. You'll turn me into jelly."

"I think I'd have to do rub a little more to do that." I didn't keep the suggestiveness from my voice. Continuing the foot massage, I began to kiss her upper legs. "There's something I need to do."

"Hmmmm?" She mumbled dreamily as I reached the soft skin of her inner thigh.

I breathed in her lovely almond scent before tearing myself away. "I need to check your bottom."

"Oh!" She sounded startled by the course correction. "Why?"

"Part of my responsibility. That was intense and..." I didn't want to overload her with information. It was best to teach her slowly.

"Should I?" She motioned with her hand and I nodded.

Clara stood and turned, raising her nightgown and putting me face to face with her rear. I sucked in a deep breath as I took in the purple bruise decorating her left cheek. Above me, she strained to see as I traced it with cautious fingers.

"Does it hurt?" I asked, torn between fear and elation.

She shook her head. "Not really. I have a lot of padding there."

The joke was meant to lighten the mood but it only reminded me of how perfect she was and how much I enjoyed spanking her. Silence stretched between us as I marveled at my work. It should feel wrong to take pride in it. It didn't. I should hate myself. I couldn't.

"X?" she called to me with the delicacy of a lamb approaching a lion. "I loved it."

I closed my eyes and let those words wash through me, cleansing me of all the shame I'd battled since I'd been pulled from a bondage club years ago and told I was a disgrace. She loved it. Not me. *It*. This moment we shared. She loved submitting and I loved claiming her. The scales had settled, centered on our love and this newfound intimacy.

Still, there were other considerations. "You might not if you saw what it looks like."

"Then show me," she said simply. The answer had been there all along, staring us in the face while we chose to remain blind.

We went to the bathroom and I took a mirror from the drawer, helping her angle it so she could get a glimpse in the larger mirror. When she caught the reflection, she gasped.

My breath hitched, waiting for her to speak, but I didn't expect her reaction. Her smile spread like honey over her lips —sweet and slow. I couldn't breathe as her eyes found mine in the mirror. "It's so pretty."

"You don't mind?" I asked. Pride swelled in my chest, straining against my ribcage.

"I feel sexy," she whispered. Her eyes flickered away and she bit her lip. "Is that wrong? I'm new to this."

"You are very, very sexy, and I'm very proud that I made you feel that way. I didn't know how you'd respond," I admitted.

"Didn't you, though?"

I had hoped. I had imagined it in my darker moments. But did I know? My desire and my certainty were always inextricably mixed where Clara was concerned. I could never separate what I wanted to do to her with what I believed I could.

"Don't keep yourself from me," she commanded and I nodded my promise.

"There have to be rules." I kissed her neck, enjoying how demurely her lashes fluttered at the touch. "Limits."

She whimpered as though I'd caged her too soon. "Later."

"This needs to heal," I continued.

"Please." Her arm hooked around my neck and I wondered if she'd let me go.

"There are other ways I can take you to that place and you'll still have these pretty marks for us to enjoy for days, Poppet."

"Yes, please."

"It's late," I pointed out.

"I'm not tired."

"If only I had..." My thoughts slipped to bindings and bars, clamps and whips. It would be a bit harder to procure those items discreetly, but I looked forward to introducing her to it all. I would show her how strong her body was by breaking it and building it anew.

"There are a few things in the closet," she said with a sheepish smile. "I don't know what half of it is."

"When you said you were going shopping, I didn't think..."

"They were delivered." Her eyes widened when she saw the disapproval on my face and she added, "By a very discreet service."

"We'll discuss it later," I growled. A possessive part of me wanted to be the one to pick out these items, but I couldn't deny I was relieved to have something to work with. "Go sit on the bed."

The bag was lined with velvet, and my mouth turned down when I realized how she'd procured these items. We would definitely be discussing this later. Still, I now had a nice set of items, including the one tool I wanted most.

Clara studied the long, silver bar as I brought it to the bed. I pointed to the headboard. "Up there, sit against those pillows."

She hoisted herself onto the bed and waited with bright eyes.

"Take your nightgown off, and show me your cunt," I ordered, slipping easily into the darker side of me. I could trust this part of myself with her. I knew that now.

She tugged it over her head and tossed it away. There was a split second of hesitation—a beautiful, lingering innocence —as she opened her legs. I drank in the sight of her, spread and waiting, while I took off my shirt. Anticipation built between us as we took in each other's bodies without touching.

"There is only one rule," I began, holding up a finger when she started to protest. "You are going to ask me to stop. I won't. You're going to think you can't take more. You will. Only your safe word will stop me. Do you understand?"

She nodded, but it wasn't enough.

"I need to know you understand what I'm saying. I'm going to take control of your pleasure. Your body will fight me. That moment before you come? When your muscles fight it, trying to hold on to the ordinary before giving away control? You will live in that cycle until I'm satisfied. I'm going to fuck every thought and every feeling from you —*however* I see fit. If you need it to stop, you *will* use your safe word. If I'm hurting you, you *will* use your safe word. This won't be about pain. Do you understand? Speak."

"Yes, I understand." Her tongue darted over her lower lip and I fought a groan.

I moved to the side of the bed and laid the spreader next to her, enjoying how she stared at it. It was a long, metal cylinder with cuffs attached at either end. Dropping onto the bed, I moved between her legs and cuffed the bar to her ankle, pushing her legs wider apart, then I did the same to her other leg.

"Oh," she whispered.

"You have no voice," I reminded her. "You've given it to me."

She nodded and the eagerness of the gesture sent a rush of blood to my pants. "Once I start, you may answer, and then you may beg." I picked up the bar and ducked under it, hooking her knees on my shoulders. I licked her thigh, savouring the salt of her skin. "There are no limits to pleasure. Your body thinks there are but it won't after tonight. I won't be through until you come with a single touch."

Clara swallowed, pressing her lips tightly together.

"Pretty Poppet. You're already following the rules. Do you want me to fuck you now?"

"Yes, please."

There was no need to torture her with further foreplay— she was already dripping—but torture was part of the fun. Bending forward, I kissed the apex of her seam while pushing a finger inside her.

"Oh fuck," she cried as I hooked it and began to massage. She was so close.

I could be merciful. But this wasn't about the first orgasm. It was about all the ones that would follow.

"Don't hold back," I coaxed her. "There's no need to hold on—there are so many more coming."

Her channel clamped against me, her knees fighting to shut against me as she came on a single finger. I let the pleasure ebb away, relishing how her porcelain skin glowed pink.

"You're so lovely when you come. I want to see it again."

She whimpered, her legs shaking and straining as I replaced my finger with my tongue. Her hands fisted the sheets as if holding on for life.

"No, no, no. It's too much," she moaned as I licked along her trembling flesh. Every flick of my tongue earned a jerk of her body. Her hands gave up the sheets and grabbed hold of my hair. She tugged it but I didn't stop. Instead, I settled my mouth on her swollen nub and began to suck.

"I can't," she said, panting desperately.

She could, but I was in no position to argue with her while I was feasting on her clit. This time she thrashed, banging the spreader against my back as she came. Her body arched up and she cried out before slumping backwards.

"One more," I urged her, "and then I'm going to fuck you properly."

"No."

I didn't argue with her. Her resistance only fed my hunger to show her she was wrong. I would never give her enough pleasure. Loving her was my life's purpose, and I would do it in every way I could find.

She grabbed a pillow and held it to her face as I pushed two fingers inside her spasming cunt. My tongue traced her engorged clit as I plunged in and out. The sensations were overwhelming her now. She couldn't process them, and neither could her body. It would take more to push her over this final time. Running my thumb along her drenched sex, I hooked it lower and pushed inside the tight pink pucker.

She threw the pillow at my head—and missed—before another climax ripped through her. I continued to tongue her as tiny aftershocks shook her. When I finally lifted the bar over my head, she'd gone completely still. Agonized bliss hung on her face and I smirked.

One by one, I unbound her legs, rubbing the marks where she'd fought against the restraints. Clara didn't open her eyes as I crept up the bed next to her.

"Poppet, you're going to ride my cock now."

The slight nod of her head told me she heard me, but that she was incapable of speech. Sliding an arm under her, I urged her onto my lap. She collapsed against me as she strad-dled me, murmuring something that sounded a lot like "jelly."

But despite her overwhelmed state, she responded to my light touches as I lifted her over my shaft. Her arms circled my neck as I helped her sink inch-by-inch onto my cock. Her body took control, acting instinctively as I rocked against her. The movement of her hips was slight, growing with urgency as I sped up our pace.

"All of that, and you still need my cock," I grunted, thrusting hard inside her. "Because I say you need it. What do you need?"

"Your cock," she whimpered, clinging to me.

I lifted her hips and she responded by dropping over it again. "That's good. It made my cock so hard watching you fight me, watching you come again and again. Now what do you want it to do? Tell me, Clara."

"Fuck me," she sobbed, nearly choking me as she

bounced up and down on my shaft. "I want your cock to fuck me."

"Hold on, Poppet." My arms hooked under her flipping her onto her back. Pushing onto my arms, I thrust inside her. "Look at me."

Her eyes opened, so full of love that I nearly came.

"You. Are. Mine." Then I filled her with the proof.

CHAPTER 16

CLARA

I was dreaming of Alexander's mouth when a shrill thief stole him from me. Pulling a pillow over my ears, I fought being taken from him. The world dragged me to consciousness against my will, and I struggled to sit up. I blinked blearily as I began to process Alexander sitting on the side of the bed whispering into his mobile.

"Give me a moment. I'll be there."

"What's going on?" I yawned. "Why am I surrounded by pillows?"

I finally managed to extricate myself from the small fort my husband had built around me.

"I wasn't certain how you'd be comfortable."

I tossed one to the floor. "I think you had every angle covered."

"That was the goal, although I don't think you've moved once." He circled around the bed and kissed my forehead. "Go back to sleep. I need to deal with something."

"What's wrong?" My mind snapped on instantly. I grabbed Alexander's arm.

He pried himself loose with a hollow laugh. "Nothing you need to concern yourself with."

"Try again."

He heaved the sigh of a man who knew he'd lost this round. "Brex is bringing Sarah into the house. Apparently, she's worse than last night."

I'd ventured out of the house yesterday to a larger than usual crowd of reporters hanging around our gates. One look at the trending stories told me why. I couldn't imagine that she would be worse than that. I wriggled out of bed, my eyes scanning the floor for my nightgown. I pointed to it.

"There's no reason—"

I delivered a glare that shut his protest down. He picked up the nightgown and handed it to me. "I'm getting your robe."

There was a deliciously dark possessiveness to how his gaze raked over me as he said it. It sent my thoughts to a few hours earlier. I still felt the slick proof of his attention between my legs and the sensation woke up another part of me—one that didn't want to put on a robe and see to his prodigal sister.

Alexander held out my robe. Unfortunately, duty called.

We heard her before we saw her. For the second time, I was grateful that Edward had suggested we give her a suite on a different floor. If she'd come through my home making that ruckus and waking my baby, she'd find the welcome mat pulled out from under her.

"A cunt from Devonshire!" She cackled as we caught up with the group. Brex and another man were supporting her as she stumbled along, her ankles betraying her with every step

"Can you imagine? And another one is gay. I should have seen that, actually."

Brex had the look of a man who had seen war and suddenly missed it. He was easily two times her size, and most of that was muscle. Given her remarkable impression of a boneless heap of a person, it was proving a struggle to keep her upright. Georgia stalked into the room looking more disgusted than usual as she apprised the situation.

"Why are you here?" Alexander snapped. "You're Clara's bodyguard now."

"He called me." Georgia hoisted a thumb at Brex.

"You didn't answer the first call." Brex tried to shrug and nearly lost his grip on Sarah, who seemed to notice us for the first time.

"Oh! Alexander. I was looking up old boyfriends, so I could move on and grow up and make you proud or whatever shit you wanted—and I discovered that I must go find new boyfriends." Her finger wagged in my direction. "Not every girl gets a Prince Charming."

"I'll keep that in mind," I said, crossing my arms over my robe and wondering how to sort this mess.

"Two nights in a row?" I recognized the unnervingly even tone in Alexander's voice. He'd turned himself off emotionally. It was what he did whenever he had to mete out a response to a situation.

"I have ten years to catch up on." She lunged away from Brex and veered into me. I caught her with Georgia's help.

"Let's not do it all at once," Georgia suggested, handing her back off to Brex.

He seemed to consider the situation and made a decision. Instead of continuing to help her, he ducked down and threw her over his shoulder. She tried to kick him, but her aim was lousy.

"Put me down!" She smacked his back. "Put me down! Put me..."

"I think she passed out," the other security guard said gratefully. Judging by his round eyes, he was new to this gig. I could only hope he was loyal. Not that selling this story would be an option. I doubted she'd kept a low profile wherever she'd been.

Brex carried her to the bedroom, and her involuntary entourage followed. As soon as we reached it, he dumped her on her bed.

I stopped, shocked to discover she'd managed to tear the place apart in such a short period of time. Clothes were strewn everywhere along with books and magazines. It looked as if she'd dumped the content of every drawer and shelf on the floor and then done snow angels in the middle of it all.

We couldn't ignore this behavior. We couldn't all go along pretending that she was an adult, or that we could catch her up on what she'd missed. Doctors were going to need to worry about more than physical therapy, and until her head was on straight, we needed to keep her busy.

I stomped over to her bed, determined to deal with it in the morning. At the moment, her needs were much simpler. The acrid scent of gin and being nearly nine months pregnant didn't mix well, but I forced my stomach to obey me. I pointed at the door. "Out!"

"This shouldn't be your problem," Alexander said.

"Are you going to undress your sister and put her to bed?" I planted my hands on my hips and waited for his answer.

This seemed to get through to him. "Georgia and I will take care of it."

"Someone should stay with her," the rookie security guard said, eyeing the chair in the corner.

Alexander rounded on him. "Do you think I'm going to let you sit in a dark room with my drunk sister?"

He backed up recognizing the alpha male in front of him. "I was just pointing out..."

"That someone needs to stay with her?" Georgia's glare could peel paint from the walls. Alexander wasn't going to trust a man, but he was in no shape to sit here himself. The sooner we got him out of the room, the better. "I'll stay with her. Happy?"

No one looked happy about any of it, but Alexander jerked his chin in agreement.

"You and I need to talk." Alexander shot Brex a look. I couldn't tell which one of them was angrier, and since the object of their fury was deep in dreamland, they redirected it at each other.

"At least she isn't wearing much." Georgia observed, looking at Sarah like someone was forcing her to unwrap an unwanted gift.

I'd already resigned myself to this fate. "I'll get her shoes."

I sat on the end of the bed and began to unbuckle the strappy heels. She'd probably drank too much trying to dull the pain they caused. Georgia urged her up, ducking as Sarah flailed wildly, half asleep and mumbling to herself.

"If she hits me, I'm hitting her back," Georgia warned me.

"Consider it an official duty." Sarah had only been home a few days but she was clearly vying to be the next Royal scandal. Alexander had enough to deal with between Parliament and Jacobson. If his sister kept this up, public favor would skew even more heavily against us. We couldn't allow that to happen.

"She's going to be trouble," Georgia said as if reading my mind, and I nodded.

"I thought Brex would be able to handle her." I knew just enough about his military training to know that he didn't shy away from life and death situations.

"Brex isn't going to last much longer," she informed me. "Alexander keeps putting him in impossible positions. How is Brex supposed to handle an adult woman who never matured past sixteen? He can't say no to her. He can't ground her."

"Neither can Alexander." It was the crux of our problem. We'd invited Sarah back to London without considering how to help her acclimate to life. We were all tiptoeing around the fact that she wasn't a twenty-six year-old woman—not mentally at least.

"Honestly, I don't know what Alexander should do. But pretending it's everyone else's problem isn't going to solve it."

"I just keep trying to think of how she must feel." Maybe that was the key to figuring this out.

"I do imagine how she feels. It's what keeps me from smacking her."

"I wondered how you were doing it." It might have been all that kept me from doing it myself. "She just keeps going back to where she was before that night. Back to the clubs. Back to drinking."

I could only hope drugs weren't involved this time, too.

"It's like she's searching for something. Like she's going to find herself there." But someone was going to have to make her face reality: she wasn't going to find the ten years she'd lost there. They were gone forever.

"She sure knows a lot about London nightlife," Georgia said, examining a stamp in the shape of a posthorn on the back of Sarah's wrist. "She's already found the hottest club in town: Lot 49."

"I'm guessing we have Pepper to thank for that." I was going to write her a personal thank you note soon, complete with a heartfelt post-script to get a fucking life.

"Brex said she met someone he didn't know there, like a date. God, help us if she's discovered Tinder."

She didn't waste any time. Then again, she'd had so much time taken from her. The trouble was that she still had the experience of a child, but her brother and his friends weren't around to keep her in check. She was roaming the streets of London with a half-cocked idea of what she'd missed and far too much self-confidence.

Georgia finally managed to get Sarah's dress over her head, and she fell back onto the mattress in her underwear. We stood on either side of the bed, debating what needed to happen next.

"I think that's good enough."

"I could stay with her," I offered. It wasn't really Georgia's job, and I'd be in the bathroom half the night anyway, thanks to his little majesty using my bladder as a punching bag.

"If you stay, I'll stay and then we'll both sleep like shit." That settled the matter. She walked across the room and plucked a pile of clothes off a chair. "Did you get my delivery?"

"Yes." I was suddenly grateful the lights were out. "Thank you."

"All the more reason for you to go back to bed."

I tugged the coverlet past her heavy legs until I had enough slack to pull it over her. Sarah's eyes opened as I tucked it around her. The moonlight caught their glassy surface, illuminating her confusion. "Poor little princess locked up in a room." Her hand strayed from under the blanket and skimmed over my stomach. "Would you lock your princess up?"

I took a step away and stared at her, my hands closing protectively over my stomach. Georgia was at my side, angling herself between my body and the bed.

"She didn't mean anything by it," I said, willing myself to believe it. Is that what she thought? That they locked her way and forgot her? I knew the truth. They'd never given up on her. That was the key to helping her now—proving to her that they'd never given up on her.

"I've got her from here." Georgia never looked away from Sarah, who'd yet to fall back asleep. Instead, she'd fallen silent, her eyes lifeless like a doll's.

"She just needs to know the truth. That her father loved her. That Alexander was trying to protect her." She'd come back to London on the defensive, and we'd responded in a similar fashion.

Georgia nodded, but she didn't look convinced. "That might be true, but you should talk to your husband. I think his sister should find somewhere else to stay."

"We'll make it work. Maybe a different wing of the house so that she doesn't wake up the baby—"

"Clara," she stopped me, "I don't think you want her in your house at all."

I TIPTOED INTO THE BEDROOM A FEW MINUTES LATER and found Alexander awake, staring at the ceiling. He was still wearing the clothes he'd thrown on when we'd gotten the call.

"I'm going to fail her," he said when I climbed into bed next to him.

I placed a hand on his chest, not wanting to interrupt him but letting him know I was listening.

"She should be able to handle this. She should be a normal twenty-six-year-old. She should have gone to university. Maybe gotten married. None of those things happened, and I don't know how to help her choose to be an adult."

"What happened to her isn't your fault," I reminded him. Alexander may have kept the secret but he wasn't at fault for the events that led to her coma.

"It was my friend who gave her the drugs."

"And you were trying to get her home."

"While I was drunk." He turned on his side to face me. Reaching out, he brushed a finger down my cheek. "I've been laying here wondering what it would be like if I'd been the one in that coma. I never would have met you. I wouldn't be King. I'd be a boy still."

"Maybe I would have fallen in love with Sarah," I teased, but the joke was as flat as the air between us. "What-if's are only a gateway to madness."

"Yes, but even though I know all of this—even though I *understand*—I'm still angry with her. I've had enough..." he trailed away. "Get some sleep. You must be exhausted, and we have the games this weekend."

I kissed the back of his palm and snuggled into the pillow, but sleep evaded me. I knew what he was going to say: he had enough to worry about. I wouldn't add to that stress by sharing Georgia's opinion.

But now I knew I wasn't alone in how I felt about Sarah's return. It was the one thing none of us were saying.

I wished she'd never come back.

CHAPTER 17

CLARA

It was strange to be at the Sovereign Games as an audience member. How had it only been months since I'd hosted the first event? Weeks since I'd handed the reins to Edward after learning the truth about Anderson Stone? It felt like lifetimes had passed. So much had happened, and, yet, I found myself crammed in a tent making small talk with familiar faces that I'd once met but obviously forgotten.

Relief washed over me when I spotted Henry in the small crowd, particularly since his mother was nowhere in sight.

"You look lovely."

I checked my fascinator, grimacing so only he could see. "I'm afraid I've never gotten used to the hats. Don't tell anyone or they'll kick me out."

"You're secret is safe with me," he assured me.

I still relied on advice from Belle when it came to events like this. She'd insisted I wear the new green dress from Tamara's and then sent over a peacock-plumed fascinator that would have looked stunning on her, but that I suspected made me look ridiculous. I couldn't help feeling as though a bird had landed on my head. I kept this thought to myself, knowing even a friend would find it scandalous coming from the lips of the Queen.

Henry's wool officer's jacket, on the other hand, fit in with the old money ensemble here. He nodded to people as they passed. I imagined he never forgot their names.

"More relaxing to be on the sidelines, I imagine," he said, after greeting a few distant relatives. He eyed me up and down. "Or maybe not?"

"I don't miss having one more thing to do." I patted my stomach. "This is taking up most of my time."

But that wasn't true. Drama was taking up my time. Alexander's troubles with Parliament and our new family member made a high-risk pregnancy feel less important than it probably should have been. Instead, I used it as an excuse.

"And there's the other complication," he added.

"Complication?" I asked. "There are a lot of complications in our lives. You are going to have to be more specific."

"Anderson."

"Oh, that." I turned toward the jumping competition, wishing he wouldn't bring it up.

"I suspect it wasn't just the pregnancy that took you away from us," he said meaningfully.

"It was the pregnancy, mostly." And it was. The baby's health and focusing on keeping my stress low meant that I'd needed to step away. But a big part of managing my stress was staying away from Anders and the tension he caused between me and Alexander.

Maybe it would have been different after I found out the truth. I suspected that Alexander was more anxious about his brother and wife unwittingly becoming friends than he was about Anderson's confusion regarding his feelings towards me. My husband knew my heart belonged to him. Then again, Alexander had shown a jealous streak before.

"I was concerned Alexander might demand it," Henry murmured, clapping at some feat on the field.

"He didn't." It was time for a change of subject. "Are you enjoying your time in London?"

"Usually, I enjoy London, but my mother is not..."

"So, you're not?" I guessed.

"It is the lot of the caretaker, I suppose. The weather doesn't seem to suit her." He waved at the lingering fog that had descended mid-afternoon.

"She never had issues here before. She seemed quite capable." At least, she'd been capable of giving a tongue lashing. She'd had no problem making sneering, derisive remarks to me ever since I'd known her.

"I'm afraid her health is failing, and she's grown quite forgetful, although that isn't stopping her from being as demanding as ever," he added conspiratorially with a slight smile. "But it is hard. She left one of her medications—for her heart—at home and insists that we go to the doctor there. She won't allow me to call the doctors here and pick up a new one. I don't think she likes being seen as dependent on anyone. Who can blame her for feeling that way?"

"I have a doctor's appointment tomorrow. Call them and you can pick it up from me after. Then just slip it in her bag and she'll find it. Save her pride," I suggested.

"You're an angel," Henry said with a laugh.

"I don't feel like much of an angel," I said.

"Well, a devious one, but I like it. You'll need wits to survive this life."

"I know," I said softly.

"Trouble adjusting to all the changes?" he asked sympathetically. "I've wanted to come by, but I thought it best to give you some time to adjust. I wasn't sure Sarah would be ready for company."

"It's strange to have her in our lives."

"And living in your home," he added. "That must be difficult."

"It's not that we mind," I began dutifully.

"But you do," he stopped me. "That's completely normal, Clara. You're young. You have a family. Alexander sprang this on you. I don't understand why he kept it from you."

"You knew, didn't you?" I asked him. "You told me about the estates. You pointed me in her direction."

"Alexander, much like Albert, is his own worst enemy. When I realized you didn't know, I knew it was only a matter of time before you found out and the longer you went without knowing..."

"The angrier I would be." He wasn't wrong about that. No one could have guessed that Sarah would wake up and make the need for honesty timely.

"When I heard she woke up, I felt terrible. It wasn't my place to say anything."

"You were trying to save Alexander from himself." It was a trait the people who loved him seemed to share.

"I am sorry you found out that way."

"You were right." I realized he'd gotten the wrong idea. "I needed to know, and at least Sarah wasn't alone when she woke up."

"Alexander told me he thought it was you who brought

her back. He said you were light that always guided him out of darkness and you must have done the same for her."

"He never told me that," I admitted.

"Then I'm glad I did, because you should know how he feels," Henry said. "How is she adjusting?"

"I assume you've seen the papers. She's the life of London."

"I was trying to be delicate," he confessed.

"She's sixteen, but it's not her world anymore. Everything has changed and grown but her. I didn't know what to expect. I suppose I still don't, but I'm worried about her." I spilled this to him because I'd been bottling it up since the night I'd tucked her into bed three sheets to the wind.

"Give her time," he advised. "Have you considered..." He trailed off as his mother strolled up to us.

Mary, who had always reminded me a bit of a bulldog, was stooped and thin. I'd seen her a few weeks ago, but the change in her appearance was dramatic.

"Why are you talking to her?" Her beady eyes darted nervously between us. "I told you to stay away from her."

"Mother," Henry said in a warning tone.

"She has no idea—"

"Mother, Clara is the Queen now. You will have to start treating her with respect."

"You think I'm the disrespectful one?" she hissed. "I should tell her. Then—"

"That is enough." Henry grabbed her elbow and steered her away, mouthing an apology to me.

I pasted a bland smile on as a few passersby watched the exchange. I was accustomed to Mary's hatred for me, but it never made it any easier. She blamed me for her older son's death and she hadn't liked me much before that either. There was no incentive for me to continue trying to win her over. It was a lost cause, and I'd run out of energy.

Looking around, I wished for the hundredth time that Alexander would arrive. He was running later than he'd hoped, though he'd warned me that might be the case. Somehow he managed to squeeze in a few meetings with potential allies in Parliament. It was far more important for him to take those than be at the games. Meanwhile, I felt alone, battling pregnancy brain and an inferiority complex. With Edward running the show and Belle absent, I didn't have any friends to save me.

I ordered a club soda at the bar only to spot someone who looked more miserable than me. Anderson Stone was here and he'd been cornered by a woman. That probably happened to him a lot and normally it wouldn't be my place to save him; it might send him the wrong message. But it wasn't just any woman who'd sidelined him. It was Sarah. The most eligible girl at the games had found the most eligible bachelor.

But what she didn't know could hurt all of us.

Anders' face lit up as I drew closer, making me feel even worse. I'd gone in with the priority that I would keep my distance from him. Now I was walking right to him.

"Clara," he called when I was within earshot.

Sarah's head swiveled, her face dripping poison at the sight of me. "Oh, *you*."

Sarah obviously wasn't as keen to welcome spring as the rest of us, because she'd dressed in black from the wide-brimmed hat she'd donned to the wedge sandals on her feet. With her looks she would have stood out in anything, but the funereal effect of this ensemble made her a force of gravity. Everyone in the tent cast subtle glances her direction. Then again, she was also the girl who had come back from the dead. Maybe the outfit had been a fitting choice after all.

"How are you feeling this morning?" I asked sweetly. The little twat needed a reminder that I'd been the one coddling her drunk ass in the middle of the night.

"Fine. I can hold my liquor." Then again, she probably didn't remember. Alcohol was the ultimate blackhole.

"It didn't seem like it last night," I muttered before I could stop myself.

If looks could kill, Sarah's would have me torn me to shreds and left me bleeding out. "I'm fine, really." She waved me off with a hand. "You can go back to gestating or whatever it is you do."

Anderson's mouth opened, probably to defend me, and I couldn't allow it.

Instead, I opened my own and said exactly what I was thinking. "I ensure the line of succession doesn't pass to a Royal cunt. That's what I do."

I shouldn't have said it.

Anders physically stepped away, looking as if he might burst something trying to keep a straight face. But the insult broke Sarah, who looked like I'd hit her over the head with a brick. Flustered, she turned and stomped away.

"I see you two are getting along," he said.

"She's the sister I never had."

"Don't you have a sister?" he asked, confused.

"I do. I *like* that sister."

"I see." He kicked the grass with his toe, daring to glance at me. The gesture made him look more like a nervous school boy than a famous race car driver. It was at odds with the artfully unbuttoned shirt and messy, blond hair. He was trying to send a message that he was wicked and reckless, but I knew better. "I take it she doesn't know about..."

"No, she knows about you," I fibbed.

"But..." Anderson turned the shade of blank paper. I thought he might pass out, so I grabbed his hand.

"I'm joking."

Relief washed over his face. Then we both realized we were touching. I dropped his hand and forced a laugh.

"I couldn't help it," I told him. "If I don't joke, I cry."

"How are you?" he asked, moving a little closer to me.

I was aware of his body in a way that I normally didn't react to most men. I often had security guiding me, but this was different. Because Anderson had lowered his voice and his eyes, which I realized now were the same blue as Alexander's, they blazed like my husband's. I couldn't deny that he had feelings for me. I couldn't make them go away. No matter how much I wanted them to.

Because I'd lost more than a friend when he'd confessed how he felt: I'd lost the chance to know him as a brother.

"Pregnant," I said. He needed a reminder that I'd made my choice long before we'd ever met. "That pretty much sums up my life at the moment."

He moved to grab a champagne flute off a passing tray, casually putting the distance back between us. At least he took a hint. "You haven't had that baby yet?"

"I have about four weeks to go," I whispered.

"Thanks, I'll be sure to change my bet. The pot is up to, like, five hundred quid."

"Please tell me you're joking."

"Seriously, how are you?" he pressed. "When I saw that press conference..."

His jaw tightened and I saw that day through his eyes and what he must have thought when I ran out on Alexander. He needed to know that any hope he clung to was wasted. "We're working through it. I was angry."

"You had a right to be."

"But we'll be fine, Alexander and I."

"I'm glad to hear it," he said, sounding anything but.

"There you are," a friendly voice said in my ear as an arm dropped over my shoulders. "I saw one sister storming off, so I knew the other sister couldn't be far."

"What does that mean?" I asked Edward. "I have been nothing but welcoming to her."

"I overheard her earlier telling everyone what a monster you were—that you made her give her old room up, because it wasn't hers anymore," he said dramatically.

I gasped, my eyes narrowing. "In that case, I just called her a Royal cunt to her face. And now I'm feeling less sorry about it."

Edward snorted, not the least bit offended by what I'd said to his true sister. "We have different ideas of hospitality. Don't worry. She wasn't telling anyone who mattered."

What mattered was that she was telling anyone at all. I was about to point this out when Edward turned his attention to Anders. "It's good to see you."

"You, too." Anderson looked even more uncomfortable than when Sarah had been flirting with him.

"I know Alexander can be a bit much," Edward said, continuing with what sounded like a well-rehearsed speech, "but you have a couple normal members in your family. Well, mostly just us." He gestured to me and himself in turn. "My husband is normal. So, three normal family members."

"I don't want to make this a thing," Anderson said slowly. "I've got my mum and my life. I'm just not like you lot. No offense. I don't need..."

"Another family."

He'd made that clear to me before, and I understood. But part of me wanted to clear up a few things with him. I hadn't been born to Royalty. I hadn't been raised in this world. We had a lot in common. Pointing that out would only complicate matters more.

Edward's face fell, but he recovered quickly, nodding. "I just wanted to reach out. If it ever changes or you need something, I make a lovely chess pie and I can usually wrangle a title in a pinch."

"I'll let you know." This actually got a laugh out of Anders. "Now, if you'll excuse me," he paused, biting his lip as he looked at me. But whatever he wanted to say, he kept to himself.

"Why do I get the impression he wouldn't mind if *you* called?" Edward murmured as Anders walked away.

"Don't start," I warned him. I'd confided to Edward and Belle about Anders' crush on me. "Sarah was trying to sink her talons into him. I had to save him. She needs to know."

"Do you want to tell the ice queen?"

I frowned.

"I mean ice princess. Clearly, you are the ice queen." He bowed slightly and I smacked his shoulder. "Where's your husband? Why don't we make him do it?"

As we turned to watch the dressage event, a skill I couldn't fathom the point of, I was about to tell him that

Alexander was on his way. Instead, we came face-to-face with him.

"Oh, he's here," Edward swallowed, adjusting his bow tie.

It was obvious from the look on Alexander's face that he'd been here for a while.

CHAPTER 18

ALEXANDER

The afternoon fog lifted when I spotted Clara and sunlight flooded the tent. It felt more like a portent than a miracle, giving who she was speaking to, however. I ignored a number of greetings as I weaved through the crowd. I had no interest in drawing attention to myself. Deeply rooted jealousy, the type that wasn't easily weeded out, drove me towards my wife and brothers.

They were laughing. As Anders left, Clara and Edward put their heads together and whispered. A vise gripped my heart, but I squared my shoulders and continued towards them. Anders hesitated midway between them and me, looking over his shoulder. But he didn't turn around.

That's right. She's mine.

I willed him to keep putting distance between himself and her. Unfortunately that sent him colliding with me.

"Anderson." My salutation was a half-step above a growl.

He responded in the same tone. "Your Majesty."

"You do realize that's a title, not an insult?" I brushed a piece of lint off my sleeve and his eyes zeroed in on it. Did he know that's what he was to me? An inconvenience? An annoyance?

"Of course, *sir*," he added.

"You were speaking to my wife." Meeting his eyes was like looking into a mirror. I'd never hated my own reflection so much.

"I was talking to a friend," he corrected me. His right hand clenched into a fist.

This time I wasn't rising to the bait. Fighting him would only give Clara more doubt. Enough people had nearly come between us—Anderson included—I didn't need to drag one there.

"Find another one," I advised him.

His nostrils flared as he shook his head. Pushing past me, he got in one last dig. "Edward was right about you."

What the hell did that mean? I didn't bother to ask. Clara might not see Anders as a threat but he wasn't an ally either. I couldn't afford to allow him to mess with my head.

I'd lost Clara to the crowd during our exchange, and I found myself searching a sea of hats looking for her. A few feet away the crowd parted, revealing her and Edward just as they turned in my direction.

I didn't catch what Edward said but I seized the moment, strolling up to them. Leaning down, I kissed Clara, earning a murmur from people surrounding us. Her hand fluttered to my wrist and when I drew back, her eyes questioned me.

"You just missed Anders," she said softly, her words an olive branch. A reminder.

There was nothing to hide and nothing to fear.

"Actually, I didn't," I said stiffly.

"Alexander, are you...?" She trailed away, seeking help from Edward with a pleading look.

"It was a long morning." Capped off by walking into a scene from my nightmares. I kept that bit to myself.

"How were the meetings?" Edward asked.

"Can I get one of those?" I pointed to his champagne flute.

"That good?" he said dryly. "Let me find you one."

"Where's Norris?" Clara asked, scanning the crowd.

"Want to make certain my nanny is nearby, so I mind my manners?" I snapped.

"I want to ask him to speak with Brex," she said curtly. Reaching up, she smoothed my tie and sighed. "You can't lose it every time you see Anders."

Someday I might not, but not until he'd given up his interest in Clara. It wouldn't do any good to tell her that. Instead, I focused on her question. "Norris is sweeping the perimeter. I'm afraid he'll never quite trust anyone else to do it."

"I always feel safer when he does," she admitted.

She'd never told me that. Then again, Norris had been protecting her since the moment I'd brought her into my life. Truthfully, I felt better when he did as well, especially since my heart was walking around inside this tent.

"Sarah's here, and I want someone to keep an eye on her," Clara explained.

There was a Cambridge who did need a babysitter, and we both knew it. Sarah had been courting the paparazzi since her arrival back in London. She'd actually asked to see the tabloids this morning like she was proud of her behaviour.

"Shouldn't Brex be watching her?" I asked.

"I think he's avoiding her," Clara admitted.

"He's her bloody bodyguard."

"And a good one," Clara said. "He's probably protecting her from himself. If I had to put up..." Her eyes flashed up to mine as though she'd only just realized she was saying these things out loud.

"Go on." My mouth twitched at my wife's horror. "It's nothing I haven't thought."

She shook her head, nearly losing her fascinator in the process. Clutching it, she adjusted it, muttering a few colourful words under her breath. "Sorry. Losing my hat, cursing—not very regal behaviour."

"Oh, but, Poppet"—I leaned closer so that I could smell the citrus notes of her perfume—"I prefer my queen wicked, remember?" I brushed my lips over her ear so swiftly that no one would spot the movement.

But the effect was unmistakable. Her breath hitched and pink stained her cheeks. Clara's responsiveness triggered my own and I turned my body towards hers, moving just close enough that she could feel the hardness of my cock.

"You look beautiful," I told her in a low voice and she closed her eyes as though she could feel the words caressing over her skin.

She did. The richly-coloured green dress she wore was a strange combination of modest and sensual. The cut covered her to the neck but the fabric did nothing to hide the graceful curves of her body. Against her pale skin, it made her gray eyes brighter and brought out the subtle red highlights in her hair.

Clara swallowed, her fingers lingering on my tie, and looked away. "I think we lost Edward."

"We don't need him," I muttered, pressing subtly closer.

"There are dozens of people here," she whispered.

"I'm not making a move," I promised with a wicked grin, "I'm giving you a sneak preview of things to come."

She licked her lips, looking slightly dazed. Then her knees buckled slightly. I caught her elbow in time, but the stumble caught the attention of everyone around us. Wrapping an arm around her waist, I fought to control my annoyance at the crowd forming around us.

Norris materialized at my side and began moving the gawkers back. "The Queen needs a moment. She's simply overheated."

"Sorry, Poppet," I murmured, walking her toward the bar. "I shouldn't get you so worked up."

"How do you fit your ego in this tent?" she asked dryly. "It's getting warm. I dressed for this morning's temperature."

The temperature wouldn't even register as balmy. It was quite cool despite the sun's appearance, but I didn't argue with her.

"Water, please," I asked the attendant.

"And I'm the one who's causing trouble?" Sarah's voice cut through the air. She leaned against the bar, sucking the olive off a toothpick before dropping it back into her martini glass. "I'm having friends over this evening."

"Use a state room," I ordered her. At least she wouldn't be out on the town. There would be no press to catch her acting out inside Buckingham. I studied her for a moment, taking in her black dress and blood red lips. "Why are you dressed for a funeral?"

"Good afternoon to you, too," she said, rolling her eyes. "It's a protest."

"Of what?" I asked.

"Inhumane treatment." She smirked as she studied Clara, who was sipping her water with wary eyes.

"Did you thank Clara for taking care of you last night?" I asked. Next to me, Clara flinched, placing a hand on my arm. I ignored it. "My pregnant wife shouldn't have to put you to bed at three o'clock in the morning."

"I didn't," Sarah said, her voice dripping with false sweetness. "I wouldn't want to mess up her plan to replace me."

"What are you talking about?" I pressed a palm to my forehead, feeling the beginnings of a headache.

"She told me the truth. That's it her job to keep the crown from passing to me." Sarah moved a little, angling her head so that her hair swung like a curtain between us and the rest of the world. "But she's wrong about one thing: a Royal cunt already stole the throne."

Clara's grip on my arm tightened, but I was too shocked to respond. As Sarah sashayed out to watch the next dressage competitor, I started after her, but Clara stopped me. "Let her go."

"She called you—"

"Exactly what I called her earlier," she said calmly.

My gaze which had been following my sister pivoted to my wife.

"I had to get her away from Anders somehow," she said with a shrug.

"Colourful choice," I muttered. "Come on."

"We can't leave," she said as I led her out of the tent.

"I want you to rest—*away* from half the aristocracy. We won't go far." The equestrian events were being held on an estate on the outskirts of London.

I watched Clara carefully as we walked the slight distance to the property's Tudor-Gothic estate, Bingham House.

Opening the front door, I held it for my wife, who surveyed me with dancing eyes.

"You act like you own the place," she said.

"I probably do," I told her. "Or it's in trust or something."

"Do you think we should be here?" she asked, glancing around as though we might get caught.

"I suspect no one will challenge me on our presence," I said dryly, pointing to a King's Trust placard hanging by the door.

"That's your problem. No one challenges you."

"That isn't true." I backed her against a wall, dipping my mouth to her ear. "You do."

"Let's not get caught shagging by the maintenance staff." She ducked away from me, but I caught her hand and dragged her into a parlour.

"I will stop trying to get in your knickers if you promise to rest." I guided her to a sofa that was far too ornamental to be much use. "This will have to do. I don't think anyone's redecorated this place since the Victorian era. Of course, there might be a bedroom."

"What happened to staying out of my knickers?"

"You can't blame a man for trying, Poppet." I sat on the sofa, swinging one leg up and patted the space between my legs.

She eyed me with suspicion, but as soon as she settled against me, she sighed happily.

"You know what I'm looking forward to?" I asked her,

running a hand over her stomach. "When the baby arrives and we can tell everyone to sod off."

"I'm not certain that paternity leave applies to the King." Her palms slid down my thighs as she relaxed further into my body.

This was how I wanted her—calm, content, and completely safe. When I'd realized I wouldn't be able to go with her to today's event, I'd nearly cancelled my meetings. With Jacobson free, the thought of my wife attending a public outing without me terrified me. But I couldn't keep her locked away if I wanted to keep her. Instead, I'd tripled the security we'd sent ahead and failed to mention it to her.

"At least I'll be home," she said, guessing what I was thinking.

"Where I can take care of you."

"We don't have to be home for that." She nuzzled into the crook of my neck. "You're doing fine right now."

"There are many components to taking care of you." I kissed the top of her forehead, the chaste show of affection somewhat undermined by the hand palming her breast. "And you want me to stay out of your knickers, so I'll need you at home."

"You offered to stay out them," she said, her body arching to press against the fingers kneading her nipple through the fabric of her dress. "I never accepted that offer."

"In that case…" I gripped her hip with my other hand, urging her ass against my cock. "Allow me to demonstrate how attentive I can be."

Drawing her skirt up, I stroked her thigh, relishing the small whimper she made as she spread her legs in response to my touch. My fingers dipped under the lace of her panties, delving into her folds.

"We shouldn't, X," she said, even as her hips began to circle against my touch.

"Shhh," I hushed her. "Everyone here serves at the King's pleasure, and I serve the pleasure of the Queen."

I would never get enough of her—touching her, listening to her, holding her. Most of my life I'd been impatient, moving recklessly from one passion to the next, and reacting to crises with equal abandon. I wanted to be a student of her body. I wanted to study every inch of her skin, record every sound she made, catalogue a thousand different ways to make her come.

"Do you touch yourself like this when I'm not around?" I nipped her ear.

"Sometimes," she whimpered, her breath speeding up.

"Tell me what you do." I slowed my fingers, keeping her climax from her.

She pushed against my hand, her answer coated in desperation. "I close my eyes."

"And your hand does this?" I continued my assault on her swollen nub.

"Yes," she moaned.

"But not like I do?"

"No." She shook her head slightly, her teeth sinking into her lower lip.

"What else?" I pressed, reducing the pressure again and earning a frustrated grunt from her.

"I think of what you do to me and what I want you to do," she confessed.

"Are your eyes closed now?" I waited for her nod. "I'll do the work but you tell me what you imagine."

"Ropes," she breathed, and my balls tightened as memories of her bound body flashed to mind. "I can't move. You've tied me up and I show you how much I love it with my mouth."

Fuck. I'd wanted to study her and she was giving me my first lesson.

"What is your mouth doing?" I asked in a strained voice.

"I'm sucking you off." She groaned and buried her face against me, her limbs contracting in inevitability. But I wasn't done with my education. My fingers paused, wanting more of her fantasy, so that I could make it come true.

"Why do you need to be tied up, Poppet?" It was a test with no wrong answers.

"Because of how you look at me."

"How is that?" I wanted to know. I wanted to see it through her eyes.

"With love and pride," she whispered. "I feel safe and beautiful and owned."

"You are." Every nerve in my body fired, ignited by her words. "And very soon, I will tie you up and make that a memory, not a wish. Do you want that?"

"Yes, please." Her lips brushed over my chin, angling for more contact. I'd been dangling her off a cliff and she was ready to fall.

"For now, hold on."

She hooked an arm around my neck as I began to roll my thumb over the point of her desire. But she didn't close her eyes. She locked them with mine, shuddering violently in my arms as I released her. When she finally stilled, I kissed her cheeks and nose.

"Why did you look?" I asked.

"Because I don't have to imagine when you're touching me. It's all I need."

For so long I'd thought I looked at my wife with depravity, wanting to possess her. I'd fought that urge without ever seeing it from her perspective. I'd never needed to fear my darkness, because our love was born from shadows. She'd never needed to tame the beast, because she'd never feared it.

CHAPTER 19

CLARA

There were a number of unfamiliar cars parked behind the gates to Buckingham when we arrived home a few hours later. We'd stayed to help Edward award winners of the day's events. After the longer than usual drive, the sun was melting from the sky, twilight moving swiftly behind it, and there was a party at the palace.

"Did I miss a memo?" Georgia asked from the front.

"I told her not to go out."

"It seems she brought the club here." Norris turned the Range Rover into the garage with practiced ease, but his voice sounded weary.

I couldn't blame him. I'd been planning a shower, a shag, and sleep.

But we had a teenager in the house now.

"She said it was a few friends," I reminded him as Alexander helped me out of the car. All of them stopped to stare at me. Georgia and Norris looked torn between amusement and annoyance. Alexander looked betrayed.

"I left that bit out on purpose," he muttered.

"Because he knew it was a stupid move," Georgia clarified. "You two might want to brush up on raising an adolescent or we can all just keep on pretending she's an adult."

"Or we can ship her to diplomatic duty somewhere," I said.

"Only if we're angling to start a war," Alexander said. "I'll deal with her. Georgia take Clara to our rooms and make sure none of our *guests* have wandered too far off the standard tour."

"I should come—"

Alexander silenced me with a kiss that made me forget what I was saying. "Go to bed."

"I want to go to bed with you," I whispered against his mouth.

"Oh hell, you two have done your duty to King and Country," Georgia broke in. "You're on your second heir to the throne. Aren't you tired of—"

"Miss Kincaid," Norris said softly.

Calling her by her formal name was enough reprimand. Georgia marched toward the house.

I followed after her. Every time I thought she and I were getting somewhere, she reminded me exactly what she thought about me. "That's my ride." I kissed him one more time. "Hurry up."

"That will depend on if we're dealing with a house party or a full-blown orgy," he said.

Georgia was waiting for me by the back entrance, tapping her foot impatiently.

"Do you have somewhere to be?"

"Actually, I do," she huffed. "I need to find Brex and slap the shit out of him."

"Brex?" I repeated.

"He's supposed to be keeping her in check. Alexander made that clear. And there's no way all her friends have security clearance. Brex is going to get fired."

"And that would bother you?" I knew I was dancing a bit too close to the fire but Georgia had never opened up to me this way.

"Why do you care?"

"I'm listening," I explained, drawing out the word. It was like a foreign concept to her. "It's what people do when another person's upset."

"I'm not upset, I'm pissed." She rounded on me, pointing an accusatory finger. "And it's not what people do. It's what friends do."

"Okay, it is," I admitted, about to clarify that I didn't flatter myself as being her bosom buddy.

"We're not friends. Friendship fucks things up."

I had a feeling we weren't talking about us or friendship anymore. Since I'd met Georgia, I'd considered her a stone cold bitch. At first I'd seen that as a character flaw but I was starting to see it was armor. Underneath it she was someone else entirely. Maybe that woman wasn't my friend either, but I suspected she wasn't as much of a hard-ass as she wanted me to believe.

When we reached our rooms, she insisted on doing a full sweep. I didn't try to stop her. I knew all too well that a party often opened the door to enemies as much as friends.

I peeked my head into Elizabeth's room to discover she was already sleeping. The night nurse waved to me quietly.

"What's wrong with you?" Georgia asked when I went back into the parlor.

"I hate days like this, where I'm too busy being Queen to be a mother. It makes me feel guilty."

"Look, if you feel guilty about not doing enough for your kid, then you're already doing better than ninety percent of parents out there. Trust me," she added.

"You're not nearly as bitchy as I thought you were," I told her without thinking.

"Is that right?" She snorted, shaking her head. "You're not nearly as uptight as I thought you were, but maybe you just finally got a good enough spanking."

I winced at the off-color reminder that she knew a lot more about my private life than I knew about hers.

"See? I told you I was rubbish at the whole friends bit." Georgia jammed her hands in her pocket. "Everything is good here, but I'm going to send someone to stay outside the door just in case."

"Thanks." I considered what she'd said about us not being friends. Maybe she couldn't see us that way because she'd never actually had a real friend. "Are you going to find Brex?'

"Yes. He better hope I find him before Alexander does."

"Just a question as a friend: Have you ever thought that maybe you're in love with him, too?" I asked her softly.

Georgia froze, her fingers on the knob. "I don't do love," she said harshly, "and I don't do friendship."

She slammed the door behind her.

"That went well," I said to the empty room.

The night was turning into a disaster, made worse by the

fact that we had actual problems to deal with. I couldn't imagine what Alexander would do when he found Sarah, but I knew what needed to be done. This was a family matter, and I wasn't about to sit here and let him handle it alone. I also was tired of shouldering the burden ourselves.

I retrieved my handbag from the table and fished out my mobile. Edward answered immediately.

"Miss me already?"

"Get your ass over here."

"Is that an official order or a friendly request?"

I heard David in the background and did my best to ignore the twinge of guilt. His husband had been schmoozing aristocrats all day and now I was taking him away again. "And bring David. Another voice of reason can't hurt."

"Do I want to know what's going on?"

"It's time to deal with your sister."

MUSIC POURED FROM THE BALLROOM, WHICH WAS ONE of the better places to throw a party, I supposed. I'd filled Edward in on the details, but I didn't wait around for him to arrive.

Brex caught me at the door, blocking me from entry. "I wouldn't go in there."

"Full-blown orgy," I muttered under my breath.

"What?" His eyebrows shot up.

"Nothing," I said. "Is my husband in there?"

"Yes."

Then I was going in. I pushed past Brex, who didn't try to stop me in the end. As soon as I was in the room, I realized why he'd tried to keep me out. It wasn't an orgy, but it was damn close. I didn't recognize a single person in the room. It looked like Sarah had gone to the nearest club and issued a blanket invitation to anyone who would follow her home.

Suddenly, I was thankful Georgia had done the security sweep.

I scanned the room, searching for my husband, but if he was in here, he'd blended into the crowd. Brex appeared at my side. There was no way we could hear each other over the noise, but the implication was clear: he wasn't going to allow me to walk around here alone.

I wanted to ask him if Georgia had found him, but it didn't seem like the place. Then, when he turned his head, I spotted the start of a bruise on his cheekbone. I couldn't help but wonder if that was courtesy of her or my husband.

All around us, people in various states of undress were grinding against each other. I'd long been of the opinion that the monarchy needed to lighten up, but this was pushing things a bit far.

The first familiar face I found was the last one I wanted to see. Pepper hadn't heeded Alexander's decree for her to stay out of our house and she was surrounding by a group of *old* friends. It seemed the Royal Brat Pack had nothing better to do on a weekend than crash Buckingham.

Pepper's full lips curled into a sneer when she spotted me and she leaned down to whisper in a redhead's ear. For the life of me I couldn't remember if it was Amelia or Priscilla, and I couldn't care less. But as much as I loathed these leeches, they were part of Sarah's inner circle before the accident. Most had pretended at friendships with Edward after, but only to get invited to the country and events. They were now on my personal black list, but they were here and they probably knew where Sarah was hiding —unless Alexander had dragged her out already. Steering Brex toward them, I reminded myself that I was the Queen.

"Your Majesty." Priscilla dipped into a mocking curtsy.

The trouble was they were the ones who needed to remember I was the Queen.

"Where's Sarah?" I demanded.

"Around." Pepper laughed, obviously infected by whatever sudden-onset adolescence Sarah had brought back with her to London.

I was done.

Done with sniveling, condescending bitches. Done with people treating me like Alexander's mistress instead of his wife. Done with strangers in my home.

Done.

And I was queen, which pretty much settled the matter.

Stalking up to Pepper, I grabbed her shoulder, leaning into her face. "Where is Sarah?"

She moved to shove me away, and Brex was next to me instantly.

"Don't touch." It was a succinct threat made all the more menacing by how he towered over her.

"She started—"

"The Queen can do as she damn well pleases," he informed her. "Personally, I'd love to let her kick your scrawny ass up and down this ballroom, but I have the line of succession to consider."

"Oh, let's not forget, she's pregnant." Pepper rolled her eyes dramatically.

"I don't think you understand your place here," Brex said. "That may be because you have no place here."

"We were invited by Sarah," Priscilla stepped in. Maybe it was years of royal intermarriage, but she obviously had no sense of self-preservation.

"This isn't Sarah's house." Not anymore. She'd worn out her welcome.

"And it's yours?" Priscilla spat at me.

Brex and I exchanged a look. How dumb could you get?

"Yes," he told her. "She's the Queen."

"I'm a Princess." Priscilla puffed up her chest as though this was a fact worth acknowledging.

"And she is *the* Queen," Brex repeated. "You seem to be struggling with this. Do you want me to draw a diagram?"

I'd never wished to have a pen and paper handy so much in my life, but before I could tell him to wait here while I retrieved one, he motioned to a man in the corner.

A moment later, four men in suits flanked us.

"These guests need help finding the exit."

"We are not—" Pepper's protest died on her lips, her gaze caught on something by the door.

I followed her stare in time to catch Sarah sneaking out of the room, clinging to a familiar blond.

"Son of a bitch," Pepper said.

For once, Pepper and I agreed on something.

"Sarah's more forgiving than I am," she said.

"Get them out of here," Brex ordered. The lot of them stomped away, tossing dirty looks at me. I recalled how they'd treated me when we'd first met. Catty remarks and comments laced with double meanings. They'd made it clear that I didn't belong in their circle.

They were right. My place was well above them.

"Should we do something about that?" Brex hitched a thumb toward the door they had just disappeared through.

"Unless you want to help Alexander bury a body, then we need to get him out of here before the two cross paths," I told him.

He jerked his chin, not looking terribly concerned at the prospect of digging graves. I filed that information as far back into my gray matter as I could.

Sarah was headed in the direction of the courtyard from the look of it. I allowed Brex to part the sea of drunken debauchery before me, wondering why on earth everyone hadn't been kicked out yet. And where was Alexander? As soon as we reached the gallery, I gulped down fresh air.

"Are you okay, Your Majesty?" Brex asked.

"It's been a long time since I've smelled that much sweat and liquor and desperation in one place." I rubbed my stomach.

"Miss it?" he asked.

"Not even a little." I tilted my head. "My guess is the courtyard."

God help her if she took Jonathan back to her bedroom.

Laughter caught my ears as soon as we opened the door. The small interior courtyard contained a colorful variety of exotic plants. It had its own gardener who specialized in each species' particular needs. I loved to walk through it, but after tonight it would never be the same.

Not after seeing Sarah pressed against an exterior wall and Jonathan's pants around his ankles. Between the leafy plumage around them and the sounds they were making, I almost thought I'd stepped into the jungle.

"Should we..." Brex began in a low voice.

"Let them finish?" I shrugged, not bothering to afford the same courtesy. "I don't think they care either way."

"Bloody hell," Sarah yelped, pushing Jonathan off her and shoving at her skirt. He stumbled, nearly tripping over his pants as he tried to pull them up.

"Party's over," I informed her.

"Just because you're too stodgy to do something like—"

I held up a hand to stop her. If she thought Alexander and I hadn't done the very same in the courtyard and every room of the house, she clearly needed to catch up on her palace gossip. "Let's go." I swished a finger in the air. "Collect your panties and your dignity."

"What is going on?" Alexander's deep voice boomed through the quiet courtyard and everyone stilled.

"Brilliant," I muttered, shooting Sarah a look that told her to shut up. "I was just telling Sarah that it was time for her friends to leave."

I rounded on my husband and grabbed his sleeve, hoping to drag him out before he saw who Sarah was with.

"What is wrong with everyone?" Sarah whined. "I haven't been shagged in ten years. A girl has needs."

"You...what...who?" Alexander was already near the point of an aneurysm, so I continued my futile attempt to remove him from the situation. It was too late. He looked around, his eyes landing on Jonathan Thompson. "*You.*"

I wasn't Jonathan's biggest fan, either. He'd completely screwed over Belle at university, and he'd proven to be a first-class wanker at every opportunity. But Alexander hated him and he had good reason. Jonathan had been the one to give Sarah drugs the night of the accident.

"How dare you set foot here? And touch my sister—after what you did?" Alexander roared.

"Help," I called to Brex. He came and took Alexander's other arm but paused when Alexander continued.

"You drugged her. She nearly died. She lost ten years of her life and you come into this house and *fuck* her?

Brex dropped his hold on Alexander's arm with a look that said he was about to go get the shovels.

"Stop this," I demanded. "Jonathan is leaving."

"He is not." Sarah planted her hands on her hips. "You two might not be friends anymore, but newsflash, I took the drugs. So it's up to me if I want him to stay—and I do!"

"There you are!" Edward called striding out to join and skidding to a stop.

"Gang's all here," Sarah muttered, crossing her thin arms over her chest.

"You look like a women but the second you speak—" Alexander started.

"X!" I grabbed his chin and forced him to look to me. "I need you to leave and let us handle this."

His eyes burned into me, muscles ticking along his strong jaw. I didn't know if he was more offended by the challenge to his authority or the situation.

Before I could convince him, Jonathan stepped closer to us. He'd taken off his jacket and he was rolling up his sleeves.

"Let him go, Clara. It's time we dealt with this." He flexed his wrist.

"You need to leave." Brex moved toward Jonathan, but Alexander shook his head.

"The last time I kicked your ass wasn't enough?" he said to his old friend. "Maybe you like getting knocked around."

"I've never tried it. What does your wife think of it?" Jonathan taunted.

My blood froze and I found myself unable to move. Edward grabbed my hand and tried to pull me toward the gallery, but I was stuck in place.

"Oh my god, he beats you." Sarah clapped a hand over her mouth, but instead of looking like she was horrified, it looked like she was trying not to laugh.

"Not like that, baby girl," Jonathan sneered. "Alexander here likes to tie girls up and whip them. That's why Daddy sent him to Afghanistan, isn't it?"

"Is that true?" Sarah asked, looking at me like I was a complete stranger.

"It's a dirty family secret. But, hey, maybe I'm wrong. I saw that pretty thing you used to mess around with is working your security. Maybe they've got an arrangement."

Alexander's fist cracked into Jonathan's cheek a moment too late. I felt the crunch of bone like it was my hand making contact. The sound vibrated through me.

Jonathan reeled backwards, no match for Alexander's strength.

But it didn't matter, the damage was done.

Brex who'd kept to the side to allow Alexander to handle the situation, now stood open-mouthed. He was putting the information together. An uncomfortable silence descended, only to be broken by Sarah's shrieks over Jonathan's injury.

"Get her out of here," I begged Edward. "Take her somewhere. Anywhere."

"The Tower of London?" David suggested.

Normally, I would laugh at this but I was acutely aware of what Jonathan had done, even if he wasn't. I didn't care what people thought about Alexander and I's private life. That was our business.

Sarah didn't resist Edward when he pulled her toward the door. The moment he stepped through it after her, a new figure emerged. Georgia assessed the scene before her, not really knowing the true damage that had been done.

"What is this, Brex?" she demanded, strolling over to him, her eyes on Jonathan.

Brex's dark eyes looked from Georgia to Alexander. He didn't speak. Instead, he reached inside his jacket and unholstered his gun. Without a word, he dropped it on the ground in front of my husband and started to leave.

"Brex?" Georgia called after him, her voice quivering. He paused for a second then continued out the door.

Georgia might not do love, but that didn't mean she didn't feel it. Her eyes sought mine, full of questions. I wanted to hug her, but I was pretty sure she'd like that even less than being called my friend.

"I'll explain later," I offered instead.

She squared her shoulders and addressed Alexander. "We've gotten nearly everyone off the grounds. We catalogued each person as you requested. Norris is wrapping things up."

"Catalogued?" I repeated.

"My sister issued a blanket invitation to half of London. I want to know who was here." Alexander rubbed his bloody knuckles. "Now get this one out."

"Alexander—" Jonathan said, but Georgia grabbed his collar and hauled him inside.

We stood alone in the courtyard. I couldn't think of anything to say. He'd faced an old friend who'd brought demons to our door. Another friend had just walked out. What could I ever say?

"I told him what Georgia was into," Alexander confessed. "I warned him, but he fell for her anyway."

"But you never told him how you knew?" I already knew the answer to that question. I wasn't even certain why I asked.

"He knows now. He knows what I am." Alexander hung his head. "Christ, it never occurred to me that people might think Georgia and me..."

"I don't." That's what mattered. "I know you. The real you."

"You've become close with Georgia," he noted, lifting his head to regard me. "Ask her to show you her scars. You don't know what I'm capable of."

"You're not going to scare me."

"That's where you're wrong. You say you love the monster—that you aren't afraid. You should be."

"So we set limits and safe words and boundaries." I refused to follow him into this cycle of self-recrimination. "If you need to take me back to our room right now and work this out, I'll go. I'm not afraid of you."

Alexander took a step away from me, shaking his head, horror-struck by that suggestion. He raised a hand. "Do you see how it's trembling? I'm full of rage and I would love to hit something. But that will never be you. Not like that. I will never touch you while I'm angry. That's a hard limit—for both our sakes."

I nodded, wondering how I could soothe the war raging inside him. The answer was so simple I'd almost missed it.

Reaching out I took his trembling hand and laced it through my own.

"I'm right here, X," I reminded him. "We can do anything together."

He looked like he wanted to believe me.

CHAPTER 20

ALEXANDER

I t was past midnight before I received the all-clear that the palace was free of guests. Clara dozed in a chair near the office fireplace, waiting for the rest of the group to meet us. There was no point in putting off the inevitable any longer. We'd tried. No one could say otherwise. But three days with Sarah was all the taste of hell-on-Earth I needed to know that another arrangement had to be made.

Norris entered the room, drawing off his tie. "I need a raise."

"Consider it done," I promised.

I didn't know what I'd do without him, and I hoped to never find out. As often as I bristled against his advice, I trusted his counsel and more than that I trusted the man himself. Having him by my side was as close as I would ever get to being in two places at once.

As soon as I'd seen the scope of Sarah's stupidity in inviting so many strangers into the Palace, I'd turned to him. Norris, as always, had a solution. The benefit of having a gated home and an entire Royal guard coupled with a more discreet private security force was that no one was able to leave without going through us. That had taken time.

I'd thought it was time well spent until I'd found my sister shagging Jonathan bloody Thompson. And then? All hell had broken loose.

"Scotch?" I offered Norris and he nodded. It was a sign of the calamity of the night's events that he accepted.

"I'm off the clock," he said as I passed him a glass.

Never in all the years I'd known him had he said that. I swallowed my drink quickly. "You don't have to stay."

"I'm here as a friend. I..." he hesitated for a moment, "I need to be able to speak freely."

"And not as my advisor?" I leaned back in the chair, contemplating what that might entail. Norris always spoke freely as far as I knew. He'd told me off for being a wanker. He'd taken Clara's side more times than I could count. If he'd been holding back...

"You're here as family," Clara said sleepily.

"You don't pay family," Norris reminded her gently.

"Don't fool yourself. We're in the family business," she said with a derisive snort. "We're all paid to be a family and you are definitely our family."

"She's right," I added. "You've been more of a father to me than mine ever was, and you know it."

"Should I come back after you're through with the circle of love?" Georgia asked, leaning against the doorframe.

I gave Clara a sharp look, but she didn't even blink.

"I asked her to come," Clara said. "This involves her now."

"Our past—"

"Let's wait for everyone," Clara stopped me.

Edward and David arrived last, although I couldn't fathom why. "How long does it take to send a girl back to her room?"

"I don't have as much practice with that as you," Edward said dryly.

"And said girl was practically climbing the walls," David said.

Edward glared at his husband over the horn rim of his glasses.

"What?" David held his hands up. "She was. We had to find someone to sit with her."

"Then she's—" I shook my head. Of all the stupid, irresponsible things to do. "I should have hit Jonathan harder."

"He didn't have drugs on him," Georgia said, quickly adding, "if it makes you feel better."

"It doesn't," Clara and I answered at the same time.

"Maybe I should get Elizabeth," Clara said thoughtfully, biting her lip.

"We have a guard inside her room and outside her room and one sitting in your parlour. Elizabeth is safer than the Crown Jewels," Edward promised her soothingly.

"Now that's settled," Norris said, sipping his Scotch, "where do we begin?"

"With the truth." I dared a glance at Georgia, uncertain how she was going to take this part. "What Jonathan said about me, about how I met Georgia. It was—"

"We know," Edward said, delivering me from actually saying it.

"You do?" I didn't know what to make of that. "For how long?"

"Since Dad ranted about it to Grandmother Mary every time you pissed him off, which was frequently."

"After I got back from Afghanistan?" I couldn't believe he'd known for all this time.

"Since he sent you," Edward corrected me.

"He talked about it in front of you? You were a kid."

"I was old enough to know I was gay and Dad was old enough to know it, too," Edward said, his tone both bitter and resigned. "Most of the time he treated me like I was a potted plant—of no consequence and someone else's problem. I overheard a lot of things."

"But not about Sarah?" Clara asked.

"I guess he did," Edward said slowly. "I didn't understand it when he talked about taking care of her. I think he was a little more careful with that information than..."

"My perversions?" I finished.

"No kink shaming," David jumped in, his mouth splitting into a grin. "Your brother's a bit more submissive in the bedroom, but I—"

"I'd like to be able to look at you all in the morning," Norris interrupted with a heavy sigh, "without all the imagery."

"Sorry." David grinned sheepishly, and I couldn't keep my own lips from twitching.

There was one more thing that needed clearing up, though. "Sorry, Norris. One last bit to clear up. As far as Clara and I go, our relationship—"

"Is no one's business but our own," she broke in. "But to put your minds at ease, Alexander has never harmed me and our relationship is completely consensual."

"Change the subject." To my surprise the plea came from

Georgia. "Shag and dominate and whatever, but leave us out of it. Now what do you want to do about your sister?"

The room quieted. It was telling that we were all more comfortable owning up to our private secrets than dealing with the Sarah issue.

"She needs to go." There was no room for discussion in Clara's voice. "I know I said she could stay here, but..."

"Where will she go?" I asked.

"She does have the emotional capacity of a teaspoon," Georgia pointed out, "and about as much life experience."

"Windsmoor?" Edward suggested and we all stared at him. "What? She'd probably feel comfortable there."

"She was unconscious during most of her time there," I reminded him. "I doubt it feels like a second home."

"There are several options in London and nearby. Rose Cottage. Frogmore House. The list continues," Norris said.

"You've given this some thought." I studied him for a moment, wondering if this was what he needed to speak freely about.

"We all have," Edward joined in.

"It's only been a few days." I felt like a traitor sending her away so soon—even though I didn't want her here, either. I looked to Georgia for support. "You said it, she's not capable of living on her own."

"Yes, but I'm with them," she said slowly, shrugging her shoulders. "I don't think she should live here. I told Clara that last night after..."

Clara's warning glare cut her off and I turned to my wife.

"After?" I prompted.

She sighed, continuing to stare murderously at Georgia. "Sarah was drunk and talking nonsense. It wasn't a threat."

"A threat?" Norris repeated. He stood and began to pace the room.

"Not exactly," Georgia said. "I just think she's angrier with you then she's letting on."

"She's trying to hide her anger. We do have a problem," I said dryly.

"It was nothing," Clara said firmly. "But we can't have parties and strangers here. We have children." She patted her stomach as if to remind me that our responsibilities were about to double.

"I know that." I frowned.

"Then you know what you need to do," Norris said. "Someone choose a place for her and pack her bags."

"That won't help her grow up," Edward pointed out.

"Maybe she can live with you," Georgia said sweetly.

"No!"

"Exactly," Clara said. "She needs help adjusting. Probably some freaking therapy, too, but if we're fighting with her all the time, we can't give her that."

"And what about the Jonathan thing?" Edward dared to ask.

It took restraint to even hear his name. "That's her mistake to make, but I want to know if she's on drugs—and I want to know if he's involved."

Norris nodded, and I realized that try as he might, he was never really off the clock.

"Okay. We'll make the arrangements, and we'll need to assign a new security head to her," I added.

No one seemed to want to discuss Brex's departure. He'd walked from the job before, but I didn't know if I'd ever get him to come back.

"I'll talk to Brex," Georgia offered. "I'll explain. He has the wrong idea."

"He doesn't, though," I corrected her gently. "I should have told him about it. It's part of his job to know anything compromising."

"We're hardly compromising shit anymore," Georgia said.

"He still should have known," Clara agreed with me.

"He'll come around," I said, but this time I didn't know if he would. I'd been around both of them long enough to know there was something between them. It wasn't until tonight that I'd realized Georgia returned his feelings.

"No, he won't. Not while I'm here." Georgia might love him, but she would never allow herself to be happy. She wasn't built that way. Someone had broken her too much for that. I could only hope it wasn't me.

"There's one more issue." Clara took a deep breath, then her eyebrows furrowed. "Ouch! Sorry! The baby is wide awake and elbowing me."

"The issue?" Georgia prompted. She hated when she had to deal with Clara's pregnancy. It's why I still found Clara's decision to ask her to be her primary bodyguard confusing.

"Anders," Clara said, her eyes darting to me.

"What about him?" I said calmly.

"Sarah was throwing herself at him earlier," she explained.

"I assume he didn't get her phone number," I said in a flat tone.

"He didn't know what to do."

"He'll steer clear of her," Edward said. "He doesn't have much interest in the family."

"She should know," Clara insisted.

"What good will that do? She's volatile. Unpredictable. She's a fucking teenager."

"I don't disagree, X, but she's your sister and that makes Anders her brother."

"In case you failed to notice, he doesn't want to be our brother." I didn't have all that much interest in having him around either. Not while he harboured feelings toward my wife. I trusted Clara, but I couldn't stomach watching Anderson covet what belonged to me. "He has his own life. Our father saw to that."

"I still think she should know," Clara said stubbornly.

"I'm glad someone does."

It took me a second to figure out who'd spoken. Everyone in the room studied each other. It wasn't until a panel next to the fireplace began to open that I realized my mistake.

Sarah had grown up in these rooms. Many things had changed, but the fundamentals had not. She stepped into my office, her mobile still turned to flashlight mode, and slid it shut behind her.

There was no sign of the manic behaviour she'd exhibited earlier, according to Edward and David. She oozed fury in a terrifyingly rational way. That, coupled with her ability to navigate the dark secret passages that connected my grandmother's suite to the King's study, told me we'd been played. I couldn't imagine why. Unless she'd wanted this all along.

"The benefit of losing ten years and having...what did you call it?" She looked at Georgia. "The emotional capacity of a teaspoon? Is that I still remember my childhood games. Hide and seek—don't you remember, Alex?"

Her words stuck all the more when she called me by my old nickname. "No one's called me that for years."

"They wouldn't, would they?" she seethed. "You grew up, unlike me. You have your secret meetings and make decisions about *my life*! Your American wife wants me gone and that's that. You never asked me if I wanted to come back in the first place. But I suppose I shouldn't be surprised. You could have pulled the plug on my life support years ago, but then that's one less life for you to control, isn't it?"

"I don't want to control your life." I stood and moved to stand before her. "I want to control my own and I can't do that with you here."

"Where do you want me to go?" She laughed as if considering the possibilities. "Maybe my new brother will take me in. But wait! He hates you, too. I wonder why?" She tapped her finger thoughtfully on her cheek. Then she tilted her head to Clara. "Thanks for stopping me before I fucked him, by the way."

"Anderson knows he's our brother," I said.

She cocked her head, smirking like I was missing a joke. "Are you sure that would stop him? He obviously wants to fuck his other sister. Then again, Clara doesn't share his blood, so maybe that's the line he draws."

"Norris take my sister to a guest room—one without access to the corridors," I said through clenched teeth, "and fire the guards who were watching her."

"Yes, Your Majesty." He held his arm towards the door, but Sarah shook her head.

"Even poor Norris has to bow down to you." She crossed to the door. "Lock me up again. I'm used to it."

When she was finally gone, we sat in silence. There was no point to speaking because we were all thinking the same thing: how much bigger could this mess get?

CHAPTER 21

CLARA

"So you two made up?"

"Mostly," I confirmed. I'd caught Belle up on the major happenings on our way to my appointment. She'd been in Scotland over the weekend and missed most of the drama.

As usual, she latched on to the detail I thought least important. "So, why isn't Alexander here with you?"

"Don't start." I couldn't handle one more abrasive woman in my life. My mother had been calling all morning, Sarah hadn't graced us with her presence, but her outrage could be felt through the whole house, and Georgia had barely spoken in the car. She was sitting in the waiting room with a homicidal look on her face. "I need soft, gentle Belle right now."

"She disappeared when the heartburn showed up," she informed me. Sighing at the downturn of my mouth, she shifted gears. "Okay, *no judgement*, but if you two made up, then I think you should tell him."

"I tried, but I wanted to enjoy some time with him before he...'

"Lost his shit?" she guessed.

I nodded. "And I did tell him about this appointment. He wanted to come, but he has to meet with the Prime Minister."

"King and Country always coming before those fragile females," she muttered.

"How are you feeling?" I asked pointedly.

"Fine." But the answer was short and her smile tight.

I was about to press her on the matter, sure she was keeping something from me, when Doctor Ball came in, followed by another man, the specialist I'd seen a few weeks ago.

"Not much longer to go," Doctor Ball said with the forced cheerfulness of a man about to ruin someone's day. "You remember Doctor Rolland."

I nodded in greeting, wondering if his presence meant they'd found something else.

"About five weeks." Not that I was counting the days. The last few weeks of this pregnancy had flown by. I was both anxious to meet my child and on edge about what came next.

"In two weeks I'll begin seeing you weekly," he reminded me. "I will arrange to come to the palace to make it more discreet. We will need to do a full examination today as a baseline, although I don't expect we need to worry about dilation. The baby seems to be sitting quite high."

I appreciated the consideration. Unlike many women in Britain, I'd chosen to have our first child in a hospital, which had turned out to be a wise choice. This time I had to go into hospital, and the press would be camped out as soon as I arrived. I didn't fancy them following me to all my appointments, but they would note the increased frequency and then the media speculation would become unbearable considering what I was already dealing with.

"That's why I'd like to do a quick scan," said Doctor Rolland. "We'll need to do one more when we get closer to the actual due date, but we should make some decisions now."

"Now?" I repeated, keenly aware that my husband wasn't here. We were running out of time and now it was on me to make the call on the baby's care.

I'd prepared for a scan by wearing a blouse, but a full examination meant getting a little more exposed than I'd planned. The doctors excused themselves to the hall and I began to undress. Belle, who'd kept up a stream of chatter to distract me, fell silent when I slipped off my skirt.

"What?" I asked, turning to her in alarm.

"Nothing." She averted her eyes, picking up a magazine with feigned interest.

"Belle," I said, then slowly I realized what had caught her attention. I'd left that part out of the story. "It's not what it looks like—"

"It looks like you've been a naughty girl." She bit back a smile.

"Okay, then it is what it looks like." I strained to try to get a glimpse of my backside. "Is it bad? I don't want the doctor to think..."

"You'll be fine," she assured me. "He'll be wrist deep in your treasure, he won't even notice."

I grimaced at the visual she painted. "Thanks, I think."

Shimmying onto the paper-lined exam table, I did my best to keep my rear pressed to its surface as I covered my lap with a sheet. The doctors came back in, and Belle held my hand as Doctor Rolland squeezed ultrasound jelly onto my abdomen.

"There's your baby," he said, angling the screen so we could both see. "Did you find out the gender?"

I shook my head. "I think it's a boy."

"We'll try to keep that a surprise," he promised me, "but we'll stick with he for now. I'm going to take a few measurements and then we'll discuss what I find. I want you to relax and think about how soon you're going to meet him."

I stared at the screen, love flooding through me. He was getting so big, and it wouldn't be long until I held him. Maybe I would have been able to let my mind wander, imaging that moment, if worst case scenarios didn't immediately follow. It was difficult to relax when the purpose of the visit was to determine what was wrong with the baby. "Is he okay?"

"He looks very happy, if a bit cramped," Rolland said gently.

"Have you two picked out names?" Belle was always good at drawing my thoughts away from the worst.

"Only about ten, so we need about twenty more," I said dryly. Royal naming conventions made it both easier and harder to choose.

"Tell me and I'll give you suggestions. Smith and I are fighting constantly. He likes the name Charles—can you imagine? Charles," she repeated, screwing her face up like it tasted sour on her tongue.

"That one is not on our list." She'd managed to get me laughing and the baby seemed to respond, stretching like he could hear me. "William for a boy and Alice for a girl, I think. Alexander likes Alice more than I do."

"Alice and Alexander is darling," Belle noted.

"It is," I said softly, trying it out myself. "Alice and Alexander. He wants another little girl."

"And you?"

This was where I gave the standard mother-to-be response, but it held so much more meaning. The words clumped in my throat. "Healthy. I want a healthy baby."

So much for distraction.

"William is adorable," Belle said. "We can call him Wills."

"Wills," I echoed her. I imagined meeting Wills. How Elizabeth would fawn over the baby—she'd taken a more active interest in her dollies over the last few weeks. As time passed, he'd toddle after, trying to mimic everything she did. I saw a whole, joyful life stretching ahead of me and suddenly, I wasn't afraid.

I was determined.

Nothing would take it from me. I had access to amazing medical care. I had resources.

Belle and I continued to discuss the numerous other names the baby would have. She rather liked adding Edward in as a middle. "Annabelle would make a lovely middle name."

"I'll keep that in mind."

When the doctor finished the scan it was time for the more uncomfortable bit. As he'd expected, there was no progress, which was a relief.

"I don't even have the nursery ready," I admitted.

"Ohhh, that's the fun part," Belle said. "I'll help."

"Alexander wanted to do it, but..." I hadn't brought it up to my husband in ages. He'd put together Elizabeth's room with the help of his brother as a surprise. At the time, when he was still leery of becoming a father, I'd seen it as a sign. I didn't want to read into the lack of room prep now. He had been busy, but the dread inside me questioned if he knew something was wrong with the baby. If we'd been resisting planning for his arrival because deep down, *we knew*.

"I will remind him," Belle said as if to put an end to that line of worry.

After I was dressed, both doctors returned, wearing borrowed smiles, to discuss the scan with me. As soon as Rolland spoke, I understood his mood.

"Doctor Ball informed that he already went over our initial concerns, and the good news is that I've discovered no further issues."

'No further issues' meant we still had the one. "But the baby's heart will need surgery?"

I spoke because I needed to face it. Until now, I'd terrified myself with what could go wrong and then calmed myself by saying it was too early to be certain. It was no longer too early.

"Yes." Rolland's voice was soft and kind but there was a heaviness that didn't match dragging at his eyes. "We'll need to administer some medicine at his birth that will help keep his ductus arteriosus open to help him breathe. After that, we'll need to keep him under observation until we determine how soon we can perform the operation."

I'd read about the condition and I knew that the operation was usually done within days to weeks. "How soon?"

"Ideally, as soon as I can perform it is best. We want the baby to have time to bond with his parents, but then it should be done right away," Rolland said.

"It's in the baby's best interest that we schedule your

cesarean in advance. I would prefer you don't go into labor at all," Doctor Ball said. "Being able to control the situation will mean more control over the outcome. I'd like to set that date today and adjust only if you're showing signs of early progress."

Tears blurred my eyes as I realized he wanted me to pick out the baby's birthday.

"I understand that you may want to discuss this with your husband." It was no secret that Alexander was involved with his children. He'd never missed a single appointment when I was pregnant with Elizabeth.

"She needs to tell him first," Belle remarked, surprising the doctors.

"The King isn't aware..." Doctor Rolland trailed off when he realized he was voicing his thoughts.

"Not yet. He's been busy. It is my body, after all." I clung to my bravado like a shield. The truth was that I didn't need anyone else telling me that I needed to come clean.

"And we will respect patient privilege regardless of who the patient is," Ball said significantly.

"Of course." Rolland agreed, but he looked uneasy about the prospect.

"I will tell him. Tonight," I added. "May I call you to schedule the date tomorrow?"

"Of course." Ball made a note on his clipboard, then shoved his pen in his pocket. "The nurse will schedule our next visit at your home, and she has Mary's medication. Make certain that Henry reads through the side effects, please."

I'd nearly forgotten about picking it up. I felt more like a bobblehead than a human as I nodded again. It was all I could do nod and accept what was coming.

Belle walked beside me in the hall, taking the medication the nurse tried to hand me, and forcing answers from my lips to her questions. Tuesday. The doctor would come exactly two weeks from now. Yes, I had the office number to schedule the birth. No, I didn't have any questions.

I had answers—answers I didn't want.

"Clara, everything is going to turn out all right," Belle promised as we reached the waiting room. "You and Alexander are fighters. This baby will have that in spades."

"What's wrong with her?" Georgia assessed me as we met her in the lobby. It wouldn't escape her notice that I was upset, but could she tell something was wrong?

"Baby will be here before she knows and she wishes Alexander was here for the scan," Belle lied smoothly.

I could tell from the way her eyes pinched that Georgia didn't believe her, but she didn't press the matter and I didn't tell her the truth. Maybe we weren't friends, after all.

I WENT STRAIGHT TO ALEXANDER'S OFFICE WHEN WE reached Buckingham, bypassing Belle's offer to have lunch in favor of getting the bad news out of the way. I'd dreaded telling Alexander, but I no longer had any capacity to worry about anything other than the baby. His door was closed.

I could risk walking in on a confidential discussion with the Prime Minister or I could wait outside. Seconds ticked by like days. Of course, now that I was ready, I would have to wait. When the door finally opened, I was surprised to see Henry standing before me.

"Oh, I thought you were meeting with Prime Minister Clark," I said to Alexander, not containing the bitterness I felt at discovering his important meeting wasn't what I'd thought.

"He did," Henry assured me. "We were discussing young Sarah."

"What about her?" I asked carefully.

"It's possible she will come to stay with Mary and I for a while. If she'll agree..."

"Naturally." Mentally, I began packing her bags. I didn't care if she demanded the Crown Jewels, I'd agree to almost anything to get her out of here.

"Your appointment went well?"

I was still caught in the fantasy of watching a car drive away with Sarah, so I merely mumbled, "Yes."

"You must need to speak with Alexander. I'll be going."

His farewell jogged me from my daydream. "Wait!" Opening my bag, I retrieved the bottle of pills that I'd been given for Mary. "As promised."

"She's an angel, Alexander," Henry called into the office. He took the medication and kissed my cheek. "Get some rest. You seem tired. This will all be past you soon."

Alexander didn't look up as I entered the room. He looked weighted to the spot by thoughts. I wished I could lift that burden from his shoulders. Then again, maybe I could. There was a place we could go together to be free for a few moments. Desire coiled at my core at the thought of release.

But once I revealed what was going on with the pregnancy, I'd be lucky if he touched me. There was no way he would accept my submission.

"What did Clark have to say?" I asked, moving to rub his shoulders. He leaned into my touch, his groan half pleasure, half frustration.

"The meeting lasted five minutes. I should have come with you."

I was glad he hadn't. I needed to tell him before he found out that way, but I kept this to myself.

"How was the doctor? I'm sorry that I wasn't there, Poppet." He caught my hand and pressed it to his lips.

I decided to work my way into my confession. "He thinks we should schedule my cesarean," I said as his mobile buzzed.

"Is that necessary? We'd discussed trying for natural birth. The risks—" He was cut off by another buzz of his mobile.

"That's the thing—"

He began to read his mobile. "Christ, I'm sorry. Give me a moment."

I knew the small number of people who had his direct number meant that every call was important, and clearly someone was trying to reach him. I also felt like I was dangling off a cliff one-handed, however, and waiting for him to rescue me.

The conversation was short and Alexander's voice brutal.

"What's wrong?"

He held up a finger and I fell silent as he pulled up the message he'd been sent. I leaned over his shoulder to see the screen as a news story flashed onto the screen. Reading the headline, I forgot why I was here. My fingers clamped onto his shoulders as my brain start spinning. We both knew what we had to do next.

Or more importantly, who we had to call.

CHAPTER 22

ALEXANDER

I read the headline over and over, trying to process the betrayal. In the end, it wasn't all that difficult. Scanning the attached article, I discovered that the press had managed to get most of the facts correct in the few hours since Sarah's post had gone viral. It would be a refreshing change if the news wasn't intended to divide my family further.

"How could she?" Clara breathed over my shoulder.

"You wanted to tell her," I reminded her flatly.

None of us had told Sarah the truth. She'd overheard it and the first thing she'd done was spill the secret to everyone who would listen. It was proof that we couldn't trust her.

It took a few minutes before Norris arrived. Everyone but Brex was gathered within the hour. I considered calling him. I needed people I could trust, but amends would have to be made before then. There wasn't time for atonement now.

Clara sat in the corner chair quietly, watching the scene unfold before her.

"Who allowed Sarah to be on social media?" I demanded.

Norris stopped mid-pace and looked down his nose at me. "It is not forbidden. It's understood."

His implication was clear: it was another matter we'd failed to discuss with her. Another way we'd failed to prepare for her return to her previous life. In the time that she'd begun, social media had morphed from innocent pastime to a megaphone for the loudest voices. It skewed elections and connected terrorists. The family had taken a proactive stance against it. There were official channels. None of us had our own accounts.

Which is why none of us had thought to check if Sarah had. We'd handed her a phone without realizing it was more dangerous than a loaded gun.

"Has anyone contacted Anders?" Clara asked as I stewed over this.

"He's unreachable," Norris said regretfully. "She posted late last night. It took the larger outlets longer to get their stories out, but it gave everyone plenty of time to track him down."

"They're in Silverstone?"

I loved my wife for caring so much, but I hated that I had to watch her care about the man who would steal her from me without a second thought.

"The good news is that they assumed he went back to Silverstone," Norris informed us all. "He stayed in London with a friend. That's the most we know. We're attempting to track his mobile signal."

So, he'd had the good sense to turn off his phone—that was something. He had some experience with the paparazzi as a driver, but it wouldn't prepare him to handle how frenzied they could become. He might be my brother, but his unofficial status meant he wasn't protected by the various legislations that had been enacted to keep the leeches at a slightly safer distance. That would have to be rectified. If the stubborn arse would finally allow me to intervene on his behalf. Now that the world knew the truth, he would have to accept that.

"We could deny it," Georgia said. "The press spin wild stories all the time."

That was true, but it had been all too easy for the intrepid reporters to dig up enough facts to make it a more than viable theory. Anderson's mother had worked for my father after my mother's death. She'd disappeared only a few months before giving birth. Then I'd been photographed brawling with him weeks ago. It all pointed to the truth.

"We could, but we'll never kill the story," I said.

"We can contain it more by making it a non-story," Norris said.

I flattened my palms on my desk, drawing a deep breath. There was only one way to do that. "It's not a story if we acknowledge it."

"Like hell it isn't!" Georgia's eyes flashed to Clara for support, but she was absorbed with her mobile.

"Scandal is like a dead body. The smell dissipates once you deal with it," Norris explained. "It only lingers if you try to ignore it."

Clara hadn't chimed in on this charming analogy. Rather she was looking increasingly upset, her hand rubbing the baby absently as her thumb scrolled through her screen.

"This is unbelievable." She slammed her phone onto the table in disgust.

"If only," I muttered. "Then we wouldn't have to worry about this at all."

"This paper is reporting that we chose Anders for the Games because he blackmailed us," she huffed, clearly offended on his behalf. "They've already forgotten that he was one of the most successful race car drivers we have. He was famous before we even approached him! If we'd left him out then they'd be saying we were trying to hide it."

I didn't point out to my wife that if she hadn't asked him to participate in the Games, this likely would never have happened. I would have gone on keeping my father's secret. No one would be any the wiser and Anderson Stone wouldn't be in hiding somewhere in London. He wouldn't even know and he wouldn't be in love with my wife.

The trouble had started entirely with the Games, a fact I was not going to bring up.

"You're quiet," she accused when I didn't respond to her rant.

"Trying to figure out what to do." Standing, I crossed to her and took her phone. "The stories are going to drive you crazy."

"Keep it." She glared at the phone like it was a snake. "I'm tired of the lies."

That was the trouble with lies built on truth, they wounded deeper than deceit itself. We were all reeling, because we'd each participated in this cover-up and we'd all be held up to scrutiny.

"We need to issue a press release," I decided.

"Not another press conference," Georgia grumbled.

"I think we've all had enough of those. A press release, but not until we find Anders."

Norris and Georgia left to check the progress on finding Anders, leaving me with my wife. I knelt before her, resting my cheek on her lap.

"Remember when I proposed?" I asked softly.

"You offered me all of London." I could hear the smile in her voice. It was reassuring that she still found that memory joyful.

"Have you changed your mind yet?"

"Not yet," she promised, brushing my hair from my forehead. "We'll deal with it."

"How?"

"Like we always do. We'll confront it and we'll overcome it."

"That will take forever," I pointed out. We were still weathering the public outcry over Sarah. At least in her case, most people were more interested in watching her every move as she adapted to life after her coma. I could only hope Anders didn't provide such colourful entertainment for those that would start watching him.

"You didn't let me tell you the rest of the plan," she said. "While we deal with it, we have lots and lots of sex."

"This plan is looking up." I nuzzled closer to where she carried our child. "And a baby—which is the best distraction."

"And a baby," she echoed. "A distraction for the press?"

"No," I said sharply. That thought had never occurred to me. I would never use my children that way. "It's the best distraction for me—holding our child, watching you care for her."

"Or him."

"Or him," I agreed, albeit grudgingly.

"Belle likes William," Clara said, filling my mind with prettier thoughts than I could, "and Alice."

"William or Alice. The baby will be here soon." I turned my face up to her. "You were telling me that the doctor wanted to schedule the cesarean."

"Yes, but it's weeks away." She waved it off. "We can do it later."

"It can't be here soon enough," I said and meant it.

ONCE CLARA HAD TAKEN MY ANGER FROM NUCLEAR TO simmering, I decided I couldn't put off the inevitable any longer. Anders hadn't been located yet, but I knew exactly where the other party in question was. A little past noon, Clara laid down for a nap. I fought the urge to follow her into our bedroom and lose myself in her for a few hours.

I made it to Sarah's room before I remembered that I'd asked Norris to place her elsewhere. Whipping my mobile out, I dialed him.

"There's still no news," he answered.

"I presumed when I hadn't heard anything," I said dryly. "Where did you put my darling sister?"

"I don't think that's a good idea."

I could see him, wherever he was, coming to complete attention. He must have known I would eventually hunt her down. It was time she faced what she'd done.

"Norris, tell me where she is."

"I will take you to her," he offered.

"You're busy, and I am in complete control. I only need to speak with her."

"Alexander—"

"I'll call Georgia." I hung up on him, which meant I was on borrowed time. Wherever he'd stashed her, he'd be on his way. I'd played the odds and headed out of the North Wing. It was unlikely that he'd put her near my family after last night's confrontation. That limited where he might place her. The staff rooms were out of the question. I could only imagine the damage she could do spinning stories to the employees.

Georgia was on my side. I knew because she answered with three words. "The Belgian Suite."

"Thank you." I ended the call and stuck my mobile in my pocket, ignoring an incoming call. He wasn't going to talk me out of going there.

I had no doubt that Sarah had insisted on the Belgian Suite, which was reserved for important foreign dignitaries, impeccably decorated, and well-secured.

If she thought that good locks would keep me out, she would find out how wrong she was. But she didn't try to keep me out. She was waiting for me, doors unlocked.

"It took longer for you to come after me than I thought." She sipped tea at the small breakfast table.

"Get dressed," I snapped. "It's disgraceful."

"There's our father." Her hand cupped her chin and she stared at me like a welcome ghost. "He's coming out more and more, isn't he? He would have tracked me down ages ago, though."

"You're leaving," I told her. "It's up to you if you do it in your robe or not."

She pulled the lapels of her red silk dressing gown together and frowned. "Where will I go? How will you control me?"

"I obviously can't control you," I ground out. That was the problem.

"That's where you aren't like him." Her head fell back and she stared into the ceiling like she was watching her memories. "He never realized that. He hated that."

"You were sixteen then. He could control you and—"

"He was our father. Blah. Blah. That's a tired excuse. You're the King now, Alexander, or so everyone insists on telling me. I have to admit your wife seems to be the one in charge." She dropped her gaze, peering at me with a poisoned smile. "Is that why you have to tie her up? So you're in control of someone?"

She dangled the insults overhead waiting for me to snap at them, but I didn't. "I'm not playing a child's game. These are lives you're messing with, and it ends now."

"It ends when I say it ends." She slammed her fist on the table, sending her tea cup toppling from its saucer.

"You said it yourself: I am King now, Sarah. If you won't respect it, I will enforce it until you do."

All hope I'd had that my sister would return to us and bring our family closer was gone. I held no illusions anymore. She shattered them and scattered the pieces behind her. I wouldn't allow her to break anything else.

"There are real issues facing this family. I can't put up with your tantrums."

"What issues?" she cried. "I don't warrant knowing, do I? You keep saying family like I'm a part of it, but you don't want me here."

"You don't have the privilege of knowing. You want respect? Trust? Earn them and stop acting like a spoiled brat."

"Admit it," she said. "When I woke up..."

"I wished you hadn't," I roared, "and now I wish we'd let you go ten years ago."

"Alexander," Norris said sharply from behind me, but my words had struck their target.

"Get out! Get out! Get out!" Sarah screamed, sobs wracking her body.

I searched for guilt, but all I felt was the cold edge of anger driven by purpose. If Sarah wouldn't grow up, I would force her to—there was no other option.

Turning, I strode from the room, pausing to issue one final command. "Take her phone."

I hadn't turned away from my darkness. I'd turned it to fuel, but now it overwhelmed me. Instead of continuing to my office, I sought my wife. Standing by the side of our bed, I studied my wife as she slept, her lips parted and her body curled on its side.

What toll was this taking on her? I saw the stress and frustration I felt reflected in her. There was only one way for both of us to escape.

Moving into the bed next to her, I ran a finger down her spine. Then I pressed my lips to her neck, stealing her from her dreams.

"X?" she murmured.

"I need you, Poppet." It was hard to control how much. It tore at me, clawing to be released.

Her hand found the one skimming over her breast and she clutched it to her chest. "I need you, too." She paused and I felt it aching in her touch. "But are you still angry?"

"Yes." I wouldn't lie. It would undermine the life we were building.

"Don't ask me," she begged.

I understood. It was my limit. I'd set it, but now I was forcing her to be the one to respect it. She wouldn't be able to if I asked. She would submit without fear.

But I couldn't take that risk.

I relinquished her hand and slipped from the bed, determined to let go of the fury controlling me.

"Find your way back to me," she called after me.

I told her I would try.

Outside the door I leaned against the wall, already feeling more empowered. It had been the right choice and the hardest, but wasn't that the way of it? My eyes landed on the door across the hall. If it was Clara's nap time, it would be Elizabeth's.

Peeking my head inside, I startled Penny who was devouring a romance novel.

"Sir?" she whispered.

"I wanted to hold my daughter." I didn't owe her an explanation, and she didn't ask for more. She took her leave, telling me to find her later. Going to the crib, I realized Elizabeth needed a new bed. She wasn't a baby anymore. A bittersweet sadness filled me. I had so much of her life to look forward to, but it was passing too quickly.

How much longer would I be able to hold her in my arms? How much longer would she climb into my lap or reach for my hand?

I lifted her and her body flailed, instantly calming when I cradled her to me. Carrying her to a chair, I sat and rocked her slowly.

I'd always questioned if I could make a bit of difference in the world. She was my answer. There had been a time when I'd thought I could never love. Clara had proven me wrong, and then she'd given me this beautiful gift of pure love.

I had no idea how long I sat there. My time with her would never be long enough. When she finally stirred, a tiny hand, warm from sleep, pressed to my cheek.

"Daddy," she blubbered before burrowing her head against my chest, frustrated to be neither awake nor asleep.

"Wake up, beautiful girl, the world is waiting for you," I called.

She peeked up at me and giggled. The sound of it supplanted the last anger inside me. There was no room for it when I was filled with this much love.

We found Penny in the parlour, and the two went off to find a snack.

Returning to my bedroom, I knocked gently, not wanting to wake Clara if she was still resting. She opened the door a moment later.

"There you are," she murmured. Moving to the side she opened the door to our room and my eyes fell on the rope she'd placed carefully at the foot of the bed. "Let's forget for a moment together."

CHAPTER 23

CLARA

Mistakes became insanity when you kept making the same ones. After the initial shock had worn off and Anders stayed out of the spotlight, interest died down enough that Alexander convinced him to come to us. We waited for a midweek afternoon to bring him when tourists were at the lowest numbers and most Londoners were at work.

None of the precaution mattered, judging from the scowl Anders wore as he waltzed into the ambassador's entrance. I'd gone down to meet him, Alexander refusing flatly to come along. I'd planned to go outside but thought better of it when I saw the mass of people pressing the barricades outside the gates. So much for the best laid plans.

"Are you the welcoming committee?" he asked, the scowl transitioning to a smile. It was the kind of greeting most women fantasized about. Certainly, most women would find Anders drool-worthy, especially now in his black jeans and leather jacket. If he'd wanted to play down the situation, he shouldn't have dressed as the Royal black sheep.

"I have Georgia guarding Sarah in her room," I informed

him in a clipped, professional tone. "Edward and Alexander are waiting in his office."

"And they sent you?" This time he didn't sound as happy about it.

I hated that it came to this—constantly reinforcing a sense of distance between us. I genuinely liked Anders but I would never feel that way about him.

"I offered." I had been the one to convince all parties to agree to this meeting.

"So this bitch sister of his..."

I cleared my throat.

"So this bitch sister of *ours*," he corrected himself. It wasn't what I'd meant, but it would do. "Will she be there?"

"No," I said resolutely. Sarah was still in the Belgian Suite. We'd probably have to burn it with fire to make it hospitable after she finally vacated it, but we'd all agreed that including her was a very, bad idea. "She's preparing to move out."

"Didn't she just move in?" He tilted his head like he was trying to shake loose enough brain power to understand how this family worked.

"And it's going so well." I reached for the door leading into the North Wing, but he jumped in front of me to hold it open. I pressed my lips into a thin smile. "Thank you."

"So what are we going to talk about? Do I have to learn Royal protocol or some shit?" He raked a hand through his mess of blond hair.

It was moments like that which reminded me he was Alexander's brother. Neither of them could see the similarities they shared. Because the one they both had in problematic quantities was stubbornness.

"Options." I kept my answers simple and to the point not wanting to give him more to work with. He'd spun an entire imagined romance out of a few conversations.

"Is this how it's going to be?" Anders asked in a soft voice, stopping in the hall and forcing me to do the same. "Edward will act like we can all be one big happy family and Alexander will treat me like something stuck to the bottom of his shoe?"

He paced closer and paused, lowering his voice. "And you acting like a robot because you can't admit the truth?"

"What truth? Anders, I can't tell you how you feel but I can tell you how I feel."

"Then admit it. Admit you feel something." His hand reached out to brush my shoulder, but I pivoted away from him.

"I care about you as a friend." How did we keep finding our way back here?

"Because he has you confused. You're so caught up in pleasing him that you don't know what's real," he said harshly.

"I have no problem with reality. We're intimately acquainted. While you were holed up drinking whiskey in SoHo, I was here coming up with a strategy to help *you* as was Alexander." I kept my voice low. We were only a few steps from Alexander's office now and I wasn't sure if he could hear us.

Anders showed no interest in self-preservation. "Am I supposed to be grateful? He dragged me into this."

"Neither of you are to blame for your DNA," I stopped him. "There's only one person alive that you can pin that on, so go talk to her if you want to yell at someone."

"Don't drag my mother into this," he warned me. "She raised me."

"With Albert's financial help." I held up my palm before he could blow his top at this perceived snub. "I don't think you owe any of us anything. We only want to help you adjust."

"To what?" Anders laughed at me and I felt the familiar urge to slap him. It was a sensation his brother had inspired more than few times as well. "Nothing's going to change for me. I'm just the latest in whatever cock-and bull scandal your lot is handling this week."

"You're wrong." I shook my head, feeling slightly sad for him but mostly annoyed. I'd once thought the press would have no interest in me either. Even during Alexander and I's brief periods apart, they'd hounded me and dissected my every movement.

Once a Royal, forever a Royal.

"I'm afraid my wife is right," Alexander called from the doorway. I didn't miss how much emphasis he placed on 'my wife.'

"Boys let's behave," I suggested as I passed them both and stepped through the door.

They followed me sullenly through the door, taking opposites chairs from one another and then studiously avoiding looking in the other's direction. This was going to be one long meeting.

"I ordered tea," Edward said brightly. "I wasn't sure how you take it, so they brought up the lot." He held out a cup and saucer to Anders who leaned over to take them with some hesitation.

"I'm not particular. We didn't have anything fancy growing up." Anders didn't add anything to the black tea.

Edward's smile grew forced as he added milk and sugar to his.

"You could have had fancy tea with the money our father sent," Alexander said. He'd spread himself in his chair, taking up all available space as if to send the message that the chair also belonged to him. I was going to have to step in if they started marking their territories in more alarming fashions.

"Is this how it's going to be?" I asked, unwilling to play this game with them. "We agreed to meet and decide what to do together. Anders, we aren't going to tell you how to handle this, but we are going to offer advice and resources if you'll take them—and you're a wanker if you don't. Alexander, we're all aware of your standing in this room, in this family, and in this country, so stop posturing. Edward, I'll take some tea."

He poured me some out of a second pot made with an herbal blend, his lips twitching at the tongue lashing I'd just given his brothers.

"You know," he said thoughtfully passing it to me after adding extra sugar, "I'm not the youngest anymore."

I raised an eyebrow, bringing the tea cup to my lips. "No, you aren't."

"But he's hardly the baby of the family."

"I'm not what?" Anders seemed to be tracking the conversation's turns with difficulty.

"You'll get used to them. They pretty much speak their own language," Alexander said. "I suppose I'll get my own tea."

"Have you forgotten how?" Edward asked and Anders smirked.

"See?" I placed my cup in its saucer and returned it to the coffee table. "You three are already acting like family—ganging up on one another and competing."

"It must warm the heart," Alexander said.

"Now that we've gotten the pleasantries out of the way, let's discuss what's going on," I advised.

"Alexander only pretends to be in charge," Edward muttered to Anders.

"Enough," I warned him. "We've prepared a press release."

"You mean I don't have to sit through another press conference? Brilliant."

"We've had enough of those for a while," Alexander agreed.

We had been hosting them with an alarming frequency. If we could avoid another, since the others had ended in near disaster, it would be for the best.

"What are you going to say? How are we going to cover this up?" Anders drained his cup and waited.

I looked to the others, wondering if it was better coming from me or one of them. "We don't want to deny it."

"What do you mean? Look, the tea is lovely but I don't want any of this life."

"We know," Alexander said with astonishing sincerity. "I wouldn't either if I was you."

"You don't know the first thing about being me," Anders said coolly.

"I know that you've broken ribs four times, that when you crashed your first car it nearly cost your mother her house. I know that you fell in love with a girl who ran off with your best mate. I know more than you think." Alexander leaned forward and picked up the milk. "I know things you don't. That car? Our father took care of that. Just like he took care of it when you were nearly expelled from secondary school."

"What is this?" Anders hissed. "You wanted me to come here so you could prove I'm in debt to you?"

"If I know all of that and it wasn't hard to confirm these matters once we knew your name; the press will know it eventually, too. They won't let this go. The media isn't in the business of turning a blind eye to a juicy bit of news—and you have their mouths watering."

"What he said," Edward added.

"Then what?" Anders slumped in his seat.

"We issue a press release that confirms the story with enough details that there's less incentive to go digging for more."

"We beat them to the story," I explained.

"Whose genius idea is this?"

"Ours," Alexander said.

"You've been meeting and discussing how to handle my life without me?" Anders asked. He actually sounded a bit hurt.

"We did try to call," I said flatly.

"They won't go away if they know."

"No, it will probably get worse," I admitted, frowning when his eyes darted to the door like he was contemplating making a break for it. "For a while. They will lose interest."

"Bollocks," Anders said. "They haven't lost interest in any of you. They're still debating your wedding"—he pointed to Edward—"and analyzing every breach of protocol that Clara makes, and we all know what they think of Alexander."

"Do enlighten me," Alexander said.

"You're paranoid, delusional, seeing threats where there's only smoke," he said directly to Alexander. It was less a quote than an accusation.

"There's rarely smoke without a fire. Lesson one."

"All those threats are real." I took a deep breath. He hadn't reacted well to our suggestion of the press release. He was going to like the next bit even less. "Which is why we need to increase your security."

"Increase?" Anders echoed. "I have security?"

"It obviously won't affect you much," Alexander said dryly.

"I can handle myself," he said.

"My jaw remembers that," Alexander said, "but you're not up against a barroom brawl."

"What am I up against? Is that Jacobson rubbish true?"

Somehow I knew he wouldn't believe anything Alexander had to say, so I answered. "Every word of it."

"Fuck." For the first time, we'd made a dent.

"Why?"

"That's a long story," Alexander warned him. "I'm happy to tell you about it, but there are other matters to consider."

"Security guards and press releases aren't enough?"

Alexander peered at me, letting me take the lead. The next bit was my idea, and one the others weren't sold on. "We want to bring in a handler."

"A body guard? You said that already."

"More like a publicist," I said slowly. "Someone who

focuses on crisis management and will know the right thing to say when you're cornered."

"A publicist? The track has those," he started.

"It needs to be someone we know and trust," Edward broke in.

Anders narrowed his eyes but he didn't argue. "Who?"

I WAS EXHAUSTED—PHYSICALLY AND EMOTIONALLY—BY the time the meeting ended. Edward walked Anders out this time. The two seemed to be warming to each other. Alexander and Anders? They were still as tepid as ice.

"That went well," Alexander said and I glared at him. "I meant that."

"What meeting were you at?" We were dragging Anders into our family kicking and screaming because we were out of choices. I didn't flatter myself that he'd listened to us out of anything other than self-interest—and it had taken him long enough to locate that part of himself.

"He listened." Alexander held out both his hands and pulled me from the chair. "I think that's the most we can hope for at this point."

"I suppose."

"You look tired." My husband pulled me against him—or as close as he could get me these days. His hands closed over the round obstacle between us.

"One month to go," I reminded him.

"Have I thanked you?" he said suddenly.

I cocked my head, looking into his brilliant blue eyes. "For?"

"Having my baby," he murmured. "

"There wasn't a lot of choice in the matter," I teased, overcome by the cocktail of emotions this dredged up. "When you shag as much as we do, it's bound to happen."

"That isn't the point. You're still doing all the work of bringing our child into the world. I wanted to thank you for that, and in that spirit..." He laced his fingers through mine and pulled me toward the hall.

"What are you up to?" I asked as he led me toward the lift.

"I wanted to show how much I appreciated it."

We stepped inside the lift and I hooked an arm around his neck, craning my face to his. "I'm listening. What do you have in mind?"

"I wonder what's on your mind." His mouth skimmed over mine.

"I am basically a walking mass of hormones," I informed him.

"Is that so?" He swallowed, pressing the pad of his thumb to my lower lip.

I nipped it with my teeth. "It is."

"That is a shame." He tore himself away as the lift doors slid open.

"Not the reaction a girl wants to hear," I muttered, skulking behind him.

"I have something to show you," he said and before I could process what was happening, he'd backed me against the wall. His mouth trailed down my neck pausing to pay homage to my collarbone. "But after..."

My hand found his cock, stroking it through his slacks. "Are you sure?"

"Fuck, Poppet. You're making this hard." Whiskers

rasped my skin as he groaned, pushing his erection against my palm.

"That's the point, X."

He pushed away from me, his arms bracketing me. "Later, I'm going to fuck you until you forget your name, and since your cunt is so in need, you call the shots. My mouth. This"—he ground harder against my hand—"or these"—he reached over and brushed a finger over my breasts. "Wherever you want to be fucked, however you want to be fucked— as many times as you need to be fucked."

"Yes, please."

"But for now," he said, pulling his body from mine and buttoning his jacket, "let's pretend like my cock isn't about to split open my pants and you're not dripping thinking about it —and let me give you your present."

"Wait," I said, blinking rapidly, "there's an actual present? I thought that was a euphemism."

"You have a one track mind, my wicked queen." He held out his arm and when I reluctantly peeled myself from the wall, he stepped behind me and covered my eyes.

"This is a step in the right direction, but maybe a blindfold?"

"I can't imagine what you would have done if I'd blind-folded you."

"Torn off my clothes," I answered truthfully.

Alexander laughed as he brought his lips to my ear and whispered, "Save the dirty talk for later, Poppet, or we're going to have another Royal scandal on our hands."

I was about to ask what he meant when he guided me a few more steps and took his hands from my eyes.

"Surprise!"

It took a second to process the presence of my friends and family. But even when it began to sink in, I felt out of sorts. We were standing in a room I'd never stepped foot in before.

"Where are we?" I asked, turning around in the room.

"Down the hall from our room," Alexander told me.

"In the baby's room," Belle squealed, running up to hug me. "You thought he forgot!"

"And you knew!" I accused.

"Well, between bringing family members back from the dead and discovering new ones, he's had his hands a bit full. We all helped," Edward said, quickly adding, "But it was all his idea."

Alexander's hands settled on my shoulders as I stared around me in wonder. "What room was this?"

"That closet you said we'd never use," he said.

"Which is a tragedy," Belle said. "What girl willingly gives up closet space?"

Edward patted her back in sympathy. "We tried."

"We probably won't use it too much for a while, but we had the room," Alexander said casually as though he hadn't just given me the sweetest gift in the world.

He led me on a tour of the room between hugs from my parents and sister, who'd been invited for the unveiling.

"You keep insisting it's a boy, so I wanted something neutral," he said.

"So you asked Edward," I guessed.

"Exactly."

They'd landed on a warm gray palette with flourishes of silver. I paused when my eyes landed on the gilded crib. "Is that Elizabeth's?"

Edward and Alexander exchanged a look. "We moved it in here this morning. She's outgrown it."

"I know," I said softly, but it still tugged at my heart.

The walls had been repapered with a delicate silver damask that caught the afternoon light filtering through the billowing, white sheers beautifully. Rather than the doll-house that Alexander had placed in Elizabeth's room, he'd found an ornate castle and surrounded it with stuffed toys: alligators and teddies and tigers. In front of the hearth, two matching gliders upholstered in striped silk sat with a large ottoman.

"Two?" I asked him.

"It will make story time easier if we can both hold one of them," he murmured in my ear.

I swallowed against the tell-tale rawness creeping up my throat and turned to him. "I love it."

"And it's neutral, so you can add whatever you want," he continued, rolling his eyes as he obviously regurgitated some-thing Belle or Edward had sold him on.

"Stop hogging my best friend and let her open her presents," Belle demanded, attempting unsuccessfully to extricate me from Alexander's eyes.

"Stop trying to steal my wife." He shot her the side eye.

"Fine, but I'm eating the cake."

"Cake?" I pulled free of him. "There's cake?"

"Don't take it personally." Edward put an arm around his brother's shoulders. "No man can compete with cake. Not even you."

The cake was also shaped like a castle, complete with a small moat and drawstring bridge.

"Fit for a little prince or princess," my mother said, holding a cake knife, "but how do you cut it?"

"Let me." Lola plucked the knife from our mother's fingers and stood back to analyze her best course of action.

"Can you get me a minute with my sister?" I whispered to Belle.

"Madeline," Belle said, wrapping an arm around my mom's shoulder, "I've been wanting your thoughts on my nursery."

"Well, there are so many options." She fanned a hand over her chest, deeply flattered by the attention. Madeline Bishop was full of opinions, and I was going to owe Belle for sitting through all of them.

"Hey, I need your help with something," I said to Lola.

"Me?" She paused, a slice of cake balancing on a server.

"Do you know who Sofia King is?" I asked her.

"The woman who just married Isaac Blue?" Lola rolled her eyes. "I don't live under a rock. I wept that day along with every other woman alive. Belle went to their wedding. I don't know how she controlled herself. I would have objected."

I'd met Isaac and while he was certainly charming, he had nothing on my husband. I didn't tell Lola that.

"I had Belle reach out to her but she's taking a permanent vacation," I explained.

"Wasn't she some type of celebrity fixer?"

"Uh-huh." I nodded, wondering how much I needed to tell her. "She basically deals with crisis and reputation management."

"That's how she landed Isaac," Lola said, pushing a slice of cake a bit too forcefully off the server. It landed with a splat. She frowned at the mess and set it to the side. "I could have turned him around!"

"Exactly!" She'd gotten there without me, but she didn't see it that way.

"While I appreciate your belief that I could land the hottest movie star on the planet with my phenomenal publicity skills that ship sailed—I heard to Fiji."

"They're in Seychelles," I corrected her.

"What is your life?" Lola asked, staring at me like I'd grown a second head.

"The point is that you could do that, right?" I scooped a bit of frosting onto my finger and licked it off.

"Sure, but I don't need a job. Bless has me plenty busy."

"I need you," I stopped her, "and I've already spoken with Belle. It would only be for a few weeks. Sofia even agreed to walk you through the situation over the phone."

"What situation?" Lola's eyes narrowed. "Who am I fixing?"

"Anderson Stone."

Her mouth fell open like a hinge had broken. I waited but she seemed to have lost her capacity for speech.

"We're going public," I said.

"With what?" Lola finally found her voice.

"It's true. He's Albert's son," I whispered.

"I knew it!" Lola stamped her foot. "Seriously, Mom said that you would—"

"Lola," I cut her off. "Part of this is discretion. We need someone to help him navigate the next few weeks. Months at the most."

"Months?" she repeated, sounding unsure.

"It has to be someone we trust. There's...there's other things going on."

She pursed her lips as if digesting what I was asking.

"You'll be paid, of course."

"I don't need money," she reminded me. "I just don't know anything about racing."

"I doubt you'll be doing too much of that," I said dryly. "Just meet him and see where it goes?"

"Okay, but only because you're my sister." She slid the cake knife expertly through a turret.

"He's pretty cute, too."

"Not my type." Lola shrugged.

Well, at least, that wouldn't complicate matters. I didn't bother to tell her that Anders hadn't totally agreed to this plan either. It was the best shot we had at getting ahead of this situation. With Alexander concerned about loyalty in light of Jacobson's release, we needed someone close to us who could handle the situation. Anyone that kept our mother in line deserved to be awarded a medal. Lola was the perfect choice.

I'd just picked up a plate for Alexander when I spotted Sarah at the door. Our eyes met and she vanished. Excusing myself, I followed after her.

"Sarah," I called when I caught up to her in the living room.

She whirled around, crossing her arms over her chest. Her face was cosmetic-free, showing how truly stunning she was when she didn't hide herself under layers of blush and lipstick. Then, I spotted the slight silver scar running from her forehead down to her cheekbone.

"It's from the accident," she said, turning it away from me.

"I brought you cake." I held the plate out to her.

"Pepper says I can't eat carbs anymore." But her gaze lingered on the cake.

"You need new friends. Preferably ones looking out for you and not your ass." I moved closer and shoved it at her.

"Edward invited me," she said, stabbing a bite with the fork. "I didn't crash."

"Look, living here might not be the best fit for all of us, but you are a member of this family. You should come to parties. I would have invited you, but..."

"It was a surprise." She slid the bite into her mouth. "It must be nice."

"What?" I asked.

"A party," she said. "People who care enough for something like that."

"Sarah your family cares about you," I began.

"So you're planning a surprise for my birthday next week?"

I fumbled for the right response, which was definitely enough of an answer.

"That's what I thought." She shrugged, but her eyes glistened as she shoved a bigger piece of cake in her mouth. "Why would anyone remember? I guess they weren't all sitting around crying every year on my birthday."

She swiped at her nose with the back of her hand muttering "stupid" under her breath.

"That's not stupid," I said gently, wishing I had a tissue.

"The other day I had to do the math because I didn't know how old I would be—and then I realized it didn't matter. Because the year doesn't matter. I'll always be sixteen to all of them," she confessed.

"Sarah, I can't imagine how you're feeling, but they're worried. You're doing all the things you were doing before the accident. They don't want to lose you again."

"They never lost me." The words were so broken that I realized she didn't believe it herself. It was merely a wish.

She'd come back and we'd tried to wedge her into our lives and pretend like nothing had changed. We had focused on the publicity and on security and we'd failed to really ask ourselves what she needed. In return, she'd reverted to how she was before the accident, acting out for attention. We'd focused on public perception more than her feelings, just like Albert would have done, so she'd done exactly what she would have done to get him to notice her.

But Alexander wasn't his father and with time, we would figure out how to make all of this work.

"You never lost them either," I reminded her.

"Everything's changed. Alex is a grown-up. I mean, no one even calls him Alex! And he's running the country *and* he's married. *Edward* is married! He's my *little* brother. And there's Anderson, and oh my God, I was flirting with him!" The confessions were coming rapid-fire now and for the first time, I knew that she was feeling as lost as we were.

"Come on." I took her by the elbow. "Come back to the party."

"I don't want to intrude," she hedged.

"You won't. You're family." For the first time, that felt like the truth.

CHAPTER 24

ALEXANDER

The numerous legislative measures Parliament had introduced to stop secret meetings and backdoor deals turned out to be a load of rubbish. I knew this as soon as I received a summons to White's, the exclusive gentleman's club. Established in the seventeenth century for the most upper of the upper classes, not much had changed. My father had registered me at birth, but I'd never stepped foot inside—until today.

That I was being called for a metaphorical spanking by the nine-member panel that had been called to examine my exercise of Royal Prerogative by a group of men keen to flaunt their own power had not escaped my attention.

We were stopped by a porter at the entrance asking for our membership names.

"Alexander, King of England, Most High and Noble," I said flatly, unimpressed by the man's dedication to appearances.

"And?"

"These are my men," I said. Neither seemed ruffled by the pipsqueak, who didn't seem to know when he was beat.

"Are they official guests? We will need to register them on the ledger," he said.

"For fuck's sake," Smith grumbled next to me.

"Mr. Smith Price, Esquire," I added.

"Norris, King's advisor." He tapped the book. "Two r's, son."

"We're meeting Lord May."

"You will want the Cigar Club. If you take the stairs, it will be on the left." He pointed to the staircase occupying a good portion of the ground floor.

"Your Majesty," Norris prompted under his breath. "There is a time to be impressed by the presence of a member. That time is now."

"Y-y-your Majesty," he tacked on weakly.

"You're going to give that boy a heart attack," I muttered to Norris as we took the stairs.

"It can't be the first time someone has put him in his place, especially not here." Smith took in his surroundings with the air of a man accustomed to both clandestine meetings and checking for the exits. Given the company he'd kept for most of his life, the behaviour was likely deeply engrained. It was yet another reason he was a valuable addition to my team.

None of us were terribly impressed by the opulent, if garish furnishings. It smacked a bit too much of old money, and I lived in a palace. A number of priceless portraits most likely listed as being in private collections hung on the walls, plaques heralding the generous benefactor loaning the piece.

Antiques from the last four hundred years of existence were crammed into every nook and landing.

"It could use a woman's touch," Norris said under his breath, earning him a glare from a grumpy passerby.

"I think the fairer species is lucky they don't have to put up with this," Smith said.

White's membership was notoriously men-only. Many other longstanding clubs in London had given in to the persuasions of the sexual revolution but here we were in the last bastion of sexism—and likely a number of other isms.

The Cigar Room had a no smoking sign prominently displayed on entry. It seemed even the misogynists had to heel to public health orders. That was fine with me. I couldn't imagine coming home reeking of cigar fumes without Clara sending my suit to be burned.

The rest of the ensemble had already gathered, no doubt to discuss strategy and drink expensive Scotch: the two things most of them were particularly skilled at.

"Gentlemen." I used the greeting loosely.

"You've brought friends." May didn't bother with hellos. He'd been a member of the House of Lords long enough to resent having to deal with the third king of his lifetime—and I suspected his least favourite.

"My council," I explained.

"This is a rather private matter, hence why we asked to speak to you where discretion could be guaranteed."

"You hold a higher opinion of your peers than I do." I unbuttoned my jacket and took a seat. Both Smith and Norris followed suit, taking up places on either side of me.

I doubted I was in danger of anything more than character assassination by meeting with these men, but Norris had prepped Smith on expectations before we left. Only after I'd explained my rationale for asking the man to be present.

Unknown to both of them it was an audition of sorts. I wasn't certain that I could persuade Smith Price to join my staff but I was willing to try.

"And who is this?" Lord Byrd whacked a walking stick at Smith's feet.

Smith bared his teeth before he answered. "Smith Price, junior barrister."

"Junior?" Byrd sniffed as though this distinction was important.

"He was being considered for King's Council before he took a sabbatical." I understood what clout meant to men like this.

May peered at him from over his reading glasses, finally abandoning his newspaper. "He's too young."

"Formidability will trump age it seems," I said coolly.

"Enough of this," said Prime Minister Clark, who looked uncomfortable by both the proceedings and his surroundings.

He didn't seem the type to belong to this group. He'd risen through the House of Commons and although his upbringing was privileged, it had not reached the upper echelons of snobbery.

A waiter appeared offering me a brandy menu but I waved it away. Smith followed my cue but didn't look pleased about it.

What he didn't realize was the subtle shade I'd just thrown at the panel. This did not escape them, however. If old men could be counted on for one thing it would be the stubborn acceptance of nonsensical traditions.

If the king didn't drink, neither did they.

Norris smiled next to me and straightened his tie. It was time to get down to business.

"You called me here," I reminded them, leaning back into the chair and spreading my arms.

"There is a vocal majority in the Parliament who have brought up concerns regarding the Royal Prerogative. Most feel your arrest of Oliver Jacobson is in direct conflict with English law."

"The last time I checked I was the head of English law," I said, tapping the leather arm.

"Figurehead," Clark corrected me. "With the Fixed-Term Parliament Act and the—"

"I didn't come here for a civics lesson," I interrupted him. "There are conditions in which I may exercise some rights that have more recently been largely forgone. Surely, the assassination of my father and attacks on the Royal line warrant my actions."

I looked to Smith for confirmation. He tipped his head, pressing his lips together, as if to say I was firmly in a grey area in this line of thought. I made a mental note to ask him how to move that firmly out of nebulous territory.

"But when the King's action conflicts with Parliament's ability to function, we have a problem." There was a carefully concealed message in May's words. "There are procedures for such a matter."

"If I may," Smith said, ignoring the shocked looks from the cadre of grumpy, old men, "we have consistent and compelling evidence that the Crown has been victim of a continued conspiracy meant to eradicate the monarchy."

"There have always been attempts to abolish the monarchy, they never make any progress," Byrd said loudly.

"There is abolition and there is treason," I said in a low voice. "Jacobson was involved in the latter."

"What about this attack on the Child Watch symposium, the one believed to target the Queen? He was in custody!"

"We're intelligent men." Smith shifted in his chair, covering his smile momentarily before continuing, "No plot of this magnitude involves a single man. In fact, we've come to suspect that Jacobson is merely a pawn in a much larger scheme."

"Who knows how deeply it's rooted wherever it's planted," I said, measuring each word for maximum impact.

"There's an implication there I don't appreciate." Byrd tapped his cane.

"I am well aware of all of these things." I was losing patience. In the past few weeks I'd sat in a number of meetings with others members of Parliament, assessing their feelings on the Crown. I had no idea where these men stood and I wasn't certain I cared. They were amongst the oldest living members of the House of Lords and therefore heralded from a time before the scales were tipped more equally. "Why did you wish to speak with me?"

"These accusations concern us. We could not simply allow you to hold one of our own with no consequences," May said to my surprise.

"You held a different opinion when we last spoke," I said, recalling our meeting in February.

"Mixed company matters." His eyes flickered to my companions, men he considered below our pedigree. "It would be wise to remember that. The House of Lords has no desire to see the monarchy abolished."

"What a relief," I said flatly.

"But we will not allow you to undermine our authority," he continued, ignoring me. "The arrest of Oliver Jacobson without the knowledge and support of Parliament could not be tolerated."

"The man killed your King," Norris said, continuing before they could contradict him, "He may not have pulled the trigger but he was instrumental in loading the gun."

Clark cleared his throat. "We would have been happy to take that stance had we been afforded consideration in his arrest."

"Prime Minister, with due respect, allow the big boys to play," May barked.

The Minister fell silent and I realized I'd been called to the Council of Ghosts. Judging from how Norris sat up sharply, he'd realized the same thing.

"Interesting," I said. Lacing my fingers together, I tried to account for this turn of events. "So, tell me, and this will decide if we continue these conversations. Did you have my father killed? I assure you I would understand if you did. He could be a right bastard."

"He could," May agreed curtly, "but no. Albert shared our vision of Parliament's role. We had no reason to be concerned over his reign."

"Is that how you decide?" Despite myself, I felt a slight shiver as I asked.

"It's a consideration," May admitted.

"And as far as I'm concerned?" I asked.

"You're young," Byrd said sharply. "Youth can be forgiven. I imagine you understand this considering your difficulties with your sister. But understanding should never be mistaken for permission."

"Noted." I stood and buttoned my jacket. "Gentlemen, this has been enlightening."

"We'll be in touch," May said simply.

I motioned for Norris and Smith to join me. As soon as we were past the doors, Smith spoke, "What was that about?"

"Not here," I said through clenched teeth. I nodded in greeting to a number of men pausing to pay their regards.

When remained silent until we reached the Range Rover. As soon as we were inside, I turned to explain to Smith. "Have you ever heard of the Council of Ghosts?"

"Yeah, but I've also heard of the bogey-man," he said with a shrug, "and I haven't feared him since I was child."

Norris watched us in the rear view mirror. "You just walked through a nightmare, son."

"Does he call everyone 'son?'" Smith asked, still nonplussed by this revelation.

That meant he didn't understand what we'd just learned. "The Council of Ghosts is the kind of bedtime story you tell little aristocrats before you tuck them in so they mind their matters at the garden party. I never believed they were real."

"Wait." Smith swiveled to stare back at White's. "Are you telling me...?"

"You just met the Kingmakers—that's the part of the story they tell the children who sleep in the palace," I said grimly. "A group of eight—obviously, Clark isn't one of them—with the authority of a shadow Magna Carta of sorts. If the Council believes a king should be deposed, that's the end of it."

"And your father?" Smith asked quietly. "Do you believe them?"

I understood what he was really asking: had we just met

the men pulling Jacobson's puppet strings? I shook my head. "There was no threat to them from my father. He was a prick but he knew who to stay in with. Although, I doubt he knew who was on the Council."

"Then why would they go to the trouble of meeting you?" Smith asked.

"It felt like they were trying to advise me in their own twisted way. God knows, Clark hasn't done much for the relationship between the Crown and Parliament." I tilted my head. "I actually expected you to be able to translate what they were saying."

"It seemed simple enough to me. I don't think they were arguing as to Jacobson's role so much as pouting over not being brought into account, and that's your problem." Smith rubbed his jaw, caught in thought. "Your understanding of how Royal Prerogative works needs some work."

"It does?" I couldn't help but find this amusing. The concept felt fairly straightforward to me: I was King. End of story.

"There are limitations, measures Parliament has enacted to make this a representative government."

"It's still one group making all the decisions," I pointed out.

"But will you win if it comes down to public opinion, because that's where you'll wage this battle. The laws are supposed to protect the will of the people, so who's more concerned with their needs: you or them?"

It felt fairly obvious to me that we were all looking out for our own interests. "I want the best for my citizens but I'll stop at nothing to protect my family. I dare any man to claim differently."

"You are not any man," Norris said.

"Hence the slap on the wrist," Smith said. "It seems to me that they want you to be more in tune with rule of law."

"How do I do that?" I snapped.

"I think they want due consideration to their opinion."

"A united front," I muttered, "with sodding Parliament."

"If you're right, though, and they're Council of Ghosts, you'd be wise to heed their concerns."

"I won't be told what to do by a group of men clinging to some ancient sense of entitlement."

"That's not why you should consider them," Smith said with a hollow chuckle. "If they are the Kingmakers—this Council of Ghosts of yours, they might be the strongest allies we can make. Whoever we're up against has resources and contacts—and we have a lot to lose."

"*We* do," I said. "If I'm going to do this, I'll need someone who understands the letter of law and doesn't mind walking its edge. I know you wanted to leave this life behind, but it doesn't seem ready to give you up yet. Come to work for me."

"That depends." Smith turned and looked me dead in the eye. "I have to know you're a man who can make a deal with the devil and not mind the heat when it's time to burn."

"You'll see me dancing in hell," I vowed.

CHAPTER 25

CLARA

"Why are we doing this again?" Belle asked as she hung up her tenth call of the morning. She'd been stationed on my sofa in a pair of yoga pants and a loose sweatshirt since breakfast, when she'd shown up complaining that she would help—if she didn't die of insomnia first.

"Because my sister needs us to prove we love her," Edward reminded her.

"I think that none of us having murdered her should be enough proof," David said, paging through a magazine. Of the lot of us, he was having the most fun. Party planning was in his blood. At least one of us was enjoying himself. I couldn't quite forget that nearly every large party I'd ever hosted had ended poorly.

"He has a point." Georgia's contribution consisted of watching us from the table, her feet propped casually on what was likely a priceless heirloom.

"Why is she here?" Belle glared at her.

I shrugged. I wasn't about to drop the f-word in mixed company. Plus, the fact that Georgia flatly refused to participate seemed to undermine any burgeoning friendship between us.

"I hate this guest list," Edward announced, "so Sarah will love it."

He passed it to me and I scanned the list of names. Half consisted of people that made me want to vomit. The other half meant nothing to me. It was on par with most Royal events I'd been forced to attend.

"You didn't ask Sarah for these people, right?" I asked. The party was meant to be a surprise. Part of me hoped she might think we'd been planning it before she reminded me her birthday was this week.

"A guest list for Sarah is easy," he said. "I invited everyone I wouldn't want at my wedding."

"You had like ten people at your wedding," I pointed out. In the end, Edward and David had opted for a simple, private affair witnessed by those closest to them. I was more than a little envious of the lack of spectacle.

"You had less," he reminded me.

"The first wedding or the second?" I asked.

"We had a guest list before we decided to elope," David interrupted. "We've been keeping a running list of twats and wankers for years. Sarah will be in her comfort zone."

"Remind me to never let you lot plan a party for me," Georgia muttered, swinging her feet down and swiping a magazine from him.

I raised an eyebrow but didn't comment. Across from me, Belle grinned, obviously thinking the same thing I was. We were winning Georgia over, whether she liked it or not.

"Should we really invite Pepper?" Belle wrinkled her nose as she read the list. Out of all of us, she had the most reason to hate Pepper Lockwood, which was saying something.

"She's currently Sarah's best friend," I reminded her.

"Can we at least put her by the loo?" she asked.

"Do you know how often I use the bathroom these days?" I shook my head. "I don't want to walk past her every fifteen minutes. The kitchen?"

"If she doesn't poison the food, she'll spit in it," Edward said absently, staring at his computer as he input the invitee information.

"Put her by the band," David suggested. "It will drown her out."

"Royal Brat Pack by the band, got it." I made a note.

Belle giggled, shaking her head. "I love that name."

"That's how I knew I'd met my soul mate," Edward said.

"Excuse me," David called with mock offense.

"We need a name," Belle said.

"You already have one," Georgia said. We all turned to stare at her. She looked up from her magazine like it should be obvious. "It's what Alexander calls you."

"Alexander has a nickname for us?" I asked slowly. Suddenly, I wasn't sure I wanted to hear it. I was currently getting along with my spouse. I wasn't certain if it would change things.

"He calls you Team Queen. You didn't know that?" She closed the magazine. "He says it to us all the time."

"Wait," Edward said, "in what context are we talking?"

"I guess it does work on two levels," I admitted.

"Whenever you go out to lunch or shopping or whatever you do," she said dismissively, "we get briefed on handling Team Queen."

"Oh, really." I'd completely lost track of where I was with the menu selections. "And how do you handle us?"

"You're going to get me in trouble," Georgia grumbled, eyes narrowing.

"That depends. Because I could call my husband and ask him, right now."

"We're to stay nearby. We're to have an eye on you but never be close enough to hear you."

"We're?" I echoed. "When we went shopping at Tamara's, it was just you."

"It's never just me." She laughed as though I was being cute.

"How many?" I asked flatly.

"Depends on where you're going. As soon as we have a location, the appropriate number of men are dispatched to cover any and all exits to a building." She paused and studied me. "You really didn't know."

"Nope," I said. "It's completely unnecessary."

"He says otherwise." Georgia hung her head for a moment, then continued, like she didn't have a choice. "Only *damaged* guards are sent."

"Damaged?" I asked in a hollow voice. What the hell did that mean?

"It means we've taken a bullet."

"Why would he require that?" Edward had shut his laptop and was hanging on Georgia's every word.

"Because he knows we can," she said with a shrug. "Step in front of a bullet, I mean."

Belle had a tea cup poised at her lips. "Wow."

"Everywhere?" I clarified.

"Right now," Georgia said. "He only lets up when he's with you."

"Because he's *damaged*," I said softly.

She nodded with dangerous eyes. "You know he'd step in front of a bullet for you. He already has."

David, who hadn't spoken up until now, broke in angrily, "You're all shit at party planning."

"He has a point," Edward said, laughing uneasily. Belle joined him. But a cloud had descended over the room.

"Excuse me." I headed to my bathroom and hung my head over my sink, uncertain if I was going to vomit or not.

"You okay?" Georgia asked from behind me.

I looked at the mirror, her reflection distorted by my tears. "You don't have to do this," I told her. "You're here because he wants you nearby."

She groaned and pushed off from the door frame. Then, Georgia Kincaid did the last thing I ever expected. She hugged me.

If I'd ever bothered to imagine what it would feel like for Georgia to hug me, I would have expected it to be quick and uneasy. But she held me tightly, letting me cry.

"We're friends, happy?" she whispered. "God, this feels stupid. I don't even know if I'm doing it right."

I pulled away, wiping at my eyes and she grabbed a tissue from the counter. "You did fine," I said, taking it from her.

"Clara, you always knew why we're there."

"I knew, but I didn't know about the damaged bit. I didn't know that he..."

"Yeah, you did," she said. "That man would die for you in a second and thank you with his last breath."

"It's not that." It was difficult to explain. "Every moment, he's worried. Even when we're together. He's always waiting for the next shot. How do you let someone love you that much?"

"I don't know. I'm not experienced in that department."

"Brex," I started.

"He's a soldier. It doesn't really count. He runs toward the fire, you know? Besides, we never..."

"You never?" I repeated, suddenly distracted.

"Some of us can control our libidos." She cocked her head toward the door. "You need some time alone, or shall we go back to planning Princess Temper Tantrum's party?"

I shook my head. "That nickname..."

"It's a work in progress," she said as we joined the others.

WE'D NAILED THE IMPORTANT DETAILS BY DINNER, BUT Alexander hadn't appeared by the time my friends said good-bye. I sought him out, but he wasn't in his office. I finally found him, wandering the grounds, deep in thought.

Alexander smiled when he saw me, and the world stopped, restarting only so it could spin around him. He'd abandoned his suit and tie, even his shoes. It was the most peaceful he'd looked in a long time. He stretched out a hand and I walked to him, one hand cupping my belly.

"How was your day with your friends?" he asked.

I started to tease him about Team Queen, but bit back the response. "We managed it all. It's true, that bit about who you know. I'm not sure how we got it all sorted."

"Feel free to drop my name."

He'd approved of my plan to host a birthday party for Sarah on one condition: the party would take place somewhere else. Booking anything in London at the last minute was a challenge. "The V&A took pity on me."

He raised an eyebrow. "You're going to spoil her."

"It's big enough. I think she wants to make a splash."

"Hasn't she done enough of that?" he asked.

"What about your meeting?"

Alexander's hand gripped mine tighter. "Not now, Poppet. Just be with me for a few minutes."

I wouldn't argue with that. We'd had our fair share of chaos in the last few weeks. If we could steal a moment of peace, we would. Spring had brought fresh flowers to nearly every bit of the Royal Gardens. "It's so beautiful. I think I discover something new every day."

Alexander inclined his head for a moment, as if considering it a challenge, then a wide grin split his face. "I know what you should discover today."

He led me along the path as the sun began to fade, giving up on another day, and handing us over to night. When he finally stopped and pointed, I gasped. The wisteria had begun to bloom around the Summer House, the purple petals swaying gently against its glass-paned doors.

"How did you know?" I asked. I always missed them. The flowers were there one minute and gone the next, like so much of nature's art.

"They were my mother's favorite. She would bring us down here to see them, and then she'd decorate Sarah's birthday tables with them."

I tucked that image away for further consideration. "We should get back. Your feet have to be getting cold."

The weather seemed to agree, because the first splat of rain hit my nose as soon as I spoke.

"Always have an umbrella in London in April," I said with a sigh. I would never learn.

"If you have an umbrella, you never get caught in the rain." Alexander bent to kiss me, his palm pressing to the back of my neck, and I forgot my objection to the weather. "Come on."

We hurried to the Summer House and let ourselves in.

"It will die down in a few minutes," he said, checking the sky.

I stared at my husband—always considering me, always protecting me—and found myself in love with him all over again. He turned, his face searching mine, and caught me staring. "What is it?"

"I love you," I murmured.

"And I love you more than anything." He stroked my cheek.

I knew that. I'd always known, but in this moment, it consumed me: the sense of belonging and completion that only came with finding the one person meant for you in all the world. I would never know why fate had matched us, but I would never stop being grateful.

"Poppet," he called to me.

"X," I breathed, pushing onto my toes to kiss him.

It started sweetly but urgency ran like a current between us. Our life would change again soon. Our life was always changing. All we had was this one moment. It was the only guarantee.

That's why he kissed me like this every time.

And as much as I hated the idea of clinging to fear, I realized now, it also pushed us to live. That was what drove us—the passion we'd felt since the first touch. It ignited me now.

Alexander's teeth caught my lower lip, but I wasn't interested in rough. I wanted to worship him. I wanted to show him that no part of him was ever damaged in my eyes. Our scars made us stronger.

"No," I whispered, pushing him against the door gently.

Alexander's eyes hooded as I unbuttoned his shirt and slipped it over his shoulders. They still shuttered against the marks that covered his powerful body, but I loved those imperfections that proved he was a man who'd fought death and won. Dipping my lips to his chest, I kissed the bullet wound that had nearly taken him from me and then the one that had missed entirely.

He drew a harsh breath, as if I was releasing something in him he didn't know he'd carried. I wanted to move lower to kiss every scar, to erase the guilt he'd allowed to fester there, but he caught my neck and brought my lips back to his.

His hands swept down, lifting my dress and I stopped kissing him only for the moment it took to shed it.

"My Clara. I want to make love to you every year when the wisterias bloom," he whispered against my lips. "And every winter by the fire and all the days between."

It was so easy to get caught up in the rush of the world around us, always planning for the next moment and worrying about making it to the next day while fearing what lay ahead. But, in that moment, I knew that every sunset prepared us for another day together.

"Love me?" I asked, and he did.

CHAPTER 26

ALEXANDER

There was only her and the distant sound of rain on the window panes. Her lips brushed over another scar and the sensation built into a vibration that roared through me turning into a growl. She would always free the beast I leashed. Only she had that power now. I'd given it to her.

"*Love me.*"

Her words asked something else of me entirely. She wasn't seeking domination or release.

What Clara needed was far more intimate. She needed to give herself to me in a way that had nothing to do with her body.

She was handing me her heart—her soul.

Her trust.

I'd earned it again, and I had no idea how. But I wouldn't betray it again. Later, I would tell her about my meeting. Later, *we* would decide what to do.

Now? Now I would love her. I would worship her. I would show her that every piece of me lived for her. I'd traded everything I was to be half the man she deserved and I would spend the rest of my life becoming the man she needed.

Her mouth continued to trace my scars, sending an unspoken message that I couldn't quite translate. I always wondered why she gravitated toward them—how she could love the proof of my weakness. But each kiss soothed a pain I always carried. Usually, her touch ignited every nerve ending. This did the opposite. A deep peace settled over me, and I realized she was giving me permission.

Permission to love her.

Permission to protect her.

Permission to need her.

Understanding flooded through me. Clara wasn't a weak woman. She'd fought me at every turn for her independence, and she'd pushed back whenever she felt I was being overprotective. At the same time, she'd given herself again and again. Choosing me when I lied. Choosing me when I failed. Choosing me when I couldn't. She'd protected me through it all. Clara guarded my heart more closely than her own. She was stronger than I would ever be.

Clara saw fear and faced it every time.

I only had my body to offer—as a shield, as protection. My heart was no match for hers. It was as mighty and beautiful as the woman who'd given it to me.

I knew then that she would continue to guard the lives of our children. She would continue to carry the burdens I could not. She would be the force behind my strength, and I would be her protector.

My hand found her chin and brought her mouth to mine. She sighed into the kiss as if she knew that I understood what she was trying to tell me. I had a message of my own to send.

My tongue slipped against hers, savouring her, knowing I would never have enough of her. Every moment she was more beautiful in ways that had nothing to do with her full lips and haunted eyes. She was beautiful in herself—in her grace, in her spirit, in her vulnerability and her strength.

Lifting her into my arms, I carried her to a polished round table in the certain of the room. I laid her across it and she blossomed like the flower carved into its surface. My hands caressed the softness of her thigh and she bloomed further, opening her body to me as she had her heart. Moving up, I pushed her skirt to the swell of life she carried. As I began to draw her knickers down, my eyes caught on the scar concealed there. I fell to my knees, pulling them free and brought my lips to that place.

She carried her own scars—ones she'd endured for me. This one was proof of our love in a way that no other could be. I kissed across it and Clara shuddered, her arms reaching to grip the edges of the table.

The final piece had fallen into place—the last unspoken words made clear. Her scars didn't show her weakness—they showed her strength.

They showed mine.

Nothing could change what we would endure for each other. Death was a price we'd pay for every moment of happiness we stole from this life.

"Do you know how powerful you are?" I murmured, my mouth moving to the apex of her womanhood and lingering there. "My crown? My life? They're insignificant compared to you. Do you know why that is?"

"X," she breathed, straining to see me. But she didn't need to see me, she needed to hear me.

She needed to understand that I was about to tell her the only truth that mattered.

"Because you are my heart. You are my soul. Without you, there's nothing. I am nothing. I'm less than a man. You've made me what I am. You are my better. You are my belief." I kissed the soft heat of her, earning a moan. "I am a king, because you are my queen."

"You're wrong," she whispered. "You made me a queen."

"No, my love, you have always been a queen. Do you know I know?" I drew my tongue along her, tasting her sweetness. A tremor rolled through her and I smiled against her slick skin. "Because my place has always been here, kneeling before you. Only a true queen brings a king to his knees."

She struggled to push onto her elbow, her eyes finally able to find mine. They locked as I began to suck and kiss. Her eyes hooded, fighting to maintain control as she continued this debate. "I was on my knees from the moment we met. You lifted me."

"You're such a queen," I said, the words moving across her cunt. "Reigning over me even now. Proclaiming the truth. As you wish, Your Majesty. You've proven my point."

"X, you—"

I slid my tongue inside her, effectively silencing any further argument. Clara groaned, sliding back to the table, as I made love to her with my mouth. Hooking my arms around her thighs, I worshipped her with my lips and fingers. I thanked her for the gift she'd given me. I thanked her for being mine until her limbs tightened, her legs closing around my head as she rode out her pleasure.

When she finally stilled, I helped her to her feet. She clung to the table and I pushed a chair back, enjoying how her body sagged languid and boneless. Taking a seat, I met her eyes and brought my fingers to my lips, sucking her taste from them. Her mouth fell open, speechless, her eyes brightening.

"Never enough," I said with a groan, wanting more of her. "It will never be enough. Do you understand? I will want you every moment of every day—in my mouth, against my skin, by my side. But tonight I want you to take your place as queen."

Clara didn't speak as her fingers found the buttons of her dress and began unbuttoning them slowly. My own found my belt buckle and began unfastening it. Her dress slipped from her shoulders to reveal her pert breasts caged by lace. Freeing my cock, I beckoned her with one finger.

"Take your place, my queen," I urged her. "Reign over me."

She crossed the remaining distance slowly, hovering over me for a moment before leaning down to plant her hands on my chest and push me against the chair.

"My king," she murmured as she straddled me. My hands found her hips to steady her, but she shook her head. "You want to be ruled?"

I nodded, swallowing against the ache in my throat and allowed my hands to fall away. She was so beautiful—so strong and sure. I would never know why I'd been trusted with her—why life had given me her.

Clara gripped my shoulders and lowered herself over me, sliding her seam over the tip of my cock until my eyes rolled from the restraint it took not to lift up and slam into her. She laughed. It was wicked and melodic.

"Patience," she moaned as she sank further. "I want to

feel every inch of you as I take you. God, you're right. It's too much and never enough." She rooted herself against me as she spoke, allowing me to finally fill her.

"There's always something missing when you're not inside me," she confessed as her hips began to rock. "Why is that?"

"Because we're not meant to be two people," I whispered, pressing a kiss to the hands still gripping my shoulders. "We're one—inextricably bound. One body. One heart."

"Always," she agreed before she took what was hers all along.

CHAPTER 27

CLARA

Someday, an angel would invent a way to get dressed for a party in under an hour. For now, by the time I'd finally tracked down my dress, pinned up my hair, and finished my make-up, we were running late. Naturally, all Alexander had to do was put on his tuxedo, but that man could put on nothing and look better than the rest of the planet.

The museum wasn't far from Buckingham, but the short drive took long enough for me to start worrying. Alexander seemed equally preoccupied, staring out his window, lost to his thoughts. Our only connection was our clasped hands. When we reached the party and made it past the inevitable onlookers and their cameras, I would relax. Everything was being taken care of, and I wasn't one to fuss. Plus, with Edward there, I knew one of us would be seeing to overlooked details, and he was the far more competent party in that regard.

When we reached the V&A, Alexander flashed me a wan smile before climbing from the Range Rover. Barricades kept the crowds away from the arriving guests. Alexander opened my door and helped me out of the car. I smiled to the crowds as camera flashes went off around us. His hand slid to the small of my back, warm and protective, as he guided me to the museum's entrance.

"You are a goddess," Alexander murmured in my ear.

I felt like one in the white silk gown that flowed loosely around me, dipping low in the back. Tamara had insisted on sending the evening maternity gown during our last shopping trip, despite my protest that I had no events that required such a fancy dress. She'd winked and told me to save it for the next one. I'd thought I would never wear it, but the party was the perfect occasion. Paired with a pair of silver Louboutins, it was elegant and sexy—and as far from the typical maternity dress as I could get.

A deep purple carpet had been placed on the steps leading into the Victoria and Albert's Grand Entrance. I'd taken the cue from royalty. Sarah was a princess whether she felt like one or not, and tonight, I would remind everyone. But the interior decor was all Belle and Edward, with one notable exception.

As soon as we passed into the large space that normally served as the museum's entrance, the entire vibe changed from buttoned up to lavishly sensual. Wisterias hung from the columns circling the room and a cocktail bar lit by subtle purple lights had already attracted a number of guests. We passed through it, stopping to greet various friends of Alexander's family.

Alexander's hand left my back only so he could take mine, as though he was afraid he might lose among the strangers. My thoughts drifted to what Georgia told me the other day about always having me surrounded unless he was nearby. Tonight his possessiveness seemed to radiate from him like a field, and I found myself pressing closer, drawn to its energy.

But it wasn't that I sensed danger. Rather, I knew my nearness soothed a jagged ache in him that nothing else could.

When we reached the corridor that split in the direction of the gallery, Alexander whisked me into an alcove and kissed me slowly, his lips savoring each movement. I gasped against his mouth, my fingers tangling into his hair. When he released me, his eyes were wild.

Before I could speak, he continued toward the party.

"What was that for?" I asked in a low voice.

He lifted my hand to his mouth and kissed the back of it. "The wisteria."

I'd done for him and Sarah, so that a tangible piece of their mother would be here tonight. But the flowers now held a different memory for me: of fogged glass doors and Alexander's hands.

There were more of the delicate blooms draped over tall glass vases on the tables in the Raphael Gallery. The modern centerpieces contrasted magnificently with the Renaissance paintings that dominated the gallery. A popular band had taken up Edward's offer to play the party and they already had people dancing in the center of the space.

Near the cake, Belle was talking animatedly to another woman I didn't recognize. I took the lead, and Alexander followed, as keen to avoid another well-meaning greeting as I was.

"Guarding the cake?" I asked her.

"Someone has to," she said. "Look at it."

It was a spectacular feat of confectionary with five different tiers, all frosted in a deep indigo and covered in dripping pearls. I was more interested in finding out whether the champagne layer or the lemon layer did more to satisfy my sweet tooth.

"I should be going. It was lovely to see you," the girl said, brushing Belle's hand in farewell and nodding to us before returning to the crowd.

I gave Belle a questioning look.

"She applied for an internship," she explained, "but she's been called home."

"Home?" Maybe that would explain why she was on the guest list.

"Her father is a Senator. She came with one of Edward's school friends." Belle said. "It's too bad. I think she wanted to stay in London."

Before I could dig for more information about the girl, the crowd parted for Smith and Georgia. The two were deep in conversation. Smith wore his tuxedo with authority, and when he saw Belle, a smile slid over his face. It faded when he saw who she was with.

"May I have a moment?" Smith asked, joining us. I was taken aback to see he was speaking to Alexander.

My husband looked to me. "If our wives approve..."

"Go and have your important conversations," I teased. "We'll stay with the cake."

"Are you certain?" he asked.

I shoved his shoulder, beaming up at him. "I'm fine. They'll look after me."

He kissed my forehead, but as he turned, I caught an

unspoken command pass between him and Georgia. I was being passed off. Now I was her responsibility.

"Do you need anything?" she asked.

"Water?" Everyone around me was drinking, but I'd yet to see anything nonalcoholic pass on a tray. It seemed unlikely that it would.

"Wait here," she ordered.

When she left, Belle moved closer, dropping her voice, which seemed wholly unnecessary given the music. "Did you see Philip?"

My eyes flashed through the crowd in alarm. I'd okayed this guest list. Edward had created it. How on earth had we allowed Philip Abernathy, Belle's cheating ex-fiancé on to it?

"I'm sorry," I said anxiously, gripping her arm. "I can have someone kick him out. I have no idea how he got on the list."

She pried my fingers free, giggling a bit too maniacally for a woman on the verge of running into the man she'd almost married. "Are you kidding? I put him on the list. He knows all these people, so I was sure he'd come. He's never missed an opportunity to kiss ass before."

"Why?" I couldn't understand why she'd do anything nice for the man who had screwed Pepper Lockwood for most of their engagement.

"This is better than a school reunion," she said, like this was perfectly obvious. "I'm hot." She gestured to her dress for confirmation and I nodded. The brilliant blue made her stand out and her gown clung to her body in all the right places, including her baby bump. "I'm pregnant." She flashed her right hand. "And happily married."

"Revenge is sweet." I couldn't help but laugh.

"It's terribly shallow of me, but I don't care," she admitted with a smirk.

Philip deserved having his nose rubbed in her happiness. Actually, he deserved a lot more than that, but since as far as I could tell, he had two emotions—bored and boring—he might not even notice.

"What does Smith think?" I asked. I couldn't imagine what Alexander would do if my ex-lover showed up.

"See for yourself." Belle raised her club soda in the direction of the bar. Smith was leaning against it, sipping a drink, and watching Philip like a hawk. "I think he wants Philip to come over to me, so he has an excuse to punch him."

"Doesn't he know you can handle that yourself?" I asked dryly. I would never forget the night that Belle had caught Philip in the act.

"He does," she said with a shrug, "but why should I have all the fun? Now if Pepper steps out of line..." She rubbed her fist with her left hand.

"You will walk away because you're pregnant," I said firmly. "No drama tonight. I need a break."

"We do, too. Smith was supposed to close on the house in —" she cut off suddenly.

"What is it? What house?" I demanded.

"It's nothing."

But it wasn't, and I could tell. "Let's get some air," I suggested.

The garden was far enough away from the actual event that few people had straggled out that direction. It was a bit of a shame since even the lights illuminating the reflection pool and the ellipse of jets had been tinted violet. The effect was other-worldly but chill, and I instantly relaxed.

"Feeling okay?" Belle asked as I kicked off my heels to enjoy a moment without their constant pinch. She scooped down to pick them up.

"Thanks," I said, hooking my fingers around them. "Honestly? I always feel out of place at these things."

"You planned it," she pointed out.

"I know." It was hard to explain that even after a few years of time spent with London's most powerful and elite, I still didn't feel like one, particularly because I'd been crowned Queen Consort alongside Alexander.

"No, I mean you planned it," she repeated. "Clara, there was a time when you would fade into the wallpaper at a party. You never would have planned one."

"I'm hiding now."

"You're taking a breather," she corrected me, turning to face me. "After which, you will return and make small talk and nod graciously and walk *hand-in-hand* with your husband."

"I know that, but I still feel like an outsider."

"Because you are," Belle scoffed. "You're the Queen. You basically went from party flunky—I love you but it's true—to above everyone. You don't belong because you were always meant to stand out."

"When did you become so wise?" I asked her, narrowing my eyes.

"Love does funny things to people. I promise not to let it go to my head," she said.

I was incredibly blessed to have my friends, because they were real. Status, money, power—none of that mattered to them. They didn't see me as an outsider. They saw me as Clara. I didn't know what I would do without them, which was the real reason that I'd dragged her outside. "Spill. What's this about a house? Are you moving? I thought you loved Holland Park."

There was enough house for a baby or two and then some, but I'd gotten the impression for months that Smith Price had plans to whisk her away.

"It doesn't matter." She shook her head. "Not since..."

"Since?" I pressed as my heart pounded a little harder. Her evasion was only more worrying.

"We're buying an estate in Scotland," she blurted out, hurrying on when she saw my face fall, "or we were. I think we still are, but it's not permanent."

"You're temporarily moving to Scotland?" I asked faintly.

"It's not far. Only a couple of hours by car and less by helicopter and you know someone who flies those," she teased, but her heart wasn't in it.

"That's why you keep going out of town. I wondered."

I recalled how much Smith had enjoyed Christmas at Balmoral. They'd returned to Scotland soon after, which had been my first clue that they were plotting betrayal. "How can you leave me here? When will I see my god baby?"

"Your god baby, huh?" Her eyebrow arched like this was in question.

"It better be."

"She," Belle said softly, the ghost of a smile flitting over her mouth.

"She?" I repeated. "It's a she?"

I forgot about being mad at her and pulled her into a hug. Belle laughed, squeezing me as we squealed. "Don't make me cry. I'll ruin my make-up."

"Sod your make-up," I said, drawing back, I glared at her.

"You can't take away my god baby and Elizabeth's best friend."

"Best friend, huh?"

"Or maybe Alice's best friend." I patted my stomach.

"Or William's future girlfriend?" she suggested.

I grabbed her hands and pleaded, "You can't move."

"It wouldn't be all the time. Hear me out."

I listened as she explained that Smith wanted the baby to have plenty of room and less stress for Belle. "The company doesn't need me in the office every day and we'll have a nanny to help. I can take meetings online and Lola can run things here."

"Lola might be busy," I reminded her.

"Anders won't need that much help." Belle dismissed this issue too easily.

"So what went wrong?" I asked.

"Smith went to a meeting with Alexander the other day. He didn't go into detail but I think it had to do with Jacobson." She paused, biting her lip. "Did he tell you about it?"

"A little." Alexander had told me that he was taking Smith to a meeting regarding the Jacobson's release. Considering the men's shared interest in bringing him to justice, I hadn't found it strange. "He seemed shaken when he came home. He didn't really want to talk about it."

"I didn't want to get him in trouble. Of course, he probably doesn't want to stress you out. I shouldn't even be talking about it."

Now I was the one who felt guilty. "I haven't told him," I confessed. "I started to the other day and then there was the whole mess with Anders. We were distracted."

"And you're avoiding telling him," she accused.

"Avoiding telling him what?" a sharp voice cut into the conversation. She held out a water bottle and I grimaced.

I'd forgotten to stay put, but Georgia hadn't missed my exit from the party, even if I hadn't seen her follow. This was why I hadn't realized that I was constantly being surrounded. I strained my eyes around the dark courtyard looking for others but all I saw were drunken aristocrats who didn't look like they'd be much use in a crisis. But Georgia would always be nearby and I should have remembered that.

It helped that she'd worn a jet black evening gown with sleeves that hugged her slender arms to the wrists. It might have been modest camouflage, except for the neckline, which cut so low that it revealed her navel. She blended well into the night while standing out. Much like Georgia, it was the perfect contradiction.

"Eavesdropping?" Belle asked, obviously trying to distract her from what she'd heard.

"Catching up with friends." Georgia's crimson smile was wolfish. "And you two are loud, anyone can hear you."

My eyes flickered around the garden wondering who had heard what. I twisted the cap off the bottle and drank it quickly.

"We're talking about baby stuff," Belle said. "No one cares."

We both gave her an incredulous look and she back-tracked immediately. She lowered her voice to a whisper. "Okay, I guess they do, but it wasn't interesting pregnancy stuff."

The other day, there'd been ten stories about what antacids Georgia had been spotted buying me in a pharmacy. This was much more interesting.

"Are we being watched right now?" I asked Georgia.

She gave me an are-you-stupid look.

"Can we go somewhere that we aren't being watched?"

"I think that's the loo and your bedroom," she said flatly.

I was glad some things were still sacred. If I had to pick, those would be the two exceptions I'd ask for. "The loo, it is."

Using the loo for a clandestine conversation turned out to involve clearing out the entire bathroom first, which made me feel horrible, and then planting guards in front of the door.

"Happy?" Georgia asked after she'd checked the stalls one final time. "Now out with it."

"It's nothing." I silently begged Belle to save me. She was usually good for a quick lie, but she shook her head.

"You might as well practice. Georgia is almost as scary as Alexander is," Belle said, crossing her arms as she leaned against a sink.

"I promise you that I am much scarier."

"Not helping," I told her. I pretended to study myself in the mirror, but since we'd been at the party for all of an hour, there was nothing to fix.

"You can't keep it from him. The doctor's going to be doing house calls soon and he's going to say something," Belle argued.

"He can't," I reminded her. "If I tell him not to."

Belle's lips tugged down at the edges. The look of disappointment made me feel worse.

"What's going on?" Georgia asked in a low voice.

I'd nearly forgotten she was here, but when our eyes met I realized I wasn't walking out of this room without coming clean.

"What's going on?" she repeated, edging closer to me,

until she'd backed me against the wall. "You're keeping something from Alexander that has to do with a doctor—are you sick?"

It took me a moment to process her sudden anger. She had me against a wall—literally. "I actually believed you when you said we were friends."

"We are," she informed me. "She's the one who takes you shopping and helps you match your purse with your shoes. I'm the one who loses sleep when you're on the outs with Alexander and walks behind you to watch your back."

Belle's eyes had rounded to full moons, and she took a small step towards us. "You should tell her. It's not going away."

And that was the problem. It wasn't going away. I couldn't cover it up or ignore it. I would have to face this—all of us would—and the moment of reckoning was nearly here.

"Pretend that she's Alexander," Belle suggested. "It will be practice."

Georgia looked as though she hated this idea, but she didn't contradict her.

"Tell me," her voice softened but the command was still implicit.

"There's a problem." I sniffled, trying to keep myself from crying. If I was going to break down telling Georgia how would I ever get through telling Alexander? I set my shoulders and willed myself to be calm, reminding myself that everything would turn out well. "The baby's heart isn't right. He's going to need surgery when he's born."

"Are you fucking kidding me?" Georgia shook her head, her mouth open. "How could you keep this a secret?"

"We weren't sure. I had to see a specialist."

"When did you find out there might be a problem?" She asked.

"A couple of—"

"I really hope you're about to say minutes," she hissed. "You've known for days?"

"Weeks," I said weakly.

"What were you thinking?" she demanded.

"You do a really good impression of Alexander," Belle said, "but I think she needs our support not our—"

"That's how you do friendship." Georgia spun to face her. "My version has slightly more accountability."

"I know I should have told him." Her reaction had shocked the tears from me. Now I was starting to feel angry.

"Even if you couldn't tell him, *I* needed to know. *Your* team needed to know."

"You answer to Alexander—" I began.

"And you," she added. "We keep secrets for a living and if the Queen has a secret, we will keep it. Do you understand? When you wanted to go to Windsor, I didn't call him. I don't repeat our conversations. But I needed to know this. How can I protect you if I don't know that there's a serious health concern with the baby? What if there was an accident and no one knew?"

"I'm sorry," I said softly. It hasn't occurred to me that my team needed to know. It had felt like a private matter, but there was no real privacy in my life anymore. Why couldn't I accept that?

"It was stupid and reckless." She shook her head. "I expected better of you. You're usually the smart one."

She stormed toward the door and Belle and I looked at each other.

"Give me a moment," I called to Georgia as she opened the door.

"There's an entire squad of fools drooling to throw themselves between you and a bullet. I need to think." She paused as she stepped out of the door. "Clara, tell him or I will."

It wasn't an empty threat, and I knew it.

"That went well," Belle muttered.

I slumped against the tiled wall, cradling the baby growing inside me. "She's right. I didn't want to deal with it, so I tried to ignore it. I made excuses for why it was okay to keep it a secret. The whole time I've been putting the baby in danger."

"You've been going to your appointments. You're taking care of yourself," Belle said firmly. "Maybe you should have told them, but there's no use hating yourself for the past."

"I have to tell him," I said, "as soon we get home."

I wouldn't ruin Sarah's birthday by springing this on her brother. Georgia knew now, so in the unlikely event the information was needed, she could pass it along.

Was that how I wanted Alexander to find out? In an emergency?

"Come on, let's find your husband. You'll feel better around him." Belle urged me back onto my feet and kept me steady as I slipped my heels on.

But I wouldn't feel better. Not until this had been dealt with.

· · ·

IT TOOK BELLE TWO PASSES TO FIX MY SMEARED
mascara. I didn't mind. I'd rather be stuck in a restroom than
smiling and pretending everything was fine.

"Ready to enter the fray?" Belle asked when I'd run out
of ways to stall us.

I shook my head and she smiled sympathetically. We
both knew that there was only one way out of here and it
meant going back to the party.

Outside the door, I paused to thank the guards, who'd
begun to look a little nervous. We'd only made it a few steps
toward the hall that led to The Raphael Gallery when a
simpering voice said, "About time," a bit too loudly.

I closed my eyes and grabbed Belle's arm before she could
confront Pepper. This night just kept getting better and
better. But Pepper, ever the sadist, wasn't about to let us off
the hook so easily.

"It's really rude to make everyone wait out here so you
two can attempt to apply make-up. Accept a lost cause when
you see it, ladies," Pepper called over, but none of the women
waiting around her laughed. Not even Sarah, who'd been
stuck waiting out here with her friend. There wasn't so much
as a nervous titter among the lot of them. Pepper frowned.

"Feeling unappreciated?" I asked her coldly. I wanted to
tell her that no one wanted her here, but tonight was about
Sarah and I wasn't going to ruin it for her. Even if her best
friend was a twat.

"I don't know," she said, her eyes narrowing. "How does
that feel? I'm sure you have experience."

"Stop," Sarah said, dragging her to the loo as others filed
in, eager to get away from the catfight.

Next to me, Belle dropped her voice, "I know what you said, but—"

"No," I said firmly. I wasn't going to let my pregnant best friend take a swing at Pepper, even if I would have paid to see Pepper's reaction.

"Please," she whined.

"What's the matter?" Pepper called as Sarah tried to hustle her past the door. "Clara got you on the short leash?"

My hands let go of Belle voluntarily, unable to hold her back anymore, because sometimes a cat fight was in order.

Before Belle could reach her, Sarah stepped between them and rounded on her friend. "You're her guest."

"I'm your guest." Pepper's lower lip stuck out a little as she battled her shock over Sarah's reaction. "I told you that these two are trash."

"Yeah, I know." Sarah took a deep breath, glancing between us and Pepper as if making a choice. "But I'm beginning to think you're the trash."

Pepper let out a strangled cry and lunged for Sarah, who looked too surprised to get out of the way. I held Belle back from getting involved, gesturing to the security guards who had already caught Pepper by the shoulders and were pulling her away. She fought them for a second before realizing it was a lost cause.

"Your Highness?" The guard prompted Sarah, waiting for instructions before realizing his mistake and looking to me.

I shook my head and pointed to Sarah. This was a decision I would leave up to her. She hesitated for a second before ripping her eyes from Pepper. "I think you should leave."

Pepper protested as they led her away from the scene of her meltdown, and Belle waved at her as she went.

"You know what happens to trash, Pepper?" Belle called. "It gets taken out."

"You enjoyed that too much," I muttered to her.

"It might have been better than the time I broke her nose," Belle admitted.

"You broke her nose?" Sarah stared at Belle in awe. "I thought it looked different. I'm sorry about what she was saying. I don't know why she hates you so much."

Belle and I looked at each other and began to spill the running list.

"I broke her nose."

"She was after Alexander."

"She broke up my engagement, but Philip dumped her," said Belle

"Then I called her out for sleeping with your dad."

"But before he dumped her, he begged me to take him back. And then I told her that."

"And she was completely banned by Alexander for selling stories to the media."

"Holy shit," Sarah said, her eyes moving between two invisible points at her feet like we'd overloaded her brain.

"Sorry," I said, clapping a hand over my mouth, "I probably shouldn't have told you all that stuff, especially about your Dad."

"I'm glad you did. That's..." she couldn't seem to come up with a word of appropriate magnitude.

"Mental?" Belle offered as we headed back to the party.

Sarah nodded. "To start with. Why did you invite her?"

"She's your friend and this is your birthday."

Sarah looked like she might start crying, so I pulled her into a hug. "By the way, we're absolute shit at parties. I'm never throwing you another one."

"Everything goes wrong," Belle agreed.

"My wedding?" I said.

"Legendary," Belle said. I shot her a look. "I didn't mean that in a good way, but you know..."

"So I should have a good time?" We'd gotten Sarah to laugh, and I breathed a sigh of relief. Just because this night was turning into another failed party for the ages didn't mean it should be the same for her.

"I, for one, would like to find my husband and make him dance with me," Belle said devilishly, "and I'm pretty sure that every single guy down there is waiting to dance with you."

We reached the gallery just as Anderson drifted into view wearing a black tuxedo. Sarah snorted and cocked her head in his direction. "Any more single guys that are also my half brothers? I'm little wary of flirting with strangers these days."

"That's the only one." I stopped myself from adding *that we know about*. I didn't want the poor girl to be perpetually single.

"Maybe we should go in another way," I suggested, looking for a different entrance.

"That's the only way that does not involve a ridiculous amount of stairs and walking," Belle said flatly. "He's not going to bite you."

"But he wants to, right?" Sarah held up her hands when we glared at her. "I'm just trying to keep up. Sorry."

"Don't let him see me," I told them as we strolled into the party.

"Sure," Edward said slinging his arms around Belle's and my shoulders. "No one will notice the three most beautiful women here walking back into the room. Excellent plan. Have you considered becoming a criminal mastermind?"

"I don't want it to be a thing," I explained.

He shook his head. "Then don't let it be."

Stepping in front of us, he held out a hand to his sister. "Fancy a dance? I can point out the available ones and steer you away from the gay ones."

"Traitor," I said as he guided her away.

"Oh, um, there's Smith," Belle said, biting her lip.

I sighed and shooed her away. Anders hadn't spotted me, so I skirted the dance floor, searching for Alexander. I was about to give up and hunt down someone with an earpiece, who would definitely know where he was, when a strong hand caught my shoulder.

"There you are."

I spun around with a smile, forgetting to account for my belly, which brushed against him.

Anderson grinned, his eyes finding the floor as he put distance between us. "I'm afraid that was my fault."

"It was...don't worry about," I said breathlessly.

"I was hoping you would dance with me," he said.

"Is that...?"

"It's your sister's idea," he said quickly. "I need to show that we all get along, so they don't think that we hate each other."

I wasn't certain that dancing with Anderson was going to send that impression, and I doubted Lola had explicitly made that suggestion. But since my best friends had abandoned me, I couldn't come up with a reasonable excuse.

Anderson and I walked to the dance floor and he put an arm around me.

"It's a bit hard to take my waist at the moment," I said apologetically.

"At my first primary school dance, the teachers went around pushing us apart so we weren't too close," he said. "This makes that a lot easier."

I laughed along with him, wishing it could always be simple and easy between us. But until he'd figured out that I was off the market permanently, I worried that wouldn't be the case. "You spoke to Lola?"

"Yes," he said, taking a deep breath. "She's a bit bossy."

"She is a handful, but she knows how to run with this crowd."

"Did she help you?" he asked.

"I sorta leapt into the deep end." By the time, I'd realized that my relationship with Alexander was more than a fling, I'd already figured out how to tread water. "I should have asked for her help. She works with Belle on her business, and she's always run interference for me when my mother gets too involved."

"It sounds like you have an interesting family dynamic." He smiled.

"And it's still not as strange as my husband's."

"Tell me about it. A year ago it was me and my mum and now?" He looked around the room. "This isn't my world."

"I know how you feel," I said, "but this isn't their world, either. You'll see. We're actually terribly boring people..."

"With private jets, family estates, and Crown Jewels." He lifted an eyebrow, calling my bluff.

I tilted my head. "Yes, but the rest of the time..."

"Thank you for the dance," Anders said, releasing me and taking a step back, "but I think someone is cutting in."

I didn't have time to ask him who before he spun me into my husband's waiting arms.

CHAPTER 28

ALEXANDER

Clara's breathless surprise matched how I felt every time I saw her. I nodded politely to Anders. It was the least I could do if he was going to show he'd learned his place. Not that I appreciated seeing my brother's hands on my wife in any context, but as I'd was unavailable, I'm glad she wasn't standing alone. She eyed me through her lashes apprehensively as I clasped her hand and we began to sway.

"Feeling guilty, Poppet?" I asked, relishing the palm she placed on my chest. Another woman might have wrapped it around my neck or touched my arm, but she kept it near my heart as if protecting it.

"Nervous," she said.

I dipped her slightly, swiftly and discreetly running my mouth up her neck before turning us. "Why would that be?"

"I was dancing with your brother."

I chuckled at her wise choice of words. She was becoming quite the politician. "And everyone saw."

"Yes," she said, sounding even more alarmed.

"Wasn't that the point?" I asked.

She cocked her head, revealing more of her creamy shoulder and I resisted the urge to bite it. "What are you getting at, X?"

"Simply, that you were meant to be seen dancing. I suppose he told you that," I said before spinning her away and drawing her back to my body.

She melted against me. "He did. Were you in on this?"

"I was informed by Norris." My mouth twisted at her disgruntled expression. Only Clara could get mad over me behaving myself. "He seemed concerned that I might start a fight."

"I wonder what gave him that idea," she said, refusing to give in to the smile dancing in her eyes.

"I thought you wanted us to get along," I whispered.

"I didn't expect such a sudden change of heart," she said.

"Let me put your mind at ease." I kept my voice low. "I didn't like seeing his hands on you. I wanted to take you away, and so I did. He had the good sense to relinquish what belongs to me, so there was no problem."

"Is that so?" She shook her head like I was being ridiculous.

"That you belong to me?" I asked. "I thought we established that fact, but perhaps you need a refresher." The hand I had on her back slipped down to grip her ass. Only for a moment, but it was all it took.

Clara bit her lip, squirming a bit in my arms. "What are you saying?"

"You seem guilty and a bit confused, and I can't help thinking that punishment might help you sort that out," I murmured, noticing how her nipples hardened at the mere suggestion of my words.

"Punishment?" she repeated. "I thought you would never touch me while you're angry."

I winked at her. "Do I seem angry?"

"But punishment?" she said, her voice peaking on the final word.

"I'm frustrated, Poppet," I told her truthfully.

"With me? Why?"

It was artless and naive, and it only made me want to take her more.

"Because you're breathtaking in that white silk that shows every inch of your body. Your nipples are hard and every man around us is eye-fucking my wife while she's in my arms." I moved my mouth to her ear, eager to catch every soft noise she made as I spoke. "They're wondering what it's like to touch a queen and they know that they'll never experience a woman like you. But that's not why I want to punish you."

"Why?" she murmured, and I knew she was as turned on by my words as I was by her body in that dress.

"Why do I want to punish you? Because you're being a gorgeous little cocktease. Because you're making me so hard that I have to keep my jacket buttoned so people don't see how hard you make me. Because other men are looking at what is mine." I paused and breathed the most important reason, *"Because I can."*

I didn't ask her if it was okay. I took her hand and led her from the party—from our friends and family and guests. There was no way I would make it through this evening without touching her, tasting her, claiming her. I nodded to one of my men who stopped his conversation mid-sentence and walked away from the guest to clear a path for us. A few more followed, blending in with the crowd until we reached another gallery. Clara didn't notice until we were suddenly alone.

She eyed the men as we passed them without a word.

"Subtle," she teased.

There were more on the other side. They'd all been briefed that I needed a moment with my wife privately. When we came into the sculpture gallery, Clara looked around in surprise.

"We're alone," she said.

"Yes." I ran a finger from her chin to her breastbone, enjoying how her nipples beaded even harder as my touch grew closer.

"You planned this," she accused.

"You did tell me where the party was," I said, feeling not the least bit apologetic. The moment she'd said the V&A, I'd thought of the sculpture gallery and fantasized about this moment. I couldn't have planned for how she would look, although I should have thought of it, or how the men would react to seeing her like this.

"This dress is terribly inappropriate," I told her. "I nearly died when I saw you in it."

"You could have told me to change." She frowned, shifting to peer down at herself.

"I like inappropriate. I like how the other men watch you —how strong and confidant you are"—I kissed her shoulder, sliding the thin strap off it —"because I know that the only man you'd bow before is me."

"You are my King," she whispered, her breath catching as my teeth sank into her shoulder.

I didn't bite hard, given her attire it would be impossible to return to the party without everyone whispering. My cock twitched at the thought. I wanted them to know. Part of me wanted to take her perfect body and show them all what only I could do to it, but I would never share her in that way. It drove me wild enough to see her walking around in this excuse for a dress.

But I couldn't allow her to leave without laying my claim.

"There's something I need to do." I slipped the other strap down, hooking it so that the entire dress hung from a single finger.

She was breathing hard, her eyes glued to my face but flickering occasionally to the cameras in the corner.

"Does it bother you?" I asked, testing her. "Knowing someone might be watching?"

Her jaw tensed and then she shook her head. "No."

"That's a good girl," I praised her, "because I make those decisions, don't I?"

She nodded, starting to catch on to the unfolding scene.

"The cameras are off. I would never expose you—never share you. You are my treasure." I angled my face so that our lips nearly touched. "But tell me, does it excite you—the thought of others watching me claim you? Showing them all that you belong to me. You may speak."

"Yes," she said weakly, sounding torn.

"Don't be ashamed. It feels good to be owned. It makes you proud, my pretty Poppet, and you should feel that way when you're possessed." I savoured the way her throat slid as she swallowed this, wondering how it felt burning inside her. "But I won't allow it, even if I would love to show you off."

Clara whimpered, and for a split second I thought she might collapse.

"I think you're overheating," I said. "Let's take care of

that." I dropped my hold on the strap and her dress fluttered to her waist, exposing her breasts.

"Perfect," I said, leaning down I caught the peak in my mouth, but I didn't suck. Instead I bit. Clara gasped, her hands gripping my hair. She didn't try to pull away. Instead she writhed against the bite until she was panting. I released it, admiring the teeth marks. "And the other?"

Another slide of the throat and a nod, her eyes bright. I wouldn't stop until the light faded and I knew she'd entered another place that only I could take her.

I caught the other one, biting down and then sucking it hard until she cried out. When I stopped she was shaking. I paused, looking her over, until I discerned it was pleasure.

Straightening, I pushed her dress to the floor. It puddled at her feet and I helped her step from it. Taking her hand, I led her to the wall.

"Do you know that I planned to take you here for days? That I pictured you standing naked amongst what others consider priceless? These are masterpieces, and you outshine them all." I turned her to face the wall, running my eyes along her backside to where my last marks had faded. Lifting her hands, I placed them on the wall, before I knelt behind her. Gripping her hips, I kissed her tailbone, trailing my tongue down until I came to the curve of her ass.

"My marks have faded," I told her, kissing the spot. "Would you like more?"

"Yes, please."

"Please what?" I wanted to hear her say it. I needed to hear it spill from her mouth as wantonly as her pleasure. The permission and the desire were intoxicating. Knowing she not only gave herself to me fully, but that she wanted it as much as I did, was the sexiest thing in the world.

"Please mark me. Please own me," she whispered. It wasn't timid but rather reverent.

"I will not stop until I'm satisfied and until you're marked properly, Poppet. I will stop only if you use your safe word. I will not stop if you scream, although"—I laughed at the thought—"the sound will carry. The guards won't let anyone in but you may consider placing your arm near your mouth."

Clara shifted her arm, dropping her to cheek to it. I loved how she responded to each suggestion like a command, her submission as natural to her now as I'd dreamed it could be. She moaned when my teeth clamped onto the soft flesh and pulled slightly. The first bite was gentle, and I wondered if the simple act would be enough to satisfy me. My palms itched at the thought of smacking her ass, defiling her amongst the art that couldn't touch her. But that sound would carry as well, and these sessions needed to remain private—a blasphemous communion more pure than any other.

When I released her, I massaged the spot before turning to the parallel cheek. This time, I bit down harder, paying attention to the skin's resistance until I knew I'd brought it as close as I could. Clara shifted in her heels and when I pulled away, her mouth was pressed to her arm, imprisoning her cries. I rubbed the spot and whispered praise, "Perfect and strong. Your skin loves it as much as I do."

I continued, aware of every flinch of her body and every whimpered cry. But there were no safe words, and with each assault, her scent bloomed in my nostrils. When bite marks covered her tender flesh, I ran my hands over them, feeling the indentations along my fingertips. Clara's head fell to the side, her breathing heavy and laboured. My cock ached from drinking in the redness that covered both sets of cheeks.

"Mine." I kissed each mark before spreading her open and dipping my mouth to run along her slick heat.

"Oh," she gasped as my tongue plunged inside her. She tasted like heaven—or as close as a man like me would ever come. I continued to devour her but this time all I cared about was her pleasure. There was no pain except the lingering sting of her submission.

"X," she called as her body continued to tremble, "I need you to fuck me. Please, I need your cock."

It was hard to refuse, even if I wasn't through with my plans for her, but I'd never been able to deny her that. I pushed to my feet and whipped my belt loose, opening my fly to free my cock. It fell heavily into my hand.

"Thank God for high heels," I said as I moved behind her. She giggled, the sound settling like a melody over my heart. Leaning against her, I drew her hands over her and pinned them together in one of mine. "A little wider."

She stepped to the side, allowing me better access, and I positioned my cock at her entrance, slipping the tip inside her.

"You asked nicely, but what did you do wrong, Poppet?" I had her at my mercy, which was the best opportunity for education.

"I spoke." She sounded crestfallen by her mistake.

"When I told you not to." I kissed her shoulder to give her some comfort. "You always have a voice with me, but when you submit to me, you only have one word."

She nodded.

"Good girl," I soothed her. "Now you have your voice back. What do you need to ask me?"

"To fuck me," she said, the edge of desperation there. I could already feel her channel tightening against my tip. She wouldn't last through one thrust. "Please will you fuck me?"

"Yes, Poppet." I wanted to slam into her. Instead, I slid in inch-by-inch knowing it would dull her orgasm into a lingering ache that primed her for another.

She cried out as I tortured her with deliberation, enjoying each pulse squeezing my cock and drawing me toward my own release. Her breath turned to pants, shallow and near panic as the climax failed to diminish.

"Now you're ready," I whispered before thrusting into her. We moved together in a rhythm that belonged only to us — a symphony of pain and bliss we wrote together.

She went limp with a strangled cry, and I caught her quickly, keeping her on her feet. Her body sagged against me, her face turning up to give me her mouth. The last bit of her to claim. I captured it with my own and erased the rest of her world and replaced it with me.

WE LINGERED IN THE GALLERY ON A BENCH, HER IN MY lap while I kissed her shoulders and waited for her to find her way back to the present. When she returned, I helped her into her dress, allowing her time to marvel at the lingering marks on her breasts. I would ask her later what she preferred, but I noted her pleasure at our newest discovery.

"Am I presentable?" she asked, coming out from the loo. I'd waited by the door, guarding her myself, unable to allow anyone else the responsibility for the moment.

"You're not just presentable," I said leaning to kiss her. "You're fuckable."

"That wasn't what I was going for." She pushed against me, "If we don't go back now, we never will—and we might be missed."

We strolled through the main hall, not bothering to smother our smiles. Rounding the corner, we met up with Edward who gawked at us.

"Where have you been? I've been looking for you for an hour!"

I examined my knuckles, remembering how I'd spent that hour. "Was it that long?"

Clara giggled, and that combined with her flushed face made it obvious how we'd spent that time.

"Obviously I need to separate you two in public places," he said with a groan. "There's a party and there's a cake and a lot of people getting grumpy waiting to eat it."

"By a lot of people—you mean Belle?" Clara guessed.

"Yes. Sarah wants the family to help her cut it."

"You two go." She held up a hand when he started to protest. "I need to sit down."

"Are you sure about that?" I asked, keeping my voice casual enough that I hoped my brother didn't pick up on the double meaning.

"Yes, go! *I'm fine*. I'll find Belle."

I refused to go ahead without her, finally parting with her only once we were back inside and in the sight of security.

As we approached the cake, my grandmother scrambled toward me. "We've been looking for you." Her eyes darted to Edward. "We couldn't find you."

I took her gently by the shoulders worried by her

disheveled appearance. I'd seen her when she and Henry had arrived, but now she looked ill. A thin sheen of sweat covered her brow and she clutched my arm.

"Why don't you watch?" I suggested. "We'll get you a chair."

"Yes, a chair." She pointed at Edward, handing off the task.

I heard him muttering something about getting punished for not shagging inside the V&A under his breath as he left.

"I need to talk to you," she said. "It's very important, I think."

"We will," I promised her, slightly unnerved. Glancing around I looked for Henry. "Let's find Henry to sit with you while we cut the cake."

"No! I need to speak with you now. I can feel it."

"Mother?" Henry studied her with concern. "Are you quite alright?"

She released her hold on me, seeming to calm a little when she saw him. "Yes, I'm going to sit down."

"That's good." He patted her hand. "Then we'll have cake."

She smiled, lifting one gloved hand to wipe her forehead. "Yes, cake."

Edward reappeared with the chair and we placed it near the cake table.

"What was that about?" he muttered.

"I think she's confused. Henry told me she's been having difficulty with her memory." It was something to look into. I didn't want to be the one to tell her she had to stay home from the parties in the future, but if they were overwhelming her...

Sarah was waiting by the table cake server in hand and a

sour expression on her face. "Can we do this? People are threatening to riot."

"You don't want me to make a speech like Dad used to?" I asked innocently.

She rolled her eyes, reminding me of all the birthdays we'd had *before*. "No, I—"

But her words were cut off as all hell broke loose.

CHAPTER 29

CLARA

I sat down with Belle, taking my time, uncertain what to expect. But most of me was still numb—except my heart. It ached with fullness. My best friend regarded me with amusement, but kept her comments to herself in front of Smith.

I was sure she wouldn't afford me that courtesy later. I expected her to drag me off to the bathroom so she could pressure me for details. But what had happened with Alexander was ours alone. I'd never been one to kiss and tell. Once I'd met him, it had been unnecessary, since what he'd done to me was written all over my face.

I felt it there now, warming my cheeks. I felt it other places, too.

Across the room, he joined his brother and sister to cut the cake. It was difficult to process that this was my family—this was my life. He'd given it to me and he'd never allow anyone to take it away.

They laughed, and I wondered at the private joke, thrilling to see them coming together. They were—

A shout cut across the room and then another. I stood as a chair was knocked over.

"Clara," Belle called, but I was already heading to the cake table. The crowd had moved in front of me, blocking my view. When I reached it, forcing my way gracelessly through the people gathered around to help. I found Edward and Alexander on their knees. Alexander's hands were on Mary's chest, pumping life into her with so much force I heard a rib crack. Next to him, Edward was calling orders.

Looking up, I saw Sarah standing behind the cake, holding her mouth. It felt as though my body was floating up, detached from the scene before me. I acted on pure instinct. Moving to her, I wrapped an arm around her shoulders and dragged her away.

It would do no good for her to see this. She turned into my shoulder, covering her eyes now as she began to cry. There was nothing to say, but I tried anyway, each sentiment sounding more meaningless than the next. "Help is on the way. Alexander is trained. It will be fine."

But it wouldn't be. Mary had looked terrible the last time I saw her. She was approaching ninety. I was offering promises I couldn't keep. I fell silent when I realized it.

It took longer than it should for the ambulance to arrive, but it always felt that way in the moment of death—like time had slowed down and forced you to savor every bitter bite. When the medics got there, the crowd parted for them, blocking us from seeing any more. That was for the best.

Spotting Norris, I beckoned him over with my free hand. He'd been absent most of the evening, no doubt checking every window in the place. He hurried over and we exchanged worried glances.

Neither of us said what we were thinking but this was becoming a habit.

"We should get her out of here," I said.

He bobbed his head, ushering us through an emergency door. Sarah gulped down air when we were outside, but it only seemed to power her tears. Norris stepped to the side and called a car.

Carefully extricating myself from Sarah, I joined him and lowered my voice, my eyes still on her. "Where are they taking Mary?"

"St. James," he said. "But..."

I closed my eyes, uncertain I was ready to deal with another wave of grief. Mary hadn't been close with her grand-children, but that carried a different kind of grief with it—one that coupled with doubt and anger in equal measure. Alexander and Edward were experienced in this kind, but Sarah...

"Should we take her?" I asked him. He pressed his ear, listening to some bit of information on his earpiece.

It was a difficult decision. The hospital would be chaotic and decisions would have to be made. I wasn't sure how Sarah would handle that. It hit me just how little experience she had in this.

"Alexander and Edward are going with Mary. I don't think that..."

Tonight we were fluent in broken sentences.

"Home?" I didn't know what we do there but sit and wait.

"Should we ask her?" he suggested.

She didn't seem capable of that kind of decision but I didn't know what else to do. The certainty that had overtaken me earlier had abandoned me now and I was left with only doubt.

We moved toward Sarah, approaching her like she was a wild animal and completely unpredictable.

"Sarah," I asked softly. "They're taking her to the hospital. We can go there or we can go home."

"Home," she said with a broken voice.

I nodded and checked to see that Norris heard me. It was the most I could give her tonight.

The Range Rover pulled into the side lot and Norris helped her inside. Closing the door behind her, he circled around to speak with me before I could follow.

"I've let Alexander know. He wants me to come with you. Georgia is going to stay here."

I didn't know if this was because she was still mad at me or something more. If she couldn't get over her anger in a moment of panic, then we needed to have a serious conversation.

Norris reached for the door handle, his eyes tightening for a moment on something behind him.

"What?" I asked, peering over my shoulder to look. "There's nothing..."

I turned back to find him white-faced, still staring at the spot. His mouth opened and one word spilled from his mouth. "Blue."

Followed by a lot of blood.

Blood that was red like the handkerchief that closed over my mouth. Blood that was red like the back of my eyelids the moment before they faded to...

CHAPTER 30

ALEXANDER

The only thing to distract me was a stack of bloody magazines a few weeks old, most of which purported to have the secret details of my own life. Hospitals were my own personal hell. I paced the room, earning a reproachful look from my brother, who apparently found reading about his own life quite amusing. David had fallen asleep in the chair next to him. Henry was wearing a similar path across the room as my own.

Tuxedo jackets, vests, and ties were strewn about—all of us eventually divesting ourselves of everything but our shirts and pants. They sat in stark contrast to the blank white walls and sickly yellow chairs. I hated everything about this place, especially its memories.

I'd been brought here on my wedding day. I'd come here after the car accident. My mother had died behind these walls. The only good thing that had ever happened here was Elizabeth's birth, but one life hardly seemed to balance all the death.

The door burst open, but it was only Georgia. She looked around the room. "Where's Clara?"

"Norris took her home with Sarah," I told her. It was best for them both to be away from this. My grandmother had been nothing but cruel to Clara, so I couldn't ask her to be here, even if part of me selfishly wanted her to be. But it was more important for her to be with Sarah.

"It's just like my grandmother to die on someone's birthday," I muttered.

"She's not dead yet," Henry said sharply.

It was cold of me to feel that way. I suspected he was as dependent on her as she was on him. He'd lived alone for so long, always the spare child until my father's death. But he'd had too little time with his mother—just like me.

The doctor came in before I could apologize and it was obvious from his tired expression. It had been obvious to me when I'd tried to revive her at the museum. There could have been a miracle of course, but they were rare in these parts.

"I'm sorry," he said, cutting to the chase. He paused and allowed Henry a moment to process this.

My uncle looked stricken himself and David jumped up to help him over to a chair.

"What happened?" I asked.

"A heart attack. There was nothing to be done. It was too much. We couldn't reset the sinus rhythm. From the looks of it, she may have been suffering smaller attacks for several days."

That was why she'd been acting so strangely. Guilt washed over me when I realized she'd been trying to tell me at the party, but why come to me?

"She seemed confused," I said.

"That's natural," the doctor said. "She may have had trouble getting enough oxygen to her brain. Some patients experience memory loss or confusion."

Memory loss. She'd come to me because she thought I was the King and she'd been cared for by one her whole life— and I'd failed her.

"She's being examined now, but our toxicologist did notice some strange things. What medications was she on?"

"General ones," Henry said. "She had one to help with her arrhythmia."

"And she was taking it?" The doctor frowned.

"Yes. Well, she missed a few days when we returned to London. Clara had to pick some up at the chemist for her," Henry said.

"Clara," I said in surprise.

"She offered to help when I shared my concern. Your grandmother was insisting she didn't need it. That she would see the doctor. Would missing a few days cause this problem?" Henry looked devastated. He hung his head. "I should have insisted."

"Do you have the pills she was taking?" The doctor asked.

"They're in her purse." Henry gestured to the bag he'd carried in under his arm like a security blanket.

"May I?"

I nodded to the doctor, wondering why we were going to this much trouble. My grandmother was an old, bitter woman who'd lived too long a life.

The doctor retrieved the bottle and studied it for a moment. "I'd like to show these to the toxicologist."

"Of course," Henry said absently. Edward had moved next to him and begun to talk quietly.

I followed the doctor in the hall. "Why do you need the pills?"

"I suppose there's no harm in telling you that there are odd traces in your grandmother's blood. It seems she may have been taking something she shouldn't," he said, shaking the bottle. "It would be useful to have her other medications."

I nodded. "We'll have them sent over. I'm not certain I understand, though. Was there a mistake? Was she taking the wrong medication? Did it cause the heart attack?"

This time he hesitated and the pause sent a shiver running up my spine. "It's difficult to say. We don't usually see this kind of thing in a simple heart attack."

"What are you saying?" I demanded. "Was it a heart attack or not?"

"Yes," he said firmly, "but it doesn't appear to have happened naturally."

"She was ninety," I snapped before the meaning of his words sank in.

"And in optimal health during her physical six months ago," he said.

"A lot can change in six months."

"Yes," he agreed, "but it's our duty to look into this sort of thing—unless you ask us not to."

He'd placed the decision on my table, waiting to see if I would take a bite. But there didn't seem to be much of a choice. If there was a possibility that this wasn't natural, then that meant foul play. It wouldn't be the first time that had happened to my family, and more proof that the Crown had cause for concern would only help my case with Parliament.

"Of course, you should investigate. We'll cooperate in any way."

"In that case, we will need to speak to anyone who handled her medication."

"That would mostly be Henry," I said, struggling to remember if my grandmother had another attendant she trusted with such matters. "I'll ask my uncle for any other household staff that might have had access."

"I appreciate your cooperation," the doctor said, "but I must warn you—this means we'll need to speak with your wife. She handled your grandmother's medication as well."

THE NORTH WING WAS DARK WHEN I REACHED IT AN hour later. The official press release could wait until tomorrow. My mobile had kept dropping my calls to Norris and Clara—an annoying quirk of old buildings that had survived the Blitz.

I went to our bedroom expecting to find Clara there lying awake. I knew she wouldn't be able to sleep until I returned with news. I wished I didn't know that from experience. But I found our bed empty.

Turning to the nursery, I opened the door to find Penny asleep in the window seat and Elizabeth curled into a ball in her new bed.

I shut the door, opening another one to panic. I went to every room in the wing, to the office. I was on my way to the Belgian Suite when my mobile buzzed.

But it wasn't Norris or Clara. It was a text sent from an anonymous number.

From within.

CHAPTER 31

CLARA

Cold. Hard. Naked.
Red. Blue. Black.

S lowly the pieces formed into complete thoughts.
The room was cold.

The floor was hard.

I was naked.

I struggled up, wrapping my arms around my body and I listened. Teeth. Mine. I couldn't control them. Then I felt it: the tremble as it rolled through me and took over my body.

The next flashes were less present. I saw the red fade of my eyelids as the rag covered my mouth, freezing the image of Norris in my mind. His mouth was covered in blood and he was trying to tell me something.

"Blue."

That didn't make any sense. A terrible thought occurred to me and I stumbled to my feet. I had no idea where I was. The room was dimly lit and there was one door. I went to it and yanked, thrown back when it opened easily.

A new word processed: corridor.

I kept my arms around my belly, protecting myself from the chill and shielding my body. Lights flickered overhead. I looked for windows and I found doors.

These ones were locked and as I reached for one I saw red.

My wedding band. I still had that.

When I reached the last door on the left, a strange sensation swam through me. The door opened to me and I swallowed back a sob when warmth rushed over my body.

There was a bed and clothes. I rushed to them and began to dress, scanning my surroundings as I did. The clothes were too small for me, but I didn't care.

There was a chest of drawers and in them more of the same clothes. I opened each one, my panic ratcheting with each discovery of the same.

There were a handful of books on a shelf: a Bible and the torn up remains of a novel. I picked up the black cover with trembling fingers, thinking of the word blue.

Blue. The Range Rover had been blue. Not black.

Not ours.

Norris had seen and they had...

The cover fell from my hands fluttering down in a swirl of black and red and white. I nearly choked. Falling to my knees, I vomited on the floor.

Sitting back, I swiped at my mouth, feeling my stomach turn again and the baby begin to kick.

And then the door opened to the face of a familiar stranger.

ABOUT THE AUTHOR

Geneva Lee is the *New York Times, USA Today,* and internationally bestselling author of over a dozen novels. Her bestselling Royals Saga has sold over two million copies worldwide. She is the co-owner of Away With Words, a destination bookstore in Poulsbo, Washington. When she isn't traveling, she can usually be found writing, reading, or buying another pair of shoes.

Learn more about Geneva Lee at:
www.GenevaLee.com

Printed in the USA
CPSIA information can be obtained
at www.ICGtesting.com
CBHW021803010924
13988CB00011B/495

9 781945 163159